DEADLY TEASE

DEADLY TEASE

A novel by

MICHELLE McGRIFF

Q-Boro Books
WWW.QBOROBOOKS.COM
An Urban Entertainment Company

Published by Q-Boro Books

ISBN-13: 978-1-933967-14-1
ISBN-10: 1-933967-14-5
LCCN: 2006936416

First Printing July 2007
Printed in the United States of America

10 9 8 7 6 5 4 3 2 1

This is a work of fiction. It is not meant to depict, portray or represent any particular real persons. All the characters, incidents and dialogues are the products of the author's imagination and are not to be construed as real. Any references or similarities to actual events, entities, real people, living or dead, or to real locales are intended to give the novel a sense of reality. Any similarity in other names, characters, entities, places and incidents is entirely coincidental.

Cover layout/design by Candace K. Cottrell
Editors: Alisha Yvonne, Stacey Seay, Leah Whitney

Q-BORO BOOKS
Jamaica, Queens NY 11434
WWW.QBOROBOOKS.COM

Acknowledgements

Clearly, at this point in my writing career I have thoughts of whether or not to continue. They aren't serious thoughts but more of a pondering, something I do on a winter day when it's cold outside and I still find myself forced to go out. I think to myself, when will I be able to stay home and write? When will my ship come in? And then I pick up that cup of hot cocoa and return to that keyboard, glancing at the clock, briefly noting that I have about another two hours before I must retire . . . if I want to be worth anything at work the next day. I take a loud slurp (I live alone, I can do that) and settle into a scene that transports me to another place, another time, and best of all, I travel for free under the identity of someone else—doing things that I could possibly never do in my real life. It brings a smile to my face when I climb between the sheets of my cozy bed when I think about it later. When I realize that I didn't need to use up any vacation time to take the trip I just went on. I realize that I didn't have to pay for cable to see the show that just played for me in my head. I didn't have to pay $7.99 for a small box of popcorn that I shared with someone else (yeah I'm cheap). I realize that my ship did come in. My ship was the love boat, the SS Minnow, the mother starship. My ship was whatever I wanted it to be, and I'm truly blessed to travel for free.

I want to thank everyone involved in my writing life, those who keep me trippin', seeing visions, and hearing voices. I want to thank those who keep my brain cells poppin' with new stories each year. Your continued support and love of my stories take my thoughts to a good place at the end of each day.

I want to thank my editors for their work, as these tired eyes don't work as well as they used to and I'll be darned if I can find my glasses half the time. I want to thank Mark, Candace, Roy, Carl, Maxine, Carla, Denise, Lil'Nataly, TL (the king of kill), my mother, my father, the lovers, the haters, the friends, and the foes, for all the help they have given me getting me where I am today.

Deadly Tease was a challenge to write, and it's not dedicated to anyone in particular, but to everyone who has written against the wind and the ticking clock.

Prologue

It was hard to pass by all the unpleasant perversions and ugliness sometimes, no matter how hard he tried. He tried with all his might to overlook the perversions, but all the effort only made him angrier. Sometimes he could block it all out, but other times, like today, it all but consumed him. Certainly, no one would call him a saint, but surely he had to be better than what was around him. Shaking his head while pressing his thumbs against the bridge of his nose, he believed he was above what was going on around him.

"So much badness," he finally cried out loudly, sounding almost as if praying. "So much badness." He slammed the exit doors and now stood on the street staring at the abandoned building across the street.

What a vibrant street this once was. He remembered being a teenager and hanging out in this neighborhood, back when it was still a decent place, a fun place, back before all the perverts came.

Looking around, his memories continued to flow, bringing mixed emotions with them.

It was a cold night, just like this one, when it happened.

"Damn fuckin' perverts," he growled, thinking aloud about that night. "Both of them—fuck 'em." He spat at the memory and then pulled the small cell phone out of his pocket with shaking hands. He hated when his hands shook because it made him seem as though he was afraid. He was never afraid. Angry. But never afraid. He needed to be civil when he spoke. He had a job to do and needed to be professional about the whole thing.

"Forgive me, Father, for I have sinned. It's been six months since my last confession," he started, sounding breathy and a little anxious. He wanted to get out everything he called to say, he wanted to keep his cool, not blurt out what was on his mind, for surely, the priest on the other end of the phone, hearing what was to be his fate, would end the conversation quickly—too quickly. He didn't want that to happen; he wanted to hear the priest out—give him a chance to explain himself. It was the least he could do before he killed him.

"Wait, my brother . . . why are you confessing?" the priest asked.

"Why not? Aren't you a righteous man? A priest?" he asked.

"Yes . . . I am. But—"

"Free of sin?" he asked.

"No, just forgiven . . . but then, we are all forgiven if we believe," the priest explained, sounding flat and almost uninterested. The man could almost see the priest, flipping through a playboy magazine, preparing himself for a night masturbation or maybe worse. . . .

"Believe in what?"

"God . . . of course."

"Do you believe that you are close to God?"

"Yes, my brother, I do," the priest said, starting to show a little pride in his tone.

"Why do you sin then?"

"We all do."

"Ah, but you . . . you feel that God listens to you."

"Yes, and I've been blessed with the privilege of helping others to be heard by him as well."

"And how do you help them?" he asked the priest, trying to keep the sarcasm from his tone.

"I walk among them."

"Ah," he said again, as if making a note. He'd walked to his car by now and had opened the door and climbed in. ". . . okay, so you dine with swine while looking for pearls."

"Not sure of your meaning, but my first thought is to say yes. I often have dealings with the lowly," the priest's voice shifted as he walked around the room. The man, from the car window, watched the priest walking around in that upper room, while speaking with him on the phone. The priest had no idea how close his caller was. The thought gave the man a quick rush and almost euphoric high.

"Then hear my lowly confession . . . please."

"Fine. I will." The priest stopped at the window and looked out. It was as if the priest looked right at the man, but it was clear the priest hadn't seen him. Just the thought of the priest looking down on him gave the man enough boldness to say what was on his mind.

"I'm going to kill a man," he told the priest now. "This man says he's a righteous man, close to God even, and from what he tells me, he feels forgiven, least that's what he told me. But then again, he is swine and perhaps his sin is truly greater than even God can overlook. Personally, I feel the man deserves to die for what he's done.

The others, all the others were just weak, but this man, his sins are bigger than even God can forgive, and so God has appointed me to be his angel of death. I shall be swift and silent. I vow to cause the man little or no pain, unless he fights me back and then—"

There was silence while the priest processed the words, placed them in perspective, and tried to pretend they weren't pertaining to him. The priest then attempted to alleviate the instant feeling of unease he felt growing in the pit of his belly. "Perhaps you should go to the police," the priest offered.

"Why? Why would I do that?"

"Because murder is a not just a sin; it's against the law and—"

"But confession will make it all go away, right? Isn't that what you do, confess and forget?"

"I don't know what you mean."

"I think you do. But then again, as a man who turns to the Bible to excuse his perversions, I'm sure you often overlook the true meaning behind scripture." The man, who the priest first thought was calling to confess sin, reached into the passenger seat of his car, opened, and then flipped the pages of his well-worn Bible, rushing to the pages he'd folded and unfolded on many occasions. The thin paper was tearing from the deep-set crease. "And he will change the natural use of the female," he began, loosely quoting scripture. "Working what is obscene, reaping the repercussion for his sins."

"I don't know what you're talking about or who you are, but—" the priest began.

"Sure you do, you all do."

"No, I don't know, and don't play games with me. Say what you're trying to say." The priest's voice rose just a little bit. "If this is some sick prank—"

"No prank. I'm The Appointed One, and you're going

to die because of your perversions. There, I've said it. You sure know how to ruin a game. Hmmm, how can I make this fun again? Oh, I know. I won't tell you when or how you'll die. That'll keep you on your toes."

The call ended.

CHAPTER ONE

Flacca and Jenessa giggled as they held each other by the arm. Both had drank too much and so their pact for one of them to at least try to stay sober was completely broken.

"I don't even want to get in a cab. Let's just walk home," Flacca suggested. Flacca was drunk and giving in to it. New Year's was the only night their boss allowed them to drink with the customers and they had taken full advantage of the allowance.

"A cab would be hella safer," Jenessa insisted, raising her hand to flag down the closest one. The driver quickly swooped up, leaned over, and rolled down the window.

"Where you fine ladies . . ." he paused, eyeing them from the legs up, realizing immediately how wrong he was, at least about Flacca, who appeared somewhat drowsy when he licked his full lips and smoothed back his hair, his hands large and knuckles pronounced, "headed?" the cabbie added, allowing the last word to linger on his tongue. Flacca giggled and winked at him. Despite the unattractive woman Flacca made, it was clear the cabbie was still attracted.

"I'm headed in all the right places," she flirted.

The driver leered wantonly at Flacca. "I bet you are," he said, deepening his voice in his attempt to heighten his seduction. Jenessa rolled her eyes at the show playing out in front of her.

"I bet you are, too," Flacca growled, leaning on the car door, allowing his voice to go even deeper than the cabby's. The driver's eyes widened, yet he didn't widen the distance between the two of them.

"Get in, baby," he insisted after the initial shock and realization had worn off.

"Not by myself, ya nasty," Flacca giggled, ripping open the back door and climbing in. "Come on, girl," he said to Jenessa who was reluctant, glancing around before she, too, climbed in the back seat. Chatter was light for Jenessa as she watched Flacca and the driver plan their night together, giving out all the details of their tryst. "You can stop right here," Flacca told the cab driver, interrupting his excited rambling about what he had in store for Flacca once he got him home. "This is where my friend needs to get out."

"Thank God," Jenessa groaned, feeling her buzz leaving.

She hadn't planned to spend the night alone, but again, it was going to be that way. The last two months had been terribly lonely; sometimes Flacca would stop by, but he often only stayed a few hours. To tell the truth, Jenessa had hoped tonight would be one of those nights Flacca stayed with her. Despite Flacca's wild ways, and conversation topics, it was always better than nothing.

Climbing out of the cab, Jenessa opened her change purse. "How much is the fare?"

The driver glanced at her and then at Flacca, who was fixing his hair in the back seat. He had great hair. "What fare, baby? It's New Year's," the cabbie grinned.

Jenessa winked and clicked her teeth, pointing her index finger at him as if the day hadn't crossed her mind, and he had just jogged her memory. "Riiiight," she said.

It was during this exchange at the curbside that the Appointed One spotted Jenessa, tall and lanky, giving off an aura of testosterone that fed his penchant.

That one will be next, he thought to himself

Why men painted their toenails, applied lotion to their heels so as to beautify their feet, shaved their legs just to slide them into nylons, always puzzled him, but then again, it all served a purpose in the end—pleasure.

Jenessa walked past him, not noticing him standing there in the crevice of the building. Her steps were light, and to a trained ear, almost confusing. Most men, no matter what, had a heavier gait. But then again, dancers were trained to be light on their feet, so it all fit. Really, it did. He'd been studying this phenomenon for months now, and although some fought back harder than others, it still added up to the same conclusion: they were all weaker than he, and better off dead.

Feeling the air thicken around her, Jenessa stopped and glanced behind her, seeing only the taillights of the cab disappear around the corner as it sped off. Her gut tightened just a little, and she immediately felt the urge to call Flacca on her cell phone. She felt the instant need to tell her to get out of the cab. Opening her bag, she dug around a minute before realizing she must have left her phone at the club. "Damn," she sighed, wondering if it was worth another hike uptown. Glancing over her shoulder, she noticed the dimness of her living room light shining through her curtain. "Nah."

Trudging up the two flights, she reached her door and opened the lock with the key she'd located while looking for her phone. She slammed the heavy door and quickly connected the chain. It was a knee-jerk response, even before turning the bolt, which she didn't always do right away. The life she lived outside of being a dancer kept her skittish—edgy, always on alert. But tonight she was tired and a little distracted. Two days off would do her good.

Jenessa passed her computer and pushed the on button out of reflex more so than desire to spend hours on the Internet. She was expecting an email. Marcus hadn't written all week. He was slipping into the "good boyfriend" category. She missed him, but his work had him tied in knots right now, and she was trying to be more than a little bit understanding, as her work, too, had put an uncomfortable distance between them.

Pulling her jacket off, she quickly reached under the short skirt and tugged at the uncomfortable appendage, adjusting it. "Now I see why guys do that all the time," she chuckled, thinking about the last time she'd seen a man adjust himself.

The doorbell rang. She left things in place and smoothed down her skirt. "It's like way late . . . must be that damned Flacca," she said loudly. "What happened?" she asked the door as she approached it. "He find out yours was bigger than his?" she asked, grabbing the chain and sliding it out of the groove, realizing suddenly she hadn't locked the bolt. But before she would slide the chain back on the hook the door burst open.

"Who the fuck are you?" she asked, groping for a weapon—something.

"I'm your salvation," he said, kicking the door closed behind him.

Her training in self-defense had her eyes moving quickly, taking in all she could, his eyes, his height, the color of his skin, his hands, the gloves he wore.

"I don't need no saving," she told him, trying to deepen her voice. She wanted to charge at him, but he was bigger and stronger. She knew that on her first assessment of the situation. Taking her eyes off him for just a moment, she was thinking how she needed her gun, so she scanned around for it.

With quick hands, he ripped her blouse. "Your breasts look good, almost real. Where did you have them done?" he asked. Her eyes locked on his as he pulled the duct tape from under his jacket and set it on the counter while backing her into the apartment.

"Sometimes it's nicer if we talk first," he said, blocking her attempt to get around him.

"What do you want me to say?"

"I want to know why you dress like a woman, why you tease men like you do, knowing you are just like them . . . for the most part."

"It's my calling," Jenessa answered, sounding sarcastic.

"Oh, okay. Well, that's a fair answer."

Now was as good a time as any to swing on him, but he was quick with his hands and blocked the punch as if anticipating it. Blocking Jenessa's attempt to kick him, he then punched her, quick and hard, right between the eyes. She was stunned and stumbled backwards against the sofa. "So you have a calling, huh? Well, so do I, and this is mine," he whispered, after leaping on her before slugging her again and again while she attempted to fight him off.

CHAPTER TWO

The humiliation was so great he couldn't even call the police, as was his normal mode of operation after a kill. He would be too ashamed to even admit the mistake he'd made where Jenessa was concerned.

He was frustrated. He'd made the mistake of a lifetime. He could have stopped before killing her, but he didn't. He gave in to the weakness of his flesh. He'd penetrated her being with full knowledge that she was not his true intended victim. But the hatred was strong and so was the resentment. She may not have been his intended victim, but with all he harbored inside, he needed to blow off some steam and he had to admit, despite it all, she did satisfy at least one need.

He'd seen her in that club. "It had to have been her," he groaned, again realizing his error where Jenessa Jewel the exotic dancer was concerned. "But she was female."

But how could that be? All this time he thought she was a man, and why not think that? All of the other dancers there were. It wasn't as if she was soft and supple like women should be; no, she looked like a man.

"There's been some trickery going here!" he yelled at the mirror. "And for that, she deserved what she got!"

She'd put up quite a fight, more than he'd expected, so he hit her with a lamp, taping her up while she lay dazed from the blow. But she quickly woke up when he entered her.

He thought about her grunts and the mumbled screams that attempted to escape from behind the duct tape while he sodomized her, but he was frantic and crazed with an evil spirit that gripped him tightly. Once he started, he couldn't stop. He watched her eyes close tightly and the tears squeeze out like a badly taped faucet. He knew he was wrong for what he did, but there was no turning back. As the eruption built inside him, he could do nothing more than grab hold of her hair as he came, twisting her neck until he heard the crack. Letting her go, he could tell by the way her head lay on the pillow in such an odd angle that he'd broken her neck

He couldn't even sleep for fretting the whole situation, and later that day, he found himself sitting in a coffee house, thinking and rethinking his next move.

"I'm so angry," he grumbled.

He needed to get some things off his chest. Pulling out Jenessa's cell phone, he dialed the number.

"So you're at the church, huh?" he asked, knowing the answer.

He was sitting at the Starbucks across the street watching him. Being a little storefront church, it had a large window in front in order to entice all who might be passing to come in on any given Sunday morning. Instead of giving their twenty dollars to the coffee counter, they could slip it into the basket at the church as it went around. Maybe if the preacher had continued to preach there instead of slowly gravitating to the Red Light District, maybe this preacher, who sat out prayer books for others to read, would have been safe. But no, he'd given in to overconfidence. He overestimated his ability to withstand temptations. He'd fallen prey to the evils of the night—the bosom of the foreign.

"Why would you ask me?" the preacher answered, looking around nervously, as if the walls had eyes and ears. This wasn't the first time the preacher had gotten a call from him, and apparently he recognized the voice immediately.

He's paranoid, The Appointed One immediately realized, while watching the preacher moving about. "Because being holy like you are, I would assume that is where you spend a lot of time."

"No, I'm not at the church," the preacher lied.

Shaking his head, The Appointed One sipped his latte and chuckled. "I guess I was wrong. Where are you then?" he asked, playing along.

"I'm . . . I'm at home. What do you want? How did you get my cell number?"

"I want to talk," the Appointed One snapped. "When someone calls you, it's obvious they want to talk, so shut up and listen. . . . Sheesh, ain't you got no manners?"

"Talk about what?"

"Okay. Here is my dilemma: I killed someone, but then I told you that the last time I called. Well, I told you I was going to. Anyway, I went ahead and did it," he said, speaking casually.

He could see the preacher pacing now, rubbing his forehead. He was a handsome man, dark-skinned with a strong build. His name was Julian Marcum. He was one The Appointed One knew would be a challenge when the time came to follow through on the plans he had for him. The Appointed One hated the thought of killing such a beautiful creature, but, just like the rest, he had to die.

"Well, I killed the sinful man, and then went to kill his accomplice, and well . . ." The Appointed One sighed in exasperation, "it was the wrong person. I've never made a mistake like that before. Well anyway, here is my problem: I could go ahead and kill the right person, but then I would still be stuck with an odd man out, if you pardon my pun and—"

"What? What are you talking about, freak?"

"You know, you're being awfully rude, considering all I was trying to do was let you know this error on my part bought you some time, so the least you could do is help me figure out what I should do next."

"I don't care what you do next. Stop calling me!" the preacher yelled, slapping the small phone closed.

The Appointed One watched now as the preacher ran around the church, opening and closing his cell phone as if debating on whether to make the call to the police. Or maybe the preacher was thinking of calling him back.

Wishful thinking, The Appointed One thought to himself, turning up his cup, and draining it. Aside from having blocked the number before calling, he knew the preacher didn't have the gumption to call the cops. That would mean coming clean with his true self, his true life. The Appointed One slid the cell phone into his pocket. "Too bad," was all he said.

CHAPTER THREE

All of the work it took to get it right, just to end up disappointed and sweaty, Portia thought to herself as she grabbed her ankles tightly, pulling her body toward her aching thighs.

"So, where's your brain tonight?" Jacki scolded.

Portia didn't answer. There was no way she was going to tell Jacki what was on her mind. There was no way she wanted to hear her mouth.

A man, Portia? You're trying to get a handle on your real life, and you're allowing a man to ruin that chance for you? Portia could almost hear Jacki's mouth already. Jacki was a little intimidating and Portia was sure she would get on her case like they had known each other for years instead of months. Jacki seemed like the type who wasn't into crushes and such—cold, a loner, and not all that attractive, Jacki didn't seem like the type to give in to enjoying girl talk, chick flicks, or pink dresses—dresses at all for that matter.

"Sorry," was all Portia managed, and then she took her position, ready to start again, loosening her shoulders and swaging her head back and forth, loosening her neck.

"One, two, three!" Jacki counted, snapping her fingers and moving behind her while the dramatic music began. They were supposed to move in sync, but when the beat started, Jacki went one way and Portia the other—again out of step.

Damn that Julian, Portia's mind wandered as she again felt herself off beat—out of sync.

Last month, Portia had broken her own rule and let Julian come to her house. They went at it like animals on her sofa. Portia had lied and said she was pregnant, and he all but ran to the bank to pull out that thousand from his secret stash to pay her off—to keep her quiet. She took two days off work, figuring it was enough to feign recovery from an abortion, and that was the end of that. But this month she was short on cash again, and on lies, too. Then again, why he was even on her mind was a mystery. *Why am I allowing myself to be played like this*? she asked herself, shaking the deadly handsome man from her brain.

Jacki wasn't cheap. These lessons were breaking her. She was going to have to find a way to get some extra money—soon. The longer these lessons went on, the more Portia began to feel the dig of debt. All she wanted now was to get out from in, from under—away from here. Now more than ever, she needed to make some space between her and the preacher man, Julian Marcum.

In the end, all this dancing was going to be worth it. She was planning to audition for a local dance troupe, and then, if she made it there, on to Broadway. She would have it made in the shade. She would be on her way to somewhere, anywhere other than where she was.

She had not shared with anyone except her cousin,

Reba, that she was taking these lessons. She wanted badly to make it before telling anyone like her colleagues. Surely they would have supported her in her venture. They were nice people and all, but what if she failed? The humiliation would be more than she could handle.

And the women at the church, she just didn't know them well enough to allow them all in her business. Maybe she felt that way about Julian, too, because for some reason, she didn't want him to know she was a dancer either.

Sometimes she wanted so much from him and other times she just wanted nothing more than to simply watch him from the sidelines, watching the way his lip would curl right before he smiled, as if his brain had to make the final decision before allowing his face to obey. Sometimes she wanted him to just get over his little commitment issues and marry her. Other times, like now, she just wanted him out of her life. He was so mysterious, or maybe he was just cheating on her. Who could know? Nevertheless, what she did know was that he was ruining her life.

What she felt for him was so confusing; it had her more tossed than a salad, which reminded her—she hadn't eaten all day.

"Portia!" Jacki yelled, snapping Portia back to the now.

"I am so sorry," Portia apologized, feeling the heat coming up on her brown cheeks.

"Look, we should call it a night," Jacki said, sounding short and snippier than usual.

Jacki, having danced professionally her whole life, had little patience for slackers. She was a serious woman, the staunch type who was not given to foolishness and seemed a lot older, even though Portia figured they were probably the same age. Maybe Jacki had issues she kept deep inside because she seemed angry and a bit pent up. Whatever the case, Jacki had little patience for her, and it was more than obvious.

"Look, Jacki." Portia rubbed her forehead, wondering where to start. "I'm low on money. I'm gonna have to drop back to only one class a—"

"One class!" Jacki exploded angrily. She wasn't fair-skinned, but when she got angry or overheated the red undertones in her complexion would give her cheeks a glow that told all. "Why not just stop them altogether? One class is not going to be enough. If I could trust that you worked out every day I would say yes, but I know you don't . . . and you won't," Jacki said, lecturing her.

"Look, I'm jogging five miles a day, plus my job. It's not like I teach geniuses who can do the work themselves. They need a lot of help," Portia exaggerated.

It was obvious that Jacki had long tuned her out because she was gathering up her things to leave. Portia dropped her head. It was a fight they had every month. Portia was getting tired of it, and she could tell Jacki was too. Portia just needed money. It was just that simple.

She dug deep in her purse to find her Visa debit card—maybe it would go through one more time before payday. Jacki could read her face and just shook her head, holding up her large hand and fanning it. "Look. I'ma give you the number of a friend of mine. She dances; she'll help you. True, her dancing is nothing like what I do here, but I mean, it will be enough for you to stay up with your practice. And who knows, maybe even get you to the stage a little faster." Jacki pulled the card from the waistband of the skirt covering her leotard, almost as if she had already anticipated this moment.

Portia took the card and stared at the address. She knew this neighborhood. It was hard to imagine any

Broadway dancing going on there. Well, maybe some off, off, way off Broadway, but nothing like the dancing she was training for.

Realizing suddenly that Jacki was leaving, Portia shoved her card toward her. "Jacki, wait. Let me try this card one more time."

Jacki shook her head. "Look, I'm late for something. Maybe I'll see you around," she said with a heavy sigh chasing her words. Hoisting her heavy looking backpack on her shoulder, she walked out.

At this rate, Portia was a long way from a Broadway audition. She felt terrible. She wondered what Julian was up to. She needed a shoulder to cry on.

Driving by the church, Portia wanted to see if perhaps Julian hadn't really lied about his reasons for cancelling their date tonight. The church was dark and by all appearances, abandoned. He'd said he was holding a late Bible class. He had lied. She couldn't help but wonder where he was.

CHAPTER FOUR

Kyle's boyfriend didn't kiss him good-bye. He just sort of let him out on the curb—cast him off would better describe it. The curb was always a couple of blocks down from the actual apartment building. Even tonight, his boyfriend seemed distracted and nervous, looking around as if they were being followed. Why Kyle bothered with such men was beyond him.

"Down-low," Kyle sighed, watching his newest lover drive off. "Shame."

Kyle was gay through and through and had never tried to hide it. Well, that's not exactly true. Most of his young life, he hid from the truth. He didn't actually come out until about ten years ago, while in college. He remembered it like it was yesterday—the look on his best friend Ian's face when he decided to just blurt it out. Ian was the brother Kyle never had. They were like twins, short of a few minor and maybe a few major differences. Kyle had a feeling that Ian knew he was gay, though. Even in high school when they both dated girls and bragged about "getting the panties" and all that, he was sure Ian had suspicions. Although Ian may have lied about his "many" female conquests, Kyle had lied as well, but for different reasons.

When they got to college, Kyle's folks swung for an apartment near the school they attended. Ian, being strapped for cash, coming from less than an affluent family, moved in. It worked out. Now Ian didn't have to work while carrying the class load that came with him having a double major. Besides, Kyle was more than happy to have him around—being the lonely-little-rich-boy he always made out to be.

The night he decided to tell Ian, Kyle was antsy and nervous. Kyle had started clubbing heavily—looking for Mr. Right. He'd started cross dressing to make his quest easier. Besides, he was a pretty man and not ashamed to admit it. So enhancing his naturally good looks with makeup and some nice fitting skirts could only help.

Normally he waited until he got to the club to change clothes from male to female attire, but that night, he wanted Ian to see him in full drag. He wanted Ian to know the truth. He wanted Ian to accept the real him. At the club, Kyle was Kyla—flamboyant and happy; at home he was just plain ol' Kyle, reserved and quiet—boring. He'd gotten tired of living the lie.

Blinking slow and long, he let just a little seduction come through when he opened his mouth to speak—to tell Ian the truth.

"What?" Ian asked, chugging from the milk carton, filling his mouth so as not to ask anything more.

"I have something to tell you," Kyle said, trying to sound nonchalant.

"What the hell you looking at me like that for?" Ian asked. "You queer or somethin'?" Ian snapped, saying the word 'queer' as if hoping Kyle would have a rebuttal.

"So you know?" Kyle asked, with a big grin coming to his lips. Ian turned away.

"Kyle, no. No, I don't," Ian answered, looking back at him, swallowing hard, gulping air.

"Yes, my friend. I'm gay," Kyle admitted Ian sighed heavily. "I think you've . . . felt it—sensed it. Your turn," Kyle said.

Ian just stood and stared, not fully getting what Kyle was inferring. Then suddenly, it came to him. He snapped instantly out his fog and focused sternly on Kyle.

"What? Me? No . . . no," Ian chuckled nervously, smoothing his blond hair which was cut in a brutal buzz style. Kyle always felt Ian looked like a marine with that hairstyle. He was white, well built and athletic, but not real bulky and had the palest blue eyes. "I uh . . ." Ian stumbled, unable to say anything else coherent.

Ian raised his hand, stepping back from him and shaking his head. "Look . . . you . . . me? Ain't happenin'," Ian snapped.

Kyle burst into laughter. "Trust me. You're not my type," Kyle admitted.

"That's right, because I'm not gay," Ian insisted, taking on a defensive tone now. Kyle was stunned a little by Ian's growing agitation. At first he thought Ian was going to accept this whole situation with ease, maybe even admit to being gay himself, but no. Ian was growing self-protective and ugly.

"Are you trying to have an attitude with me now?" Kyle asked, slamming his hands on his hips. "Because I'll kick your ass."

"Look at you," Ian scowled. He pointed at Kyle's stance and frowned. "You're a punk. Oh my goodness," Ian covered his mouth and looked off as if gathering his thoughts. "I've been living with a friggin' faggot."

"Ian, stop. Don't call me that." Kyle stepped toward him, but Ian stepped back.

"This is so not cool," Ian blurted, slamming past him into his bedroom and locking the door behind him.

Kyle couldn't help it. He started crying. It took a long time before Ian came around, and even now, all these years later, Kyle wondered how much of his lifestyle Ian had truly accepted or was okay with. Truthfully, it was Ian's lack of conversation on the topic that bothered Kyle the most. Kyle hated not knowing what he was thinking. And now—this new boyfriend, Kyle could only imagine what Ian would think about him.

Kyle honestly felt Ian wasn't as straight as he made out to be. It was impossible for Kyle to believe that Ian didn't sense something about the way things were. Ian was too comfortable with their living arrangement, too 'okay' with Kyle's feminine ways, although as the years went by, he had to admit he was far showier than he was that night and Ian was getting less and less "okay" with it.

Reaching the apartment after his two-block walk, Kyle glanced at his watch and realized he was going to be late for work—again. "Nala is gonna cut my nuts off one of these days."

CHAPTER FIVE

Lawrence always hated the start of a new year. He always felt a foreboding with the turn of a calendar year. What was the big deal about it anyway? What drove people to act like it was the end of something fantastic and the start of something so much better on New Year's Eve?

Maybe it was his life as a cop that had made him so pessimistic, or maybe it was the fact that at thirty-seven, he was single again after a painful breakup and end of a long-term relationship, and until recently, lived back home with his aged mother. It wasn't that he was a mama's boy as much as he was a late–in-life child—his mother was in her seventies already.

Lawrence's older siblings had long since left their mother to fend for herself, but he felt she deserved better. She deserved hands-on care, the kind a strong son should give, and therefore, he lived home with her, that is, until she had that stroke a few months back. She had to move into an assisted living facility because there was no one to care for her special needs. However, as soon as she signed the paperwork and moved out of the family home, his siblings came out of the woodwork, claiming a stake in their mother's life. It was ugly, and immediately, Lawrence knew there was nothing he wanted to fight over with them. There were no parts of his mother's possessions he was willing to go toe-to-toe with those greedy siblings over. He was ready to move out—move on.

"I'ma give them all that shit," Lawrence explained to his partner, Jim Beam, not too long after helping his mother get settled in the manor. They'd been partners for a while now, he and Jim.

"I hear ya on that. When my pop died, it was a catfight big time. If them broads weren't my sisters, I'da sold tickets and pulled up a lounge chair. I mean, hair flying, clothes rippin'—"

"Please, spare me. I've seen your sisters," Lawrence chuckled. Jim shrugged understandably.

"That's what I'm sayin'. Be glad you're deciding all of this now. Don't wait until ya folks pass off the scene to take care of all that stuff. It's harder then."

"Yeah, it'd be horrible if Mama was gone, watchin' her *chirrens* fight over her stuff. She'd be looking down wishing she could take a switch and—"

"You think your mama is goin' ta heaven?" Jim teased, having met Mrs. Miller—a feisty little woman who was not one to mince her words.

"I'll ignore that," Lawrence said, sounding tongue-in-cheek, "but now I'm gonna have to move. I mean, not havta, but wanta," Lawrence admitted, thinking of his limited options.

It wasn't as if he had anywhere to go. Not really. At that time, Hannah was still not returning his calls, as the breakup was still new. "There is crime in the streets,

Hannah. For cryin' out loud! I'm a cop!" he had yelled from outside of the house upon seeing his clothes out on the lawn and still flying from the second story window.

Even now, all these months later, Lawrence still wondered why he couldn't just find a woman who understood a complicated man like him. Maybe he just needed to find a more complicated woman.

Despite all the wrongs in the world, Lawrence was lovesick.

Finishing his third cup of coffee, Lawrence groaned again, not only at his thoughts, but at the pile of files on the desk in front of him.

Cold cases, everyone hated them. They were the newest craze in the department. There were so many TV shows glorifying cold cases as easily solvable. The shows made it seem as if years of lying around in a file cabinet now had caused the old cases to sprout with new and fresh evidence and leads that for some reason weren't there when the case was hot. Everyone in the department had at least three of these files on their desk

"If Chiefy brings another one of these funky old files in here, I'm gonna shoot her myself," Jim whispered over the desk. Lawrence snickered under his breath.

"Yeah, but at least if you shoot her right here, right now, that case will have a few good clues and maybe even some good motives," Lawrence chuckled.

"Yeah, might still take a while to figure out who done it, but . . ." Jim laughed even louder, realizing what he was implying about their case solving abilities or lack thereof.

"We're not that bad. This case is what . . . over a year old?" Lawrence shook the file at him.

"And, like, sooo . . ." Jim sighed heavily, holding up another so-called coordinating file, "unrelated."

Lawrence took the folder from Jim and gave the contents a closer look before shaking his head. "Think so?"

"Well, sure. It only had the same type of murder, but that's all," Jim said, completely tongue-in-cheek. The two cases were all but identical.

Two men in their late twenties to early thirties, one found in the back room of a church, the other was a transvestite who was found in an abandoned hotel a few days later. Both had been duct taped to a cot, sexually assaulted and then mutilated—penises removed, causing them to bleed to death. There had been no closure on either case, as a motive was not found. By all appearances, the murders were random.

"Random?" Lawrence said aloud, shocked at the incomplete information he found. The questioning of witnesses and family members was appalling. The detectives working the case clearly pushed the whole thing to the back of their minds—and file cabinet. "Complicated, sure . . . but random?" Lawrence asked the air.

"Exactly. Who wakes up one morning and while looking at their roll of duct tape, decides, 'hmm, I'm going dick hunting today?' " Jim said. "Got my duct tape, my really sharp knife . . ."

Lawrence burst into laughter.

"Stop playing around!" the chief barked, showing up unexpectedly. Jim jumped in a start. He hated when the chief snuck up on him that way. "Oh, and Beam," she began, "keep calling me 'Chiefy' and your ass is grass, hear?" she smarted off, flipping her blond hair in a taunting fashion, "Why haven't you guys solved these old cases?" she asked, sounding not altogether serious, taking the file from Lawrence's hand and thumbing through it.

He glanced at his watch. Just then, the phone rang. "Yeah," the chief said, answering the phone that sat in

Lawrence's reach. She could be downright bossy sometimes, he thought to himself, watching her sling her hair as if on a social call.

Suddenly, Lawrence noticed the change of expression on her face as she began scrambling for something to write on and something to write with, snapping her fingers and trying to get the attention of someone else who could tie into the call. Jim quickly ran to another desk and picked up the phone.

"Who is this?" she asked.

"Like I'm going to just tell you, just like that . . . no. You writing this down? Because I don't have a lot of time. I'm sure you're already trying to find me, if you cops are worth your salt," the caller said.

"Yeah, I'm writing," the chief said, scribbling the address she was given as soon as she answered the call.

"And it's going to be pretty ugly, what you find, because I was pretty angry when I . . ." The caller paused. "You know, when I did it."

"Was it an accident?" the chief asked.

The caller burst into laughter.

"Yeah, let's call it an accident for now. I accidentally killed him to death," he said before hanging up, while still chuckling.

After the remainder of the call was put on speaker, everyone hearing stood stunned for a moment, wondering what the chief would do or say next. "We got a body—first of the new year, on our block at that. And he just gave us a step by step," the chief said, after a moment of regrouping. "You know what that means . . . looks like we got a psycho on our hands."

Who would she put on the case? Lawrence wondered, trying to avoid her eyes. Who would be sent to the scene of a possibly gruesome murder, the first one of the year, on their block as she put it? Their eyes met, and Lawrence knew immediately she had chosen them. “Beam, Miller, you’re on it,” she said, tossing the scribbled address toward Lawrence.

Damn, early to be finding bodies, Lawrence thought.

“Happy New Year,” she said, heading back to her office rubbing her forehead, no doubt anticipating the worst.

“She digs me,” Jim whispered, as he and Lawrence left.

“Is that why we get all the good cases?” Lawrence griped.

CHAPTER SIX

Within the hour, Lawrence and Jim made it to the scene. The uniforms had beaten them there and were already taping off the area and trying to keep the crowd from building. The body was found right where the caller said it would be, in one of the empty rooms of the abandoned Madison hotel, which was atop the Asoki liquor store on the corner of Madison and Mather Way. It doubled as Victory Outreach church, a meeting place for the religiously misplaced. Those who gathered there hoped to one day find their way back to some semblance of normalcy with God as a platform. It was an awful scene, and in Lawrence's mind, nowhere near a random act of violence. Somebody meant for this man to be *really* dead. He'd been sexually assaulted, stabbed, and mutilated—his penis removed. Who knew which came first? One could only hope he was dead before being detached from his manly member.

Blood was everywhere, forcing the men to walk on their tiptoes to prevent the sticky, reddish-brown fluids from getting all over their shoes. Gloves and masks were quickly passed to Jim and Lawrence.

Being a big man, standing nearly six-foot-three, and a muscular two hundred and forty pounds easily, most would think Lawrence would be above flinching at the sight of blood or death, but he wasn't. Lawrence Miller hated the sight of blood, even his own. It all but turned his stomach. He was gentle in nature and wouldn't hurt a fly—unless of course the fly was breaking the law. He had a sensitive side, but a strong sense of right and wrong. Both of those qualities were probably what made him such a good cop.

"Victim's name is Fox," the officer read from the notes. "Deacon," he added.

"So he's a deacon?"

"No, the name is Fox?" the officer repeated.

"Hey, maybe he's a . . . no, wait. It can't be that easy. Tell me he's not a—"

"Don't say it!" Lawrence blurted, hoping to stop Jim before he started.

"A deacon named Fox."

Lawrence groaned. "Get serious, Jim."

"No Sir, I believe he's a priest," the officer said. Jim's eyes widened.

"A priest named Deacon. Now how complicated is this getting to be?" Jim added with sarcasm showing as he and Lawrence entered the building.

The two photographers snapped away, one handing Lawrence Polaroids while the other camera operator used a high-resolution digital for the lab.

Lawrence grimaced as he watched the camera man getting up close and personal with the remains of Deacon Fox, whose mouth was gaping open and eyes fixed upward, as if perhaps caught up in prayer right at the moment it counted most.

"Looks like he's having an orgasm," Jim interjected, totally disrupting Lawrence's thoughts on Deacon Fox's expression.

"What?"

"His face, look at him . . . almost blissful," Jim went on.

"Well, whatever he was doing, musta been pretty good," the cameraman with the digital camera said, aiming his camera at the crotch area, making sure to get good shots of the area that was missing Deacon Fox's male organ. "Yeah, pretty good," he repeated before he and Jim burst into laughter at the crude sexual implications.

"Let's get a sample or two of this mess, see how much was his blood how much wasn't," Lawrence interjected, hoping to sound official and busy. No, this scene was not Lawrence's cup of tea at all. The camera guy looked up at him and smiled slyly as if knowing exactly what Lawrence felt behind his weak command.

"Deacon Fox," Jim mumbled, suddenly growing serious and wandering around the small room, looking around. Jim's actions told Lawrence they were back on the task of the body they had just found. Lawrence tolerated Jim's eccentricities because Jim was usually good at a crime scene. He didn't miss much when allowed to go over the place in his own fashion, which usually included off-color comments and plenty of bad jokes. "Fox . . . Foxy, Foxy mama . . ." Jim went on in his normal rambling.

"So this is a church?" Lawrence asked.

"Yeah, but somebody didn't wanna hear no more preaching," Jim snickered wickedly.

"No, check it out—this is a church," Lawrence said, jogging Jim's memory.

"Okay, the irony is tremendous!" Jim blurted out, grimacing at the odor at the same time. Lawrence agreed, with both the irony and the stench. Just this morning they were reading files that now had them feeling as if they were in a time warp.

"Yeah, just a little much. Let's get outta here," Lawrence said, backing out of the room. "Let's see what we got out here." Moving out onto the sidewalk now, Lawrence pointed to the neon-lit building that sat in place of his pleasant childhood memory. The neon sign flickered against the morning as if it had never been shut off the night before.

These five blocks used to hold a fairly decent strip of industry. Lawrence remembered being a kid and going through this area with his folks on their way to visit family in the Palemos—a track of homes not far from there. Lawrence's dad would stop in the liquor store not far from where they had found the dead man today. Lawrence's father and uncles would always ride up to this store after tiring of the womenfolk, buy a few forties and Lawrence, being so much younger than everyone else, would have to stay in the car while they socialized on the stoop. It seemed to take forever for them to finally come back to the car, drunk and loud, handing out loose, single bills to him to hit the ice cream parlor. It was bribe money to keep their drunken secrets; however, Lawrence knew even then, that if they all weren't so wasted they would know the money wouldn't help hide anything.

Back then, in the seventies, the owner of the store was an old Asian man named Chi Asoki. He was an oddity to his neighborhood. But not anymore; now, foreigners ruled. Lawrence didn't have a problem with the foreigners coming in. He just hated change. No matter what it was.

Now Asoki's Liquor Mart stood practically abandoned during the day, yet came alive at night, doubling as a crack house after dark, and the ice cream parlor across the street was now some kind of dance hall.

"What's the name of that place?" Lawrence asked Jim, thinking aloud.

"What place?" asked Jim, his face still twisted up with disgust, as if the foul smell from the house stayed in his nose. "Oh, you mean Queer Land."

"What?" Lawrence chuckled.

"The Rainbow Room, s'cuse meee," one of the apparent patrons of the homosexual bar commented after easing his way over near them, stepping away from the growing crowd. He was showing irritation with the way Detective Jim Beam addressed his hangout.

"Ahh . . . Rainbow . . . yeah," Lawrence said with sarcasm showing in his statement. He'd been following the fads and trends and he knew what the reference to a rainbow meant now.

The pretty, young man with a face full of makeup and wearing a wig just shook his head in exasperation, and then, with a nervous drag from his cigarette, his attention was brought back to the grisly scene he had stumbled upon.

"You familiar with this place? You know what happened here, right?" Jim asked.

"Of course I do," the pretty man answered. "I've been in there."

"So, you like to hang out in abandoned buildings?"

"No, it wasn't an abandoned building, and I wasn't hanging out. It was being used as a church. And for your information, I was about to confess some stuff to Father Fox when I heard all this commotion and saw all these people." He smacked his lips, still holding his cigarette between his two fingers, and then bit his thumbnail nervously. "You just never think something like this would happen so close to you, ya know?"

Lawrence stared at the young man for a moment. He could only imagine that completely in drag, the young man had to look like the young Eartha Kitt a little—exotic in an 'interesting kinda way.' He was getting ready to ask if perhaps Ms. Kitt was the young man's persona when on stage, but their attention was drawn away by a ruckus starting up in front of the Rainbow Room. A large rock was thrown from the passenger window of a fast moving truck, busting the front window of the nightclub with a loud crash and the familiar sound of breaking glass. The young man let out a womanly scream.

Out of reflex, Lawrence ran out to the street to catch the license plate number of the vehicle. He only caught a couple of numbers. Several drag queens emptied into the street, cussin' mad.

"Are you the police?" one of them finally asked. "Cuz we gots some crimes occurring in our midst."

"Can't you tell he's a cop—got that big . . . ummm . . . gun," a tall, exotic looking woman-like person flirted while moving through the growing crowd.

She wore a kimono robe that exposed much cleavage. Lawrence caught himself staring at her for a second before suddenly feeling the tightening in his throat. He looked at Jim, who was smiling—grinning actually. Jim could tell Lawrence was about to panic.

"Okay, ladies," Jim interceded, corralling the drag queens together. "Okay, one thing at a time, one thing at a time," he instructed. "We got a stiff in that building and some stone throwers over here, so . . ."

"A stiffy?" one of the drag queens gasped. "That doesn't sound like a good thing—or does it?"

Lawrence couldn't breathe. He quickly headed back over to the dead body being loaded into the coroner's wagon across the street. He could handle that much better.

"Somebody get this place closed up," he instructed one of the uniform cops, who nodded.

CHAPTER SEVEN

After asking all the appropriate questions of the patrons of the Rainbow Room and anyone else who looked overly interested in the scene that lay out in the upstairs of that abandoned building, Jim and Lawrence climbed back into their car to head back to the precinct.

"You need to loosen up, Lawrence," Jim said.

"What?"

"Those gay guys . . . you gotta loosen up. It's not like rap music and baggy pants. Homosexuality is here to stay," Jim said, sounding altogether serious, although he was not. He looked at his notepad before looking up at him, grinning again.

"Look. I'm a Christian, man. I just don't believe that men need to be doing that," Lawrence explained bluntly.

"Come on, Lawrence. You're acting like a damn homophobic. Being Christian doesn't even come close to being your main issue with those guys. Besides, one of them was female, and I'll bet you can't guess which one."

"No, and I'm never gonna get close enough to even try to guess."

"I'm not saying that I'm like . . . into that either, but you do need to open your mind a little more—accept the differences, man," Jim explained. "Difference can be . . ." Jim paused, "beautiful." Again, Jim was being lighthearted, but Lawrence took him far too seriously.

"My mind is as open as it's ever gonna be, Jim," Lawrence said with his large hand flying up and then cutting the air on its way down. Jim just shook his head and looked out the window. "What?" Lawrence asked, questioning the silence, refusing to acquiesce. This conversation wasn't over as far as Lawrence was concerned.

"What . . . what? I'm just sayin' that you need to get in touch. You are gonna have to stop just judging things based on what you see up front, or what you think you see," Jim explained. Lawrence glanced over at Jim again, while maneuvering the wheel. *What is Jim trying to say?*

"Are you gay, Jim?" Lawrence finally asked. Jim rolled his eyes.

"Why is it always black and white with you? Just because I try to get you to think with your mind open, I have to be gay . . . or whatever. Like when we were talking about politics, I disagreed with you and suddenly I was communist. And you wonder why you're not married? Do you wonder?" Jim asked again rhetorically.

"No, I don't wonder why I'm not married and I never wondered until today if my partner was gay. Should I wonder, Jim?"

"Oh, for crying out loud, Lawrence," Jim slapped his forehead, leaving a red mark there. His blood was pumping hard, Lawrence could tell. "Drop it. Drop it," Jim insisted. "You are a fuckin' closet bigot of the worse kind."

"Now I'm a bigot, a racist? I think not, Jim!" Lawrence yelled, swerving through traffic, his driving becoming erratic.

"I didn't say racist, I said bigot. There is a difference. Look it up!"

"I'm not lookin' nothing up. You're worse than Hannah, trying to talk over my head all of the damn time! You know that! You're acting awfully womanish at this time."

"What?" Jim chuckled, trying to keep his temper under control. This type of argument with Lawrence was the norm and Jim knew not to allow himself to get too worked up. Lawrence was squarer than a box and just as closed minded. "Whatever, Lawrence, you just don't get it, and today having to question those queers just proved it."

"Whatever," Lawrence sighed, still refusing to see the correlation between the scene today at the gay dance hall and why women just didn't understand him. He sure didn't get the connection between all of it and the fact that Jim was a gay communist.

Kyle was flabbergasted and left not too long after the police cleared out. He didn't care if he got fired or not—not today; there was no way he was going back to work. He knew too much and his head was starting to hurt. Deacon had been murdered and Kyle had a feeling he knew why. He knew exactly why and it was all about jealousy and deceit. Somebody's game playing had finally ended up in murder.

The thought gave Kyle a chill.

Waiting outside their apartment, Kyle was ready to talk as soon as Ian rode up on his bike. Kyle stared at Ian's lean frame and long, strong legs a long time. Ian had let his hair grow long over the last couple of years. They'd been living together as roommates a long time, and Kyle hoped that one day Ian would be the one he could find comfort in . . . real comfort, maybe even love. Kyle wanted them to be a couple—not just roommates. Ian never really dated, so maybe they were a couple and Kyle had just missed the signs. Maybe all this time Ian was just waiting for Kyle to just say the word.

"What?" Ian asked, locking his bike.

"I need to talk to you," Kyle began.

"So talk," Ian said, rubbing his hands together. His gloves showed only his fingertips. Kyle wished Ian wouldn't cut up his nice gloves that way, especially ones he'd bought for him. "I took off early and rushed home thinking it was an emergency . . . uh, you're not bleeding, soooo, what is it?"

"You left work early?" Kyle smiled before he could catch it, causing Ian to smack his thin lips in irritation and look off before looking back him. His blue eyes were steel-like, un-nerving Kyle so much he reached into his pocket and pulled out his cigarettes, lighting one quickly.

"There was a murder across the street from my job."

"There's murders all over this city, Kyle, not just near your job. Hell, there was a murder near my job last month; I didn't call *you*!" Ian barked.

"No, you don't understand. The guy was not just murdered. He was *kilt* with a capital T. Somebody meant for his ass to feel it while he died," Kyle told Ian. "He was tortured." His hand shook so much while he smoked that Ian finally took the cigarette from him and dropped it to the ground, smashing it under his foot.

"I don't know why you still have such a dirty habit," he said, sounding cool and together before he simply curled his lip disdainfully and headed inside with Kyle hot on his tail.

"Smoking is the least of my problems, Ian. I was almost witness to a murder and you're not hearing me. I might still be in danger. Hell, if I had been up there with him, I could have been all cut up like that. Dude's dick was gone."

"And you know that how?"

"I was there while the cops were there. I was on my way to the church."

"For what?"

"Ian, stop it now, you're getting me off track from my story."

"Which is? You're just now telling me you've been going to some church and you don't expect me to be a little surprised?"

"I don't go to some church, not that church anyway. Ian, listen, stop talking and listen. What if he saw me over there?"

"Who—the killer or the cops? Did you kill the guy?" Ian asked, while opening the refrigerator and taking out the juice, drinking it from the carton, which was his own bad habit. "I wouldn't think he would come after you," Ian then said, noticing Kyle's expression. Kyle was showing hurt at his lack of caring as well as his badly aimed jokes. "Come on, Kyle. I'm sure you are not going to be a victim of some random murder just because you work at the Rainbow Room or just because you were on your way to some church. . . . By the way, why were you on your way over there?"

"My friend . . . I have a friend who, uh," Kyle stammered. Ian rolled his eyes and slammed the refrigerator door.

"There is no church over there. I know what's over there—a bunch of abandoned buildings. The street is a dump, full of nothing but a bunch of nothing. If you were on your way over to one of those buildings, I can only imagine what you were doing over there," Ian told him, sounding like a harsh disciplinarian "You're scared now?" he asked. "Well, I suggest you keep your ass out of back rooms and alleyways and shit, acting like some damn whore," Ian said flatly.

Finally, after regrouping a moment, Kyle spoke. "Is that how you see me?"

Ian looked away and then back at him. "I'm just saying lately it's been like that. You . . . you're always on the chase. I don't know how it's supposed to go with guys like you, but isn't somebody supposed to come after *you* once in a while?"

"You sound jealous."

"Anyway, Kyle, see, that's what I mean. You're always getting off the point. Never listening. That's why your ass is always in trouble. You need to—"

"What are you gonna say? I need to just settle down? Is that what you're about to say? Find some nice girl and settle down?" Kyle was following Ian around the apartment now, ranting. Lately they were arguing more and more. It was as if it was leading up to something but never getting there. Kyle was frustrated and couldn't help his part in the arguing. Ian was shaking his head. "That's what guys like you do—all that down-low shit. Well, I'm not like that," Kyle went on, digging deeper and deeper, pushing buttons left and right.

"Down-low?" Ian snapped.

"Yes, you're on the down-low. I know the signs. I see them all the time. When's the last time you got laid, Ian? No regular guy could go years and years without getting any. Who's the chick, Ian? See, just as I thought—no answer."

Ian stared Kyle down before he slammed into his room, closing the door with contempt.

"I'm gay, Ian! I admit it! Why don't you?" Kyle screamed.

CHAPTER EIGHT

The news story was so gruesome that Portia couldn't finish watching it. Clicking off the television, she flopped onto the sofa. "What's happening to people?" she asked out loud.

The phone rang.

"What are you doing?" Julian asked. Portia's heart skipped a beat. Why he had this effect on her was still very disturbing. He had offered her nothing in return for her love—nothing, yet she loved him. Or maybe it wasn't love. Who knew?

"Nothing."

"I need to see you."

"Or not," she smarted off. He was silent.

"Don't play games, Sister Hendrix. When your man wants to see you, you're supposed to respond in kind."

"My man?"

"Yeah, your man. You don't think of me as that?"

She didn't answer. The thought of her saying yes, and him correcting her thoughts would be too much to take right now.

"Let me come over."

"No, Julian, you can't come to my house. How many times do I have to tell you that? My house, my bed, is for my husband. It's to be an honorable place to—"

"Yeah, yeah, I know the scriptures, Portia. But you must admit, what we did the last time you let me in your house leaves me questioning which Bible you read from."

Stunned by his audacity, her mouth dropped open. "What did you just say to me?"

"I'm just saying, I think you've made up your own book of morals to suit you, my sista. And maybe I have, too. Seeing how badly I want you, I would sometimes be more than willing to make up a chapter in the good book if that's what it would take to be with you right now."

"It's late, and I don't know about you coming over here and—"

"If I had a key, I could just come by anytime and slip into your bed and not disturb you. I could just come over, come in and, well . . . make you cum, make you scream my name, make you . . ." he whispered. Portia felt heat rising to her cheeks. Julian was such a sexual being. She had never met anyone like him. Even when he talked dirty, he could make it all seem all right.

"Where do you want me to meet you?" she asked, slipping into her shoes. If she gave herself a moment, she would have felt foolish, but that moment was not going to be allowed, even if she had to keep him on the phone until she got to him. "Your house?"

"No!" he snapped. "Not my house. What are you thinking?"

The mood changed instantly. Standing now, she put her hands on her hips before kicking off her shoes again. "I was thinking you wanted to be with me tonight, that you wanted to see me no matter where or how, no matter—"

"I want to come to your house. As a matter of fact, I can be there in just a minute. I'm not far away."

"You're farther away then you think, Julian," Portia said, hanging up and tossing the phone onto the sofa.

Exhausted now, she headed upstairs to her room.

Portia stewed over Julian for the better part of the night. What a waste of time he was turning out to be. Here she was living a life that could easily be considered comfortable, and she was complicating it with a man, a man who didn't want to marry her. What she wouldn't give to have another chance to redo the last year of her life.

Portia and her father had lived quietly in that big old house on Bush Street, the one with the empty flowerbed that lined the driveway and sat up on a hill. She taught literacy at the local elementary school down the street, just like her mom used to do when she was alive. Her dad enjoyed his retirement—bumbling around that old house, breaking stuff and fixing it again.

The thought of her old man made her smile—his dancing, bright eyes. And then there was his smile. But suddenly, he was gone. One bad cold, complicating into pneumonia and just like that . . . It was amazing how fast it took him. And there she was, left with nothing but his memories and that old house—that broken down old house.

Lonely most of the time after her father's death, Portia had gotten into some bad habits to fill her time—TV, Internet, potato chips. The binge, however, was short-lived, and soon she decided she needed to move past all those vices she had been indulging in over the last few months and do what she knew would be best—go to church and pray. She had thought about dancing again, too. It was common knowledge, as with everything: if you let it go too long it's gone forever. She wanted help to get focused again. Chasing a dream was hard work and was easy to give up on, especially when grieving.

Finally having reached the depths of despair, she visited the new storefront church that had opened across from the school where she worked. Julian Marcum was a dark, tasty piece of smooth chocolate, tall, and well put together from any angle you saw him. He, the pastor of the church, was beyond gorgeous and from the moment she laid her eyes on him, she was a goner. With eyes as dark as Kenyan coffee, rich and mysterious, he was heavenly. He must have noticed her, too, because right after the sermon, he came right up to her, despite the fact that she sat way in the back. He introduced himself, took her hand in both of his, and held it a long time while asking for her phone number and address—to keep a watchful eye on her, of course. With that one little act, she knew they had made some kind of connection. She was lonely and the handsome, single, young pastor was all but promising to be there to comfort her. On the other hand, the right one—he preached like she had never heard preaching before, damned the wicked and heralded all righteous things on high. He knew his Bible.

All in all, Julian Marcum had raised her blood pressure, brought her back to life, and gave her a reason for living. Since attending his church and listening to his inspirational sermons, she even picked up a personal dance instructor to put a little pep in her step. And she owed it all to him.

Portia was weak and knew it, but still, falling for and entering into an immoral relationship with the pastor of her church was surely going to put her sins in the 'unforgivable' department. She always felt love would hit one day, and when it did, it would hit her like a fall off of a mountain, like the bumper of a car, or maybe just head on. Julian hadn't really affected her that way, but he had affected her to be sure.

Holding his position as pastor of that small church with much authority and prowess, many loose living members feared him. He was younger than most pastors and was not afraid to be assertive, yet charming all at the same time, which was perhaps his biggest obstacle, as many of the *sistas* had tried to get next to him. But he seemed resistant, that is until Portia came along. Still, sinning with a preacher wasn't what she had in mind when this whole thing started.

Over the months, Julian did do some wonderful things for the community—starting with the church itself. He moved his gospel to the streets, helping lost teens find their way back to a real life.

At first, he was merely a curiosity for Portia; pursuing a relationship with him hadn't really crossed her mind—it just sort of happened. In the beginning, he hadn't really made a move on her, but all the little teases and tugs at her heartstrings said more than his lips ever could. She, working at the university across the street, was in constant view of him, well, the lot where he parked his car. That was enough to give her a tingle. It just seemed like there were sparks between them from the start. At least Portia felt them.

A handsome, powerful man like Julian being interested in her was something she hadn't experienced before. He was amazing. Watching him in the pulpit was really something—impressive to say the least. She had reasoned in her heart that it all had to be good—her feelings for him. And why wouldn't she think that? She'd even begun praying again—praying that it wasn't obvious the way she came on to him all the time. And then she prayed that he wasn't coming on to her, but she feared they both were obvious.

When they slipped the first time, it was as if it was the natural thing to do, despite the fact that it happened in the back room of the church. He had put her in charge of the Sunday School, and that put her in constant contact with him. She'd given in to her weakness for Julian, and there was no turning back now. He was in her blood, and she was in dire need of a transfusion.

Now she wanted him to commit and come out in the open with their love affair. But no, he couldn't go there. Couldn't go there? Hell, he shouldn't have gone where he'd already been. What was he thinking? Did he think she was just going to give up the goodies and let him alone?

Portia's father, an agnostic with a keen sense of right and wrong, would have seen Julian as a hypocrite of the biggest kind—preaching the straight and narrow, yet looking at her out of the bend of his eye. But still, he wouldn't commit to her and sometimes he acted downright shady about the situation, like the issue he had about her coming to his house. What was up with that?

It didn't matter because she had decided two could play at that game; thus she didn't allow him at her house either.

"So dumb," she mumbled, turning over in the bed, slugging her pillow.

Portia knew something was wrong with the whole situation when she allowed herself to realize it. What was Julian up to?

Drifting off to sleep, she dreamed heavily, waking up abruptly and beyond late for work.

CHAPTER NINE

New Year's Day was a memory now, with them being three days into the year and working on new murder cases.

The call came in and they were given the call. This new murder would actually be a nice break from the "Unholy Murder" as Jim and Lawrence were calling it.

"Venus Murder just doesn't seem to fit," Jim said, thinking out loud about the title given to the case by others at the precinct.

"Whatever," replied Lawrence, still feeling a little huffed about their argument the day before.

"No, think about it . . . it just doesn't."

"Whatever," Lawrence repeated. Jim smiled knowing Lawrence was just showing an attitude.

A hotel room, a man and woman found dead in bed together. The woman was married and the man in the bed was not her husband.

What a gory scene Jim and Lawrence had walked into, meeting the other officers who had arrived before them.

There was plenty to work with and an immediate person of interest to visit. The male victim still had his penis, and so Lawrence knew this was going to be one of the easy ones. This case was hot—open and shut where Lawrence was concerned. They weren't going to waste any time on this one. Surely, there was enough blood to convict someone before the day was over and ruin his appetite for the rest of the day. But this was police work in Lawrence's opinion—clues, leads, and more importantly, suspects that were still alive to question, not like what they were in for with those cold files and all those cold clues and leads and nothing like the case of Deacon Fox. Everyone's stories in connection with the Fox murder had checked out and they had no leads or suspects jumping out at them. Despite it all, Lawrence was at least happy that the cold case they had was only a year or so old; he'd heard some of the guys at the station talking about their cold files, some of which were as old as twenty years. *There's something just not right about bothering the dead. Folks should be allowed to rest in peace.* .

"You are always so cynical and negative. I would wager that we are about to speak to a man who will be devastated when he hears the news that his wife is dead," Jim began, sounding as if he was romanticizing the situation.

"He killed her. He's probably in his house cleaning the blood and prints off the gun right now like an idiot," Lawrence interrupted, speaking what he felt was the bitter truth. Jim snickered slightly.

Now, racing through her house, Portia grabbed her lunch, and then desperately looked around for her keys. She was so disorganized. Why? She didn't know. Maybe it was all the things she had on her mind these days. The banister was broken on the staircase, the lawn boy needed to be paid this week, and she had spent her last putting that ad in the paper for someone to rent her room.

Reba, her cousin, told her she was insane for even thinking about renting out a room in her house to a stranger, but Reba had Bradley and just didn't want to understand that Portia really needed the extra income a boarder would bring in.

Portia had put up a poster at the church, but on Sunday, she had noticed it was down—no doubt, Julian had taken it down. He was so prideful. Portia could only imagine that her needing a roomer was like a slap in the face to him. He surely would not have wanted the church folks to question him about why he hadn't taken care of the Sunday School teacher's immediate material needs. What would he say?

"Doesn't matter. I plan to fix her up right nicely pretty soon here," Portia mimicked. "Are you crazy, Portia?" Portia asked herself while lifting cushions and digging around for her keys. "Why do you keep thinking that man wants you?"

Her hand ran across a hard object. It was a matchbook buried deep down in the crevice. THE RAINBOW ROOM was printed on the cover.

She stared at it for a moment before her brain jarred the fact that her father did smoke on occasion and this was no doubt just a leftover from his things. "Duh," she said, tossing the matchbook aside and continuing to dig around. Suddenly she was hit with another moment of clarity. "Portia, Julian doesn't give a damn about you," she said aloud, almost as if Reba's words had come from her mouth instead of her own. "He's the pastor of the church, and he needs a spiritually sound wife, not one who's planning to dance on Broadway," Portia told herself aloud, pulling the keys from their hiding place, which was in clear view on the desktop under the window.

Shaking her head, she rushed out. Today was going to be one of those days.

"Mr. Stevenson, we would like to speak to you if we may," Lawrence requested, flashing his badge at the crack made when the man opened the door—barely.

"About what?" the voice of Mr. Stevenson came, sounding weak and shaky.

"Your wife, sir. Can you open the door please? We—"

"Why do you all keep bothering me about her? She wanted a divorce, and I . . . I gave it to her," Mr. Stevenson answered nervously through the thin slice of an opening he'd made.

"Mr. Stevenson, we really would like to talk to you," Jim spoke up.

"What, is she dead or something?"

There was silence, and then both men watched as Mr. Stevenson's eyes widened just before he gently closed the door. They heard the chains rattling, and then there was nothing. They knocked again.

"Mr. Stevenson, we need to talk to you, and we would like your cooperation," Jim called.

"Mr. Stevenson," Lawrence's voice boomed while he knocked harder.

"You won't take me alive!" Mr. Stevenson screamed, sounding like a line from a classic gangster movie.

Suddenly, the bullets pierced the thin wood of the door. "What the hell?" Jim exclaimed.

Dodging, Lawrence yelled, "I told you!" He waited until the shooting ceased, then kicked in the door.

More shots fired. Jim rolled out of the way of the flying bullets, and then began shooting blindly toward Mr.

Stevenson, who was heading out the back window. Despite his efforts to miss him, Jim was afraid he was going to shoot the man square in the back with all that wild, frantic *get away* action he was doing.

"Why don't you just stop, dammit!" Jim yelled.

Despite the wild bullets, Lawrence charged at Stevenson, who slipped quickly under the small opening he'd made, lifting the window. Lawrence cursed bitterly, knowing the space was only wide enough for a worm like Stevenson to fit through.

Lawrence and Jim darted out the door, down the two flights of stairs and onto the street. "When I catch him I'm going to fuck him smooth up," Lawrence yelled, knowing Jim could hear him. He didn't care who else did.

Sprinting around the corner, he spied Stevenson jetting up Mission Boulevard, running blindly into traffic. Lawrence pursued him.

That's when the car hit him.

"What the hell!" Portia's heart nearly jumped out of her mouth, as the little white man carrying a backpack and gun flew over the hood of her car. She screamed loudly, missing all the details of the situation, while slamming on her brakes. Her head hit the steering wheel.

Lawrence grabbed Mr. Stevenson by the cuff of his shirt and pulled him up to his feet. He cussed the nearly unconscious man bitterly.

Portia, shaking her head semi-clear, climbed quickly from behind the wheel. She had not seen the gun fly out of Mr. Stevenson's hand when she hit him.

Reeling from shock, she saw Lawrence as nothing more than a large black man, pummeling the defenseless little white man to death. Caught up in civil duty, she jumped on Lawrence's back and slugged him in the side of the head, causing Lawrence to nearly lose balance. "Let him go," she screamed, spinning with Lawrence as he attempted to sling her off.

"Lady, you are under arrest!" Lawrence yelped, letting Mr. Stevenson go and grabbing at Portia in his attempt to get her off him.

"What?" Portia asked.

"Where do you think you're going?" Jim said through gritted teeth, slamming Mr. Stevenson, who was using the confusion to attempt another escape, against the car hood.

That was when Portia noticed the handcuffs placed on the white man's wrists by Detective Jim Beam, Lawrence's partner. She then saw the gun lying in the street, causing her to unconsciously loosen her grip. Lawrence threw her over his shoulder. "You're under arrest, lady," Lawrence spat, pulling out his gun and badge.

Portia just looked up at the angry man hovering over her. His nostrils broadened as the hot air came from them. Then everything went black.

"I need my lawyer!" Stevenson yelled, drawing the attention back to himself.

"You're gonna need a doctor if you don't shut up," Lawrence threatened, looking over his shoulder at the beautiful woman lying in the street. The crowd gathered. He used his cell phone to call for emergency assistance.

Portia was filled with many emotions, but relief at seeing Detective Miller standing in the hallway was not one of them. She wanted to slug him again just for being there.

"Are you okay? I didn't mean to dust you out like that. I mean, it's not like I had much choice," he said, starting the apology awkwardly.

"I'm not hurt," she lied, shoving past him, holding the ice pack on the back of her head.

"You shouldn't get involved in police business," Lawrence explained following quickly behind her. Finally, she stopped dead in her tracks. Spinning on her heels, she glared at him.

"Police business? Please, more like police brutality," she huffed. "Look, if you're scared I'm going to make some kind of formal complaint or something, well I'm not. If anything, I'd rather just cuss you out for being such a . . ." she looked around for a word to express her feelings about what had happened between them, and the best name to describe Lawrence for causing it to happen. Turning to him, she looked at him for the first time . . . really looked at him. His eyes were soft and caring, despite his gruff exterior; she caught herself giving in to the warmth coming from them. "I'm sure I have a concussion," she groaned, half out of the embarrassment she instantly felt. "If I'm left unable to dance . . ."

"You're a dancer. I could have guessed it. You're very graceful." Lawrence sounded like a schoolboy.

Just then, Reba came through the doors. "So you finally got that big head of yours cracked, eh?" she cackled.

"Please, Reba. I'm not up for it," Portia groaned, again placing the ice pack back on her head.

"Who is this?" Reba asked, directing the question to Lawrence.

The nurse walked by and handed Portia a prescription for pain medication. She glanced at the paper, and then at Reba and Lawrence, shoving it in her pocket without answering.

"Well, I suppose I'll get back to the streets where there are people needing real help," she heard Lawrence say before he walked out.

* * *

Real help, Portia thought, growing angrier and angrier each moment she thought about Lawrence Miller. The morning started out badly and only got worse for Portia. The trip to the ER took hours.

"And for what? To confirm that your head is as hard as I always thought it was," her cousin Reba chortled.

They pulled out of the parking lot on their way to Moorman University where Portia taught full time. Portia just smacked her lips—still stewing. The vision of the big cop blaming her for all his troubles just boiled her blood.

"What was his name again?" Reba asked.

"Who?"

"You know who."

"Oh, that cop I plan to sue? Oh yeah, I'm going to sue his ass off if this injury affects my balance or anything," Portia threatened with her finger pointed at her head.

"Okay, sista, but just remember you jumped on him, not the other way around. Besides, what injury? You landed on your fat ass and conked that big head," Reba said, smiling as they turned into the faculty lot. Portia knew she would be bothered by thoughts of Lawrence Miller—along with a nagging headache.

Already too late to save her second class, she stopped in to get her mail at the faculty mailbox. She noticed Ian Randolph, another of the part-time teachers. He, too, had stopped at his box, no doubt on his way to his class. She knew he taught a class about this time. He smiled at her, as was his usual manner, but today she wasn't even sure she smiled back. It wasn't intentional, but with a gorgeous cop to sue—yes, she had noticed Lawrence's good looks—she had a lot on her mind.

"How are ya?" Ian Randolph asked her. She barely

heard him and only nodded a response while looking through her mail.

Sure enough, there was a note from Julian. She ripped it open without realizing Ian was still standing there.

The note was from Julian asking her to meet him at the church when she got off work.

"Great, like I'm just doing nothing else," she sighed heavily. This day hadn't gone well at all. Her life could easily be described the same way—if she wanted to be so dramatic.

"Problems?" Ian asked. Portia pretended not to be as irritated as she was. The thought of Julian asking her to meet him as if all was well between them was exasperating to say the least.

"No, I . . . I just got a notification of debt that was higher than I thought. I'm not actually able to pay it," she lied. Ian's eyebrow rose with the choice of words she used. It was as if he read right through them.

"Perhaps you can work out a deal with the debtor."

"No, he's a bastard, greedy and unconcerned about my well being," she went on.

"Well, I guess you'll know better next time than to do business with the devil," Ian said, and then without further comment, walked away, leaving Portia stunned. Ian seemed to know her situation better than if she had told him herself.

CHAPTER TEN

Back at the precinct, Lawrence was fighting the mental distraction Portia Hendrix had caused. She was a strikingly beautiful woman in his opinion. Maybe not the type many men would find glamorous or even sexy, but she was fine by his standards. Her eyes were almond shaped; her mouth was pouty and perfect. She was tall, thin, and athletically built; yes, she was just fine by his standards. But it was time for work and Lawrence was forced to shake loose the thoughts of Portia Hendrix so he could focus on looking through the old murder cases. There was a link between the past and the present, and it was getting clearer and clearer with every hour spent scouring through them. Reading the reports of how Marvin Shackles, Sal Mendoza, and now the newest victim Deacon Fox, Lawrence knew they were all connected by the Appointed One—they had to be. Despite the obvious differences, no one could convince him they were not all connected.

"And what is so obvious?" Jim asked, taking a bite from his order-in dinner. It was Chinese. Lawrence hated when Jim ordered Chinese food, as he was allergic to half of the things on the plate and could never share in eating it.

"Well, it's obvious that Marvin Shackles was a cross dresser, a transvestite," Lawrence said, pointing to the pictures of Marvin's crime scene. "We have nothing to indicate that Father Fox was anything of the kind."

"I'm thinking he probably was the kind, or maybe he liked the kind," Jim interjected, showing his mind had been working on connections, too.

"What about this one, this Sal guy, no indication that he was the kind either," Lawrence said, picking Jim's brain further.

"But, look here . . . see anything interesting in this picture?"

"What besides all the blood? Ugh, what a mess this case is. Anything else we can work on besides this?" Lawrence asked, pushing the picture back from him, giving his eyes a momentary break from the gruesome pictures of the murder scene. "How can you eat looking at those?"

"Easy. Anyway, well, aside from the obvious," Jim began, after taking a big bite of something noodly off his plate, "the Bible, look at it, the way it's laid open on the table. It's almost as if he was either reading it or it was like, laid open on purpose."

Lawrence picked up the picture to get a better look, digging quickly in his desk drawer for a magnifying glass to get a closer look.

"You would think the case of a dead priest with his dick missing, next door to a gay dance hall wouldn't be this complicated," Jim remarked.

Lawrence wondered if he was being sarcastic or telling another bad joke. "I'll get this sent to the lab to blow up this picture. I want to see if maybe the page this Bible is turned to means anything."

Just then, a small, but well-built man, looking lost and afraid wandered into the room pulling up the drooping neckline of his large colorful top. Jim tapped Lawrence on the shoulder, pointing in the man's direction.

"Can I help you?" Jim asked.

"Yes. I want to report a murder . . . well, a murderer," the small man answered.

"Stop dancing, guy, and spit it out," Jim said, pulling up a chair for the young man to sit. He suddenly recognized him as the pretty man with the makeup and wig, from the scene of the crime. He was dressed a bit more casually today and looked a little different, more male. "What's your name?"

"Kyle. But my stage name is Kyla," Kyle said, showing his femininity immediately, glancing over at Lawrence to see if there would be any type of reaction. He got nothing from either man. "Yes, well I think I know who killed Father Fox. I think it was this guy who was calling him."

"First, let me start by asking how well you knew Deacon Fox," Jim said, reaching for a notepad.

"Not well," Kyle answered quickly.

"So how do you know somebody was calling him?" Jim asked.

"And if this person was calling him, and knew him well enough to be calling him, why would he do something like this?"

"Well," Kyle began before leaning in and whispering, "he was on the down-low, you know."

Lawrence immediately glanced at Jim, giving him an I-told-you type of glance, and then looked back at the feminine man. "Deacon Fox? The priest? He was gay?" Jim asked.

"Deacon Fox . . . he was my friend. I wouldn't say he was gay like that. You say it like . . . like . . . he was *gay*." Kyle rolled his eyes. "He was curious."

"You just said you didn't know him well. Now he's your friend. Which was it?" Lawrence asked.

"Yeah, and why didn't you tell us all this when we were there?" Jim asked.

"Well, because he is . . . was, um, a priest and well . . . too many folks around, and yeah, okay, so I knew him . . . pretty well, but . . ."

"And what? You were feeling some kind of loyalty?" Jim asked him, sounding a little harsh. "My God, the man was a priest. I mean, come on. You were 'friends' with a priest," Jim said, making the quotation marks around the word priest.

"Anyway . . . go on," Lawrence said, noticing Kyle's eyes and the look of slight intimidation showing. Kyle looked at him and smiled as if finding a little support in the big guy.

"Yeah, anyway, I think a woman killed him," Kyle went on, growing instantly animated.

"You think a woman did that kind of damage?" Lawrence asked.

"No, hired someone, like a hit man or something. I think there's a guy out there women hire to bump off gay men or something."

"As in 'Gay Blade,' you know—eliminator of all that's purely queer," Jim said, making quotation marks in the air again. Kyle smacked his lips and rolled his eyes as if Jim had let out the steam of his fantasy balloon. It was clear they were not making a love connection here.

"Wasn't that a movie or whatever?" Lawrence interjected. Jim nodded.

"I'm serious, guys," Kyle said, sounding snippy and tense.

"Yeah, okay, okay, so you figure this guy is ridding the streets of all the unpretty, huh? Making sure the gay line stays straight?" Jim went on, sarcastically using the word "straight."

Kyle frowned, and then reluctantly nodded, pursing his lips and crossing his legs tightly. "If you wanna say that."

"Maybe you should tell me what I wanna say," Jim said, practically growling.

Kyle went on to tell his story about the men who came into the Rainbow Room, and then after a night of carousing and swinging the "gay way," they would return to their regular lives, whatever those were. In the case of Deacon Fox, his life found him behind the pulpit. Jim and Lawrence listened on as Kyle gave his account of things: ". . . and well, I think that somebody is sick of all that *down-low* shit and is trying to rid the world of men who don't want to face their gayhood," Kyle explained, rolling his hands at the wrist. He then turned to Lawrence. "Men like you, for example, who pretend to be all macho and deep inside, would love nothing better than to—"

Lawrence stood, glaring at Kyle and then at Jim, who snickered slightly.

"I saw the way you were looking at me at the murder scene," Kyle went on, sounding as if it had been a black tie affair they had attended instead of a mutilation. "You were wondering, weren't you? Wondering if I was available. But see, I'm already dating someone and—"

"What are you talking about? I thought you were here to talk about the murder!" Lawrence blurted.

"I am. . . . Lawrence, is it? I read your card there on your desk. I am here to talk about murder; I was distracted by your aura, and well, I mean my gaydar is on and . . ."

Lawrence walked away with his eyes wide and a shocked-filled expression on his face.

"Look . . . Kyle, is it?" Jim began, talking in a low voice. Kyle had moved closer so as to hear him better—or maybe to flirt. Who could tell with Kyle. "You are headed for an ass whooping of major proportions if you keep that kinda shit up with my partner, okay? Now, stop playin' and tell us why you came in here, all right?" Jim explained flatly. "When was the last time you and the Father went to the confessional booth together? How you feeling now that he's dead? Did you kill him? Did you click out when he told you he didn't want to give up the priesthood for a little twista like you? Maybe it was somebody else he wanted more, one of the other queenies that work there at that little joint you work at. Since you know so much, who called us and told us where to find the dear Father Fox?" Jim asked, firing questions left and right.

Kyle gulped loudly and sat back nervously, showing embarrassment. "Sheesh, straight guys are no fun at all."

"You're damn right about that," Jim stately bluntly. "Now who might this woman be that you think had the ability to beat the shit out of an average sized man, tie him up, fuck him in the ass and then cut his dick off? What women do you know capable of doing that?"

"You guys are just way too uptight in here," Kyle said, as his eyes widened even more.

At that time, Lawrence came back to the desk. His expression was blank now, as if he had taken a quick walk and counted to one hundred and fifty. There was a moment of silence between them in order for things to calm down, and then Kyle continued. "Look, these men, they are pathetic—confused for the most part. It's like the hooded dudes back in the day. Half of them couldn't wait to get their hands on a piece of male tail come dark fall, am I right?" Kyle asked Lawrence, edging to the point of offending him again. "Well, Deacon was the same way—preached us all off to hell by day, but come night . . ." he looked at Lawrence, who said nothing in response, but his eyes told Kyle he'd better tread lightly down the road he was on—again. "Besides, I think those church guys think it's all fun and games to twist the scriptures the way they do, and frankly they don't bother me. I don't care what they say. It's just not serious enough to kill over," Kyle explained further.

"Well, somebody thought it was," Lawrence interjected.

"Apparently," Kyle went on, pulling out a cigarette and tapping it on his knee. Jim nudged him, drawing his attention to the no smoking sign.

He huffed and wriggled disconcertedly.

"So again, where were you during all of this?"

"Damn," Kyle gasped, having a hard time with Jim's line of questioning. "I was at the club. . . . Why you all up in my Kool-Aid?"

"You know I'm gonna check on it, Kyle . . . Kyla," Jim said. "You know I'm gonna ask every faggot up in that place where you were! So you better tell me."

"God, I was with this guy, okay? That's why I was going to talk to Deacon. I was gonna tell him that it wasn't going to work out with us, okay?"

"What's the guy's name?" Lawrence asked now, ready to take down the information.

"Oh my God, you're not going to talk to him, are you?"

"You bet your sweet . . ." Lawrence paused before saying the rest of his normal comment. He knew mentioning Kyle's ass in any way would start something he did not intend to finish.

"Stan . . . Stan Furbishon. He's a regular at the club; everybody knows him. Just ask. Matter of fact, ask Louise the bartender. He saw me smoking Stan in the backseat of Stan's car. Ugh, it was all dramatic. Louise and I got into it because Nala, my boss, doesn't allow that kind of thing with patrons, yada, yada. Louise threatened to tell Nala, ass kisser that he is. Like I care, because damn if Nala doesn't fuck whoever she can. Anyway . . ." Kyle fanned his hands as if speaking to others not present.

There was silence between the three men for a second as Jim and Lawrence gathered their thoughts. Finally, Jim spoke. "So," he began, clearing his throat, "what you're saying is that Deacon, the priest who was cut up in that church, was what . . . gay?"

"Well, not in the strictest way. I mean, he was a priest, for crying out loud, but if you ask me, being like all the way gay would have probably saved his sorry life. But no. He was bi-curious."

"Bi-curious?" Lawrence asked.

"Yeah, folks who preach against being gay all day long, yet the first chance they get they wanna try it out."

"And then?"

"And then if it's not what they wanted, they try to beat the hell outta ya like it's your fault, and hop back on the homophobic bandwagon they rode in on."

"So did Deacon Fox like it?"

"Who you askin'?" Kyle asked bluntly.

"I thought you said—"

"Shit, I was not even gonna go there, with his little ex-crack-head-got-his-ordination-off-the-Internet, Bible-misquoting ass. He was a freak with a lot of old baggage and deciding on a sexual preference was the least of his issues," Kyle huffed, smiling wickedly as if he'd gone a few rounds with Deacon recently about Deacon's orientation as well as ordination. "Like I said, I got a man, but hypocrites piss people off, ya know? And Father Deacon Fox was a hypocrite of the major kind. And that's why he was getting those calls—at least that's what I thought until he showed up dead."

"Did he ever tell you what the caller said?" Lawrence asked.

"Well, he said that some guy was calling him and threatening to kill him."

"So you think one of the other *guys* from the club might have decided to give Mr. More Hypocritical Than Thou a toss? Find out how far he'd go, and then got ticked off after the honeymoon was over and Father Foxy turns on him and starts casting stones?" Jim asked. Kyle looked at him quickly and then squirmed a little.

"You askin' if I think one of the guys who work at the Rainbow Room could have done that to Deacon?" Kyle asked and began to shake his head. "No. Like I said, Deacon was all blow, if you'll pardon my pun. But, I think you need to be talkin' to someone in his little *religious* circle." Kyle made quotation marks around the word religious.

"So, you have a lot of clergymen patronizing your joint?" Jim asked.

"You act like we discriminate." Kyle smiled wickedly

"Okay, then what about this Sal guy. You know him?" Jim asked, holding up the picture of what was left of Sal Mendoza. Kyle flinched but recovered well.

"Yeah, Deacon and Sal were friends. Sal came in from time to time, but suddenly he just stopped. I guess now I know why."

"What about Sal's wife? You know her?"

"Of course. Who didn't? She used to barrel in there about once a month and raise Cain, calling folks and their mamas out their names. We just thought maybe she convinced him to fly a little straighter."

Lawrence and Jim looked at one another. *Sometimes things drop right in your lap*, they both thought at once.

"You ever hear the name Marvin Shackles?" Lawrence asked, hoping to bat a thousand.

He didn't show Kyle the photo of Marvin, as it was more than obvious that Marvin's identity was unclear from the photograph. He was cut up so badly, that only a wife or mother could possibly know him from that picture. Lawrence was sure of that.

"Ohhh, Shackles. See, I knew you were a freak from the first time I laid eyes on you," Kyle said teasingly, hoping to lighten the mood a little. The day had darkened and so had everyone's attitudes. Lawrence's face distorted with instant irritation. "Okay, big boy. Calm ya nerves. No," Kyle chuckled. "No, I've never heard that name before. Why are you asking me?"

"Just hoping," Lawrence answered.

CHAPTER ELEVEN

Portia couldn't help herself. She wasn't about to pass up a chance to be with Julian a second time, she'd worked herself into a near frenzy all day, anticipating it, and now she truly believed she "needed" to see him, if for nothing else—spiritual healing. She was such a terrible liar and even more so when lying to herself.

She drove over to the church to see what she could see. Julian's car was parked in the lot. Having the key to the side door, she went in. Not seeing him immediately, she figured he was waiting for her in his office. Stepping closer to his office door, she could hear him on the phone.

"No, it's not going to go like that." He then chuckled. Portia had heard that kind of snicker before. He was flirting with someone. "Yeah, I like that. I told you: Kyla fits you. Nah, nah . . . never in public. No . . . meet me there, and we'll go where the evening takes us. No, I don't have any obligations; I'm totally free for the night. Well, wait, I might have a meeting in a few minutes, but that isn't gonna take long, I'll be there."

Portia had heard enough. She was fuming. The longer this went on, the more Portia began feeling his footprints leaving tracks all over her back—especially when she would allow herself to face the fact that she was still waiting for his half of her three thousand-dollar Visa bill—as agreed. The initial fling had flung and Portia wanted out. Of course, she had no clue how to end it. She was drowning. The first step would be to tell her cousin, Reba, the truth about the affair. All this time she had Reba thinking she was seeing a colleague from work. She told Reba she was seeing Ian Randolph, the math professor at the university where she taught. He was shy and quiet, but not someone she could be interested in—for various reasons. The first one: he wasn't Julian.

If Reba knew Portia was seeing the pastor of her church, surely Reba would slap her crazy, or rather, crazier. Portia knew she was caught up too deep in this mess. She had gotten herself into it before she could stop. Things went from church socials to Portia having dinner with him regularly, and within four or five weeks, she had agreed to meet him on the outskirts of town in a motel.

"I'm not really this way," Portia explained, sounding coy while covering herself in the large towel that hung in the bathroom. Julian had already climbed into bed and was waiting.

"What do you mean?" he asked.

She looked around the room, hoping the words would jump off the wall, hoping the phone would ring and it would be his wife, calling him home.

She knew better than this kind of sinnin'. She'd been taught better.

"I've only been with one other man—in my life," Portia admitted shyly.

"You're joking, right?"

"No, I'm not. I'm only thirty-two. I got married right out of high school—divorced soon after, went to college—"

"Oh well . . . I'll be gentle. Come on," he interrupted, sounding a little bored with her story. Portia always talked too much on a date. She mentally scolded herself and moved closer to the bed.

"What are you scared of?" Julian asked, pulling back the blankets, exposing his tightly packed body. He had a good build and Portia was impressed with his physique, but not quite prepared to see it all so openly and uninhibited. Rodney would always wait until the lights were off before getting out of his shorts, and if they made love during the day, they stayed under the covers while removing their underclothes.

"Take the towel off. Let me see what I'm getting."

A large smile came to Julian's lips as he climbed out of the bed and walked up to her, taking the towel from her reluctant grip. His eyes covered her body almost lecherously and Portia began to feel a bit strange standing there. But then he pulled her into his embrace and it was better.

"You're gonna use something, right?" she asked, feeling his erection pushing against her thigh. He leaned back, looked at her seriously, and then smiled again, leading her back to the bed.

He handed her the small package and lay back, fully erect.

"You can do the honors," he said.

Portia giggled nervously.

Julian liked to play games. Portia had heard about stuff like this.

Maybe this could be fun after all, she thought, while sliding the condom over his thick hard-on.

After she finished, he pulled her on top of him, entering her quickly. He was rough and talked dirty. There was no *way Portia felt 'loved' by this act of 'lovemaking'. She was being 'fucked' as Reba would say, in the purest sense.*

"Next time, we'll do some new things," he purred, kissing her behind her ear right before they walked out of the room. Her mind was still spinning—still unsure of what had just happened.

That was the first time, and she paid the tab for their little rendezvous. It went on like that once or twice a week—Julian rough and demanding, and Portia learning.

Finally, Portia told Reba about the affair—about the sex, leaving out, of course, the fact that it was Julian Marcum, the pastor of their church. Reba settled her mind on the style to which this guy—Ian—had chosen to sex her, explaining to Portia that for some men, that was just their way. But when it came to the issue about the money he owed her on her Visa card . . .

"You need to put a cap on that shit. Check please, pay da woman," she joked, with her palm outright as if waiting for money.

"I can't say that," Portia admitted.

"Then I say—end it," Reba barked. "End it now while you still have your pride and your credit rating."

Reba and Portia were first cousins, but more importantly, they were friends. It was being cousins that made her crass nature barely tolerable, and at the same time, it was the fact that Portia could count on Reba in a pinch that made them friends.

When Portia's dad died, Reba stayed with her for nearly a week. Helping her clean out his things, helping her attempt to give the old house a new feel—her feel. But Reba was married and had responsibilities elsewhere, and so their time together was usually limited.

"I can't just end it like that," Portia explained.

"Why, you liking it too much? His dick gold or something?" Reba asked, heading over the to the sliding glass door in order to enjoy her smoke. She stepped out onto the deck, speaking to Portia from outside.

"Reba!"

"I'm telling you right now: two bad words here—Visa and bill—yours," she said, with two fingers squeezed around her cigarette while she counted off. "And lack of commitment—his!"

"Please, and that's like *way* a lot of words," Portia groaned. She wasn't up to hearing her. "Besides, he told me his, um, job is really stressful and he can't commit right now—not until he gets his class schedule together," she lied.

"Oh, my Lord. And you believe that? Wake up and smell the lying, black nigga's ass; it's fulla shit," Reba said, her tone full of lecture. "You teach, too. How is his job more stressful than yours? Math is not that stressful. Two plus two, Portia—how hard is that?"

"Come on, Reba. I really like him. And how can I break it off? I see him every day," Portia went on, attempting to explain her predicament—lying all the while. Reba shook her head, taking another long drag off her cigarette, watching the wind take her smoke away.

"Oh, but off the topic: there's a dance troupe from New York coming through, and girrrl, I'm gonna audition for it," Portia bubbled. Reba grinned and then after slipping her cigarette between her lips, she held up her hand for a high five, which Portia gave her happily.

"Now you're talking good words," Reba said. "Dancing, not all the other shit. I'm not interested in that other shit. Dancin', yeah, that's what happenin'," Reba went on, flicking the finished smoke off the deck. She then reentered the house and headed back to the bubbling pots on the stovetop.

Yes, Reba was right; nobody had time for Julian's bullshit anymore. She needed him to pay her what he owed, then she could call it even . . . call it over.

Portia didn't really care that Julian wanted to keep their affair a secret; that wasn't the issue. And considering she hadn't told Julian her plans to skip town as soon as she landed a dancing gig, it wasn't as if they had real ties to one another. But now he was lying to her for no reason, cheating on her with no just cause. She wanted out.

This wasn't a pop tune, and breaking up just couldn't be that hard to do.

CHAPTER TWELVE

The phone that was used to call in the lead to Deacon Fox's body was traced to a cellular owned by a woman named Jenessa Jewel. Jim and Lawrence headed out to ask her some questions, arrest her, and then charge her with murder. It was going to be just that simple. The landlady had let them in after seeing their search warrant.

Glancing at his watch, Lawrence sighed at the sight of both hands sitting on the twelve. Another day in the life of homicide cops was about to start.

Working vice had never been Lawrence Miller's cup of tea. As a matter a fact, he hated it. The lines were always so thinly drawn on who was guilty and who was merely making a living. Homicide, at first glance, seemed so much easier to define, but as they stepped into Jenessa Jewel's apartment, still heavy with the weighted air of violence and death, Lawrence had to wonder if it was really any better.

This year starting off the way it had was not helping at

all. Here it was still new and fresh, and already they were on body number four in their precinct alone—Ms. Stevenson, her lover, a bi-curious priest, and now this woman, Jenessa Jewel. All police work was getting to be so gruesome. So many lives affected by the actions of others. *Why can't we all just get along?* Lawrence thought to himself while looking around.

"Okay, something is really wrong here," said Jim, bringing Lawrence's mind back to the scene. Jim was coming from the bedroom.

"What do you mean?"

"I think you better come take a look."

Entering the room and stepping reluctantly over to the bed, Lawrence quickly assessed the scene. The victim was female, her arms and legs were hogtied with duct tape, leaving her totally vulnerable to the apparent sexual assault that had been clearly perpetrated on her by the blood on the bed sheets. "What's that in her mouth?" Lawrence asked leaning forward, trying not to be too caught up in the blank stare of her eyes, wide open in death, a death that was clearly a few days in. They knew that by the smells and the rigormortis. Pulling out his cell phone, Lawrence called the murder in.

Before the hour was out, the apartment filled with police and the investigation began. The photographer quickly handed Lawrence a Polaroid. "Looks like maybe two or three days," he said in his casual tone, the one Lawrence always knew him to have. This wasn't their first murder scene together. It was strange how all of this was starting to seem like a social club, everyone addressing each other by first names, sometimes ordering takeout if the scene looked like one that would take hours to go over. Yes, strange as it seems, Lawrence felt as if he had just entered The Twilight Zone social hour.

"That's what I'm sayin', and that there is a dick," Jim said calmly, pointing at the picture over Lawrence's shoulder.

"And what's this smell?"

"Formaldehyde, and there's a sign of forced entry, but the door wasn't locked; it just looks like maybe the perp bogarted his way in after she opened the door," the uniformed officer said as he came into the room.

His observation was noteworthy. While he spoke, he, too, acted as if the male part peeking from her lips was not an odd sight. A commotion began in the living room and Lawrence and Jim hurried in to see what it was. The tall womanish figure with the big hair was ripping away from the two officers that were watching the front door. The strength she appeared to have was tremendous, or they were just caught off guard. Lawrence prepared himself for the impact if she made it to where he was standing. She was distraught and nearly hysterical.

"Jennesssssaaa!" she bellowed. Her voice was deep and manly sounding, catching both Jim and Lawrence off guard. "What's happened? Oh my god!" she went on. "I just saw you the other day! Oh my God, what's happened?" Lawrence was confused now, seeing the large hands flailing.

"Calm down," Jim said, addressing what he thought to be a distraught woman. "Who are you?"

"I'm his best friend," the mannish woman cried now. "My name is Flacca Flacina," he went on.

"I see," Jim went on, sounding altogether serious.

"What's happening? These brutes barely wanted to let me in. I had called—been calling for a couple of days. Today when he didn't answer I was like, damnit, I'm coming over and seeing what's what, and now I'm here and I see all this."

"Wait, wait . . . why do you keep saying he? Who are you looking for?" Jim asked.

"Jenessa. I don't know his former name, but he goes by Jenessa. Just like I gave up Ruben when I faced my true self," Flacca explained, dabbing his eyes in the corners with the tissue he pulled from her bag.

Ruben, a.k.a. Flacca, was dressed in a short skirt that exposed muscular legs, no socks and boat shoes. He wasn't unattractive, yet, not real soft around the edges. Now that Lawrence looked a little closer, it was easier to tell Flacca was a man.

"So, Jenessa is male?" Lawrence asked, joining in.

"Of course, we all are. I mean, we aren't friends like intimate friends, but like, he told me he was male, and I mean . . ." Flacca looked instantly confused. "Yeah, I've known him like two months, ever since we started dancing together. She's a him," Flacca stately flatly.

"And where is that?" Lawrence asked, taking over the questioning while Jim stepped back toward the bedroom. "The dancing, I mean."

"The Rainbow Room. We're exotic dancers, male strippers . . . What's happened? Won't someone tell me?"

"Do you know if we can find your friend? Did you know if he had a roommate or maybe a . . . another . . . friend?" Lawrence asked keeping his thoughts straight. He had a billion questions for Flacca, but for right now, he was trying to get to the main issues at hand—the resident of this apartment versus the dead woman in the bedroom.

The coroner had arrived. Flacca just about lost it when they rolled past. "Oh my god! You're gonna have to tell me something before I flip," she warned.

Lawrence decided to get the body identified if possible. It was obvious this was not Jenessa, so maybe Flacca knew the woman who had been found on the bed, and then Flacca was going to have to do some serious talking about where Mr/Ms. Jenessa was. Lawrence had some questions for that guy, and if he looked anything like Flacca, he was gonna have many. The main one being his familiarity with a priest named Deacon Fox.

"Hold on, guys," Lawrence said, leading Flacca into the room.

The large drag queen gripped Lawrence's arm tightly. He caught himself glancing at the large hand before catching Jim's eye. He already knew what Jim wanted to say. Slowly Flacca approached the bed where the sheet covered the victim. She braced herself for the unveiling.

"What the hell!" Flacca exclaimed when the sheet came back. "That's a woman."

"Is this or is this not Jenessa Jewel?"

"Well, I don't know now. I'd say yeah. . . . I mean, that's definitely his tattoo, but . . . damn, this is a woman. . . . What's that in her mouth? Is that a fakey or a snakey? And what the hell is that smell?" Lawrence was hoping Flacca would notice the appendage and maybe have some ideas about how it got there. "What the hell is going on?" Flacca exploded. "Are you telling me all this time that Jenessa was a woman?"

"Okay, we need to roll this up if your done here," the coroner interrupted, handing Lawrence the rest of the Polaroids taken. "We'll have the rest for you later, but I can say now, she's been dead a while."

Slowly they moved the stiffening body from the bed to the gurney where a body bag was waiting.

"Would you like to come down to the station with us and make a full report?" Lawrence asked Flacca.

"Certainly."

"Do you know who we could contact?" he asked then,

thinking maybe Flacca would know some of Jenessa's relatives.

"Damn, I didn't even know he was a woman, so how would I know who he . . . no, she, knew in her real life? Obviously she was in some major incognito," Flacca said, chuckling sadly and glancing again at the body on the gurney, framed under the plastic body bag.

"Detectives!" one of the officers called. Lawrence and Flacca followed the voice into the living room.

"Look, Ms. . . . uh, Misterrr . . ." Lawrence stammered now after standing with Flacca for a few more moments, while the body of Jenessa moved past them.

"Ms.," Flacca said, sniffling sadly, yet making sure a little flirt came through.

"Yeah, right. Um, I'll have one of the officers take you down to the station where you can leave a report. We need to know the last time you saw Jenessa and your relationship, stuff like that."

"You mean, like an alibi?" Flacca asked nervously.

"Just a report for now, I mean, unless you think you need an alibi."

"So, you won't be the one . . . drilling me?" Flacca asked. Yes, Flacca was definitely flirting now. Lawrence scowled, knowing Jim had overheard, despite his seeming preoccupation with searching the apartment. Jim heard everything. He was a good detective.

"No," Lawrence answered quickly, turning her over to one of the officers who immediately walked her outside.

Walking into the kitchen where Jim had gloves on and was going through Jenessa's purse, Lawrence was preparing himself for the harassment over Flacca's statement. Instead of taking advantage of an easy opportunity, Jim showed total focus on the purse's contents. "Well, it wasn't a robbery," he said, pulling out a wad of bills, over five hundred dollars worth in large denominations. Pulling out her wallet, he went through the contents. "Oh daaaaamn!" Jim gasped.

"What did you find?"

Holding up the badge of Detective Rachel Williams, a.k.a. Jenessa Jewel, Lawrence knew immediately this case was going to be more complicated than ever.

And considering the phone that made the call that led them to Deacon Fox's body was sitting right there in clear view on Rachel Williams, a.k.a. Jenessa Jewel's kitchen counter, they now had a bigger problem on their hands than just a psycho who enjoyed the game of catch me if you can. They had a cop killer.

CHAPTER THIRTEEN

It took more than five hours to go over Jenessa's apartment. This whole case was getting very messy and taking up precious time that Lawrence could have been spending home alone in his apartment sulking. It was six a.m. and he'd not been asleep in over twenty-four hours.

The body.

The phone call from her cell phone.

The well-preserved penis in her mouth.

"And frankly, I don't think it's the Father's, which leads me to wonder who else is missing one," Jim blurted, thinking aloud. He, too, was showing signs of sleep deprivation now.

"Well, Marvin Shackles and Sal Mendoza for two."

"What in the hell was she doing there?" the chief asked, still waiting for the call from Rachel's superior.

"Apparently pretending to be a man," Lawrence answered, rubbing his tired eyes.

"What about our witness or suspect—the drag queen."

"I haven't had a chance to speak with the officer who questioned her . . . uh, him, yet."

"Well, hell, what's taking you so long? Is she here?" she yelled. "You can't just hold her . . . uh, him here." It was obvious that the murder of an undercover cop was not a good thing, and this case was gonna bust wide open as soon as the media got wind of it. The chief was tense. She had called them in her office to discuss where they were on this murder case. All Jim and Lawrence's other disconnected cases had been quickly farmed out and this case, the Venus Murder case was to be their baby. "So don't fuck it up!" she warned. She wanted to make sure they dotted all their I's and crossed their T's. "I mean, if you got something saying that *Flicka* person killed our little cross dressing detective, Rachel Williams, also known as . . ." the chief picked up the file and read from it, "Male impersonator, Jenessa Jewel, then make an arrest. If you think we have a serial killer on our hands, cut Flacca slash Ruben Howard," she read on from the quick report Jim had taken right after they returned from the scene. "Just say it. Say something, damnit, so I won't get eaten alive when the press gets here," she said, slamming the report on her desk and marching out of her office, leaving Jim and Lawrence standing there. "Be ready for a briefing when I get back."

"I thought that's what this was?"

"No, I called in somebody who can add a little insight on this madness. A interdenominational religious whatever-they–call-'em person. She . . ." the chief turned back to them, stood, and smiled wickedly. "She'll be able to cast at least some light on why our victims are tied together by the Bible, albeit loosely."

"She?" Jim uttered under his breath.

"What is she, some kind of female Ghandi?" Lawrence added in the same tone, as they both watched the chief leave their first floor pit via the elevator, no doubt headed to the cafeteria on the second floor.

* * *

Jenessa, a.k.a Rachel Williams's true legal occupation was kept under wraps in the press conference. The chief worded everything she said carefully, especially all of her answers to the reporter's questions. Flacca had not revealed to the officer taking her report that he was any the wiser that Jenessa was not only a female wearing a prosthetic penis, commonly known on the street as a fakey. Flacca also appeared to have had no idea Rachel was a cop. She had an alibi for the time of the murder. The cabbie was reluctant at first, but seeing the gravity of the situation, soon admitted to having taken up Flacca's time that night, so she was let go. This would buy them a minute, at least, to eliminate some last minute change of game rules on the part of their killer. For surely if he was a serial killer, perhaps Jenessa Jewel would have made a match, but surely Rachel Williams did not.

The news began blasting the Venus Murder on every channel immediately after the report finished. It was interesting how the media managed to tie the murder of a black priest named Deacon Fox and to the murder of the cross-dressing stripper named Jenessa Jewel together with the murders of Marvin Shackles and the self-ordained minister Sal Mendoza nearly a year ago. There was a leak in the precinct, that was clear, as the chief had said nothing about the year old murders in her televised press conference a moment or two earlier.

"Very interesting," Lawrence mumbled. "But then again, all the killings were within a block or so of that club, not the best place for a preacher to be hanging out and spending time."

"Why are they calling it that?" another officer asked, watching the report that played on the small television that hung on the wall over their heads.

"What?" Jim asked.

"Venus Murder. Why?"

"Don't you know about mythology?" Jim asked.

"No. Why don't you enlighten me?" the officer smarted off, thinking maybe Jim really didn't either.

"Venus—Aphrodite," Jim retorted. The officer shrugged slightly and Jim continued. "She was born when Uranus got his genitals sliced off and thrown into the sea. There's some kind of perverse connection with that and gays. And well, it's kinda confusing, but anyway . . ."

"Yeah, anyway," the officer said, turning back to the television report, "but the guy was a priest. You'd think they'd give it like some kinda holy name or somethin', like the one you guys use—Unholy Murders. Yeah, I like that better."

"So what we got?" Jim asked Lawrence when looking over the freshly delivered lab reports as well as another thick file of cold cases that had been filtered through for similarities. They were hoping that perhaps the Appointed One had started his run even further back than Marvin Shackles and Sal Mendoza.

Lawrence sighed heavily at the thought that filled him with mixed emotions. "What's up with the Rainbow Room?"

"Don't know, but I'm sure we're gonna love it when we find out."

"What about your lady friend—Fucka?" Jim joked, choking on his own words. Lawrence nearly growled. "I mean, Flacca."

"Don't start, Jim. Do not start!"

Jim laughed even harder. "Maybe we need to get him back into the interrogation room so you can, um, how did he put it . . . drill him. Dang, you're such a stud; first there was Kyla and now, our friend, Flicka. And you had the nerve to wonder about me."

"Drop dead, Jim. I'm leaving. I've had it and I'm tired. I'm going to bed."

"You can't leave. Chiefy promised us a guest speaker when she got back." Lawrence groaned, slamming his jacket back onto his chair. Just then, the phone rang. Lawrence answered it roughly, just as the chief stepped from the elevator into the pit.

"I know you are not the priest—he's dead. But still I need to confess. Besides, I can't trust the clergy these days—not really. Not with all their bad actin'."

"Who the hell is this?" Lawrence asked. Jim's interest was immediately piqued.

"I might as well tell you now that you finally made it over to Jenessa's place that I was sorely disappointed in how long it took for you to take care of that matter. I was losing sleep over here." He sighed heavily into the phone.

"We did our job. What's it to you how long it took to find her?" Lawrence asked, motioning for the nearest phone to be tied in.

"Yeah, *her*. Optimum word being *her*." The caller sighed heavily again. "Well, as hard as it's been to face, when I killed her, I realized immediately that I killed the wrong person."

"What?" Lawrence said, fanning Jim frantically, urging him to conference into the call as well.

"You heard me. I killed the wrong person. That woman," the caller chuckled slightly, "tricked me into thinking she was a man. I would have let her go, but after realizing how she had tricked me, I figured I needed to kill her for that. But problem is, now my whole assignment is off and well, I don't know what to do."

"What assignment?"

"Oh, I'm sorry. This is The Appointed One. That was rude of me not to re-introduce myself. I just figured you knew me by now, that we are friends, colleagues, at best."

"Why did you want her to be a man?"

"I didn't want her to be a man. Don't ever accuse me of being a sodomite again. I'm not."

"But he sodomized her," Jim mouthed. Lawrence shook his head wildly, hoping Jim's words were not heard. He didn't want The Appointed One to hang up.

"I'm a Christian man with good values and morals, thus my need for confession."

"But killing people, isn't that wrong to you?"

"Not when you are appointed."

"Appointed?"

"I just wanted to let you know that I didn't mean to kill that woman. She was supposed to be somebody else. I was tricked by Deacon Fox, and I'm pretty upset about that, but then he was a tricky one, leading me to believe he was sexually involved with Jenessa like that. However, suffice it to say, that's not why I killed him. But his little game didn't help matters."

"Why did you kill him?"

"You see, sinners come in pairs. There is never an instance where only one person is wrong. But now, with Jenessa, this whole assignment is off. Well, anyway, I'll figure it out and get back to you. I'll have to call you from another phone because I think the GPS is on this one. It looks kinda newish, so don't bother trying to trace me to this phone; I'm gonna chuck it."

He hung up.

Jim and Lawrence stared at each other for a long time before they, too, released the line. "Can we find out whose phone he called from? Like he said, get the location on that phone," the chief ordered after hanging up her end. She had tied into the initial phone line after stepping from the elevator. She began snapping her fingers, as was her mannerism when excitedly handing out assignments. People began moving hurriedly about, making things happen. She liked seeing people hop to her command. "Whew . . . well, I guess that answers a couple of questions," she said to Lawrence and Jim.

"Except one—who in the hell was he really tryin' ta kill?" Jim asked.

"Maybe the real Jenessa Jewel," Lawrence answered.

CHAPTER FOURTEEN

Everyone felt the presence of something dark at the club. Every new face was closely scrutinized. Nobody left the club alone after closing.

"I hate being scared," Kyle admitted while he and Flacca rode home on the bus.

"Ask yourself: do you really know anybody anymore? There was a time when what you saw was what you got, and now look," Flacca explained.

"Just because you can't tell a real dick from a fakey, shit, don't be including me in with the deceived. I knew Jenessa wasn't a man. I could tell by her hands and feet," Kyle lied. He, too, had been duped, but there was no way he was going to admit it. "Did the cops ask you about Sal or Marvin?"

"Noo, what about them? Are they dead or something?"

"Nunya. I guess you didn't need to know," Kyle said as if he had been made privy to cop business.

"Well, with all they did ask me, you would think I killed her," Flacca sighed.

"Well, she was raped. Maybe you—"

"Pu-lease," Flacca said smacking her lips. "I'm a virgin, honey," he added.

"You ain't never had a woman?" Kyle asked, not keeping his voice down as much as he could have.

A woman sitting on the bus across from them looked over. It was obvious she had just realized the two of them were male. Kyle and Flacca were the prettiest men working at the Rainbow Room. Many thought they were female at first glance.

"What you need to know?" Kyle asked the woman rudely, jerking his neck from side to side. Flacca patted his knee. "You wanna know if I have a dick? The answer to that is none of your fuckin' business," Kyle went on. He was fussing at the woman as if she knew him.

"Kyle, stop it. You are such a fire starter," Flacca said, trying to quiet him down a little bit, "always trying to fight. I'm sorry, ma'am. My girlfriend here is just a little tense. With a killer who cuts off dicks on the loose and all, we're both kinda tense," Flacca added, sounding dramatic. The woman's eyes widened, and she got up and quickly moved to another seat as far from them as she could get.

"I'm just so sick of people always acting shocked when folks come out real with stuff. I mean, yeah, this is real, baby!" he said, slapping his padded chest.

"You wish. I only know one real pair of titties," Flacca mumbled under her breath. The both of them, knowing whose were being referred to, burst into laughter.

"You ever seen her tits? You ever seen 'em?" Kyle asked, now referring to that person.

"I told you . . . I'm a virgin," Flacca said. They laughed again.

Just then, Kyle's cell phone rang. Looking at the number, he winked at Flacca, holding up a finger while answering it in his most seductive voice.

"Yes, I called," answered Kyle, and then losing a little bit of the sexiness and sounding more like a woman with attitude, he went on. "I've had a hard week, too. You wouldn't believe what's been going on in my neck of the woods—no, forget the woods; it's been a jungle," Kyle went on. Flacca shook his head. "Meet you?" Kyle asked out loud. Flacca, again, shook his head, only this time with more determination and she mouthed the word "no." "Well, I have to take my lady friend home first, and then I'll come where you are," he purred. "Okay." Again, Kyle winked at Flacca and then hung up.

"So who is your new beau?"

"Can't tell you. Nigga is on the down-low," Kyle admitted.

"Why do you bother with men like that?"

"You have got total nerve. Like Deacon was a straight up—"

Flacca shushed him loudly. "Nobody is supposed to know about that. I told you. It was only one time!"

"Yeah. Well, don't let mutha find out," Kyle said, jerking his neck again and smoothing on his lip-gloss. "She'll have ya nuts."

"What would you do if you caught your man cheating?"

"My man would never cheat. Hide his shit, yeah, but cheat, never," Kyle admitted unabashedly. "And if he did, it would be seriously on." Kyle snapped his fingers twice and jerked his neck.

"Folks don't kill over a little thing like cheating, do they?" Flacca asked.

"Hell, that's what I think happened to Deacon. I think it was a lover's spat. I think some nasty female was all jealous and—"

"Couldn't no woman do that to him."

They both sat for a moment, pondering similar thoughts about Deacon's murder.

"You thinking what I'm thinking?" Flacca asked.

"Yeah, and it *is* scary."

"So you think you know who the killer is, too, huh?"

"I ain't gonna say a word." Kyle twisted his lips and looked over his fresh manicure.

"Umm-hmm, me neither," Flacca concurred, crossing her long legs, and then, as if drawing the same conclusions, they both sat quietly for the rest of the ride.

"I've got to eat something before I go see my boo."

"Your boo. Who isn't your boo?" Flacca teased, to which Kyle turned, sticking out his behind toward him tauntingly.

"Kiss that, why don't cha."

Catching a cab, Kyle left Flacca at the bus stop, while he headed to the meeting place he and his boyfriend, Julian Marcum, had set up.

CHAPTER FIFTEEN

Ten minutes to make a decision on whether The Appointed One was a serial killer was ten more than they needed. But that was how long the chief gave them before calling them to the briefing.

Jim and Lawrence reluctantly entered the briefing room. They were met by five other detectives chosen to work along with them on this case in one capacity or another. Two were females who no doubt would possibly end up, if needed, working undercover as Rachel Williams did when acting as Jenessa Jewel. It had come out that Rachel Williams was on a drug case. She was undercover attempting to weed out a drug lord who frequented gay bars. Perhaps she spent just a little too much time in the Rainbow Room. Perhaps she blended in a little too well, or maybe she stepped over the line with Deacon Fox. Those little details were not obvious and maybe not important at this moment. However, from what Jim and Lawrence finally deduced, she had been mistaken for a man, and this had caused her to be killed along with Deacon Fox.

The chief walked in next with a tall, statuesque, womanish person, which was the term Lawrence had taken to saying and thinking. "You can never be sure anymore," he told Jim. She had her hair pulled back in a long ponytail and wore a long, tan colored, dashiki-type garment that covered her body. It was clear she wanted to look sexless, and it worked.

"Hello, everyone. This is Reverend Marilyn Huber. She is a psychologist and minister who specializes in working religious medicine. She's like a shrink for the clergymen, for lack of a better way to describe it, right? Would that describe what you do? Oh, and she's also a specialist in serial killings of this kind," the chief said. The Reverend Marilyn smiled slightly and nodded, and then moved mellifluously to the front of the room. She only glanced at the photos that hung on the wall of the victims. Her feelings about them did not show on her face.

"Hello, gentlemen. I suppose you all want to know if there is some kind of connection between these religious men." She fanned her hand over the photos, stopping briefly at Sal and Deacon, and then fanning on to Marvin and Jenessa. "And these men." Lawrence picked up on that move right away. Perhaps she had been told who the clergy were and who the cross dressers were. Either way, Lawrence watched the woman like a hawk. She gave him a vibe that he couldn't shake, and it wasn't a good one.

"The connection is simple: they are men, confused men, who, despite their jobs, all have one thing in common—their sexual deviances," she began, and then over the next fifteen minutes, she explained the burden of responsibility often carried by clergymen and why so many led secret lives. The discussion was enlightening, but less than helpful, until she finally began to discuss the possible make-up of their suspect, The Appointed One. She apparently only had a few minutes with the file but seemed very astute on the subject, down to the very eerie details.

"As with many serial killers, who pride themselves on their work, this one is a killer who believes his work is ordained and that he has as much right to do what he does as these men he kills have to do what they do, more so, actually. My thoughts are that your killer was abused by a clergyman, possibly due to some type of physical defect that caused the clergymen to believe he was weak or unable to defend himself. So I think your suspect has some kind of physical impairment."

"Don't you think that would be impossible? I mean, how can a handicapped person do this kind of damage?"

"Easily, Detective Beam," Marilyn answered, causing Jim to instantly become un-nerved. It was clear this woman was overtly observant, as Jim had not been formally introduced to her, yet she knew his name. "Not all handicaps are incapacitated; they just often appear to be to the ignorant. Often when a person has a weakness in one area, such as sight, the body will overcompensate, in the area of hearing, for example. The same goes for your killer. Where he is lacking in one area, trust me, he clearly excels in another."

"So are we looking for someone with supernatural strength, or like . . ." Jim went on.

Everyone laughed.

"No, Detective, I'm sure your killer looks just like you or me," she said, catching Lawrence in a death grip stare down. Lawrence felt his hair rise on the back of his neck. Yes, this woman made him terribly uncomfortable.

"Wait! Nothing's been said about the cross dressers. Why is he killing the cross dressers?" Jim asked now. "And do you think he's taking any other trophies—short of the penises?" he asked.

Again, there were snickers in the room.

"Oh, the other men, they're sinners, and as you have found in your investigation, are tied in with the clergymen. And yes, I'm sure he's taking trophies, other than the appendages, as you gently put it. It's simple really," Marilyn concluded. Jim, as well as others, nodded at the obvious deduction.

"Okay, so let's get to work on this thing. The Appointed One is out there, and we need to get him before another man of the cloth dies, people," the chief announced now, again snapping her fingers. "Jim, Lawrence, I have a long list of 'to do's' for you today, and I want you right on it." As if noticing both of their countenances fall simultaneously, she glanced at her watch. "Tell you what: go home or whatever you do, and then we'll get on it when you get back, okay? I've had Drew and Smith do some preliminary stuff."

"Great," Jim said, admitting to exhaustion. Lawrence was still a little disturbed by the woman, who by all appearances, could have just as easily been a Shaman priestess. He watched her as she stood staring at the photos of the victims on the wall, as if admiring fine art.

"People like that bug the hell outta me," Lawrence told Jim as they both left the station house. "What kind of Reverend is she? Did you see the way she looked at me? She's spooky and—"

"Here we go again, Mr. Closed Mind at work," Jim fussed, knowing this was the start of another diatribe on Lawrence's belief system.

It was hard to turn off the job when it was time to go home, but Lawrence tried to do it as best he could. He wasn't like Jim, who seemed to just keep going and going. Even in the car on the way to his house, he did nothing but discuss the case and the possibilities.

Pulling into the convalescent home where his mother now lived, he parked and went in. It was Friday night, and he knew he could be somewhere else, but his mother needed him, and he was a good man.

"This is my job, too," he said in an undertone.

Reaching her room, he took a deep breath. He always needed to do that before going in. He needed to accept everything. Turning the corner, he found her room empty. Stepping back into the hall he ran into a C.N.A.

"My mother? Where—"

"Oh, Mr. Miller, she's at the social in the community room." She looked at her watch. "Oh my. Yes, it's late. But then again, your mother was having a blast last time I checked. You may want to come back tomorrow," she said, patting his shoulder and continuing on her way.

"Tomorrow," Lawrence heard himself say. Another day of work, but tonight was just another night of lonely.

On his way out to his car, he contemplated calling Hannah. He needed her. "Stop lyin'," he chuckled. "You want her body."

Looking at his phone, the case came back to his mind. The Appointed One had Rachel Williams's cell phone. There was only one place he could have picked that up, and Lawrence knew he and Jim would be visiting that place again.

The thought of the drag queens un-nerved him, "Surely, I'm not homophobic," Lawrence said to himself, thinking of what Jim called him. "Every man is equal, even when he's wearing a damn dress." He blew out hot air and shook his head. "And if one of them even thinks about trying to get next to me I'll—" *Deacon Fox, Rachel Williams, Jenessa Jewel,* he thought. "A priest and a gay stripper? Or was it a priest and an undercover cop?" Lawrence shook his head, unable to fit the jagged pieces together while fighting with his racing thoughts on his own sexuality. "Either way, one of those combinations got them both killed."

CHAPTER SIXTEEN

"Stop, Julian," Portia snapped, moving quickly from him, scooting far to the other side of the large bed. Portia was angry, not just at him, but at herself, too. Right after hearing him on the phone, she went in as if not having heard anything, suggesting they go to a hotel. She had plans to break up once they got there. She had her entire game plan set, but as soon as Julian undressed, she was unable to follow through and again ended up in bed with him.

"What?" he asked, his voice holding on to heavy seduction. His voice scared her, hearing it in the darkness. He sounded so eerie. What he was doing to her felt so . . . perverse.

"I told you I don't like all that freaky stuff. I told you that," Portia said, swinging her legs over the side of the bed. He groped for her, only to have his hand slapped away.

"I'm leaving," she said, sounding quite decided—a little late, but still decided. She had yet to figure out why she met him tonight. Maybe to get the money he owed, maybe because he had paid for the room, maybe to say good-bye. Whatever the reason, she had ended up in bed with him and it just wasn't going the way she planned.

"Portia, baby, I'm sorry. You're just so . . . so fine, and well . . . I mean, you bring out the animal in me," Julian admitted. "Makes me want all of you, every mole every hole . . ."

"Well, some holes are not for exploration. We talked about that," she interjected quickly.

The small lamp that sat on the table next to the bed clicked on. Portia had hoped to stay in the darkness a while longer, at least until she had found her underwear. Standing there naked made her feel so vulnerable.

Julian was on his knees, still erect. His face, though sweaty from the heavy foreplay, was hypnotically handsome. His eyes promised good sex, and she had to turn away to keep from falling for it yet another time. Being with this man was like a drug for her. That's what she compared it to, for surely she couldn't think of anything good or healthy to compare her need for him. She watched him remove the torn condom and open a fresh one.

"Look, I'll start over," he said, while replacing the useless latex, rolling on the new one slowly. She couldn't help it. Her lips dried and she licked them. He noticed and spread his arms wide open, offering her a taste. He knew she was not into oral sex either. Reba called her a flat-backer and maybe it was true. Sex wasn't a game, not really. It was hard enough indulging in it without any marital direction, but all this exploration was just not her thing, not without commitment anyway. Julian wanted anal sex—nearly insisting on it, tonight. He'd all but forced the issue. She had promised herself that only a husband would have that privilege. Only a husband would be granted all the consensual treats shared by two who were truly dedicated to one another. With Julian, it was straight missionary, despite how rough he got sometimes and always, always with a condom. Julian was good about that rule; Portia insisted on protection. But once or twice, the condom had broken. That was how she had gotten away with lying about being pregnant. It was just punishment for treating her as if she was some kind of cheap whore.

What was she thinking coming here? It's over. She had promised herself. He was cheating on her with somebody named Kyla. She had more than enough proof. Why was she even here!

"Come back to bed, baby," Julian pleaded, his dancing, caramel colored eyes, changing colors—lightening, as he grew more and more amorous, as his penis headed upward another inch or two. "Okay, I'll come to you then," he said, climbing out of the bed, backing her toward the wall. She soon felt its coolness against her bare backside. Julian lifted her leg high while kissing her neck, face, and mouth hungrily as he pushed himself into her with hard, quick thrusts.

Portia's mind wandered.

"I bet he never stops to think about how I can get my leg up here like this," she thought, as her mind stopped on every thought except pleasure.

A lifetime of dance lessons had made her very limber. Her mother would often find her in her room in the middle of the Chinese Splits—just down there in that position reading a book, unconcerned with the painful look on her mother's face as she imagined herself attempting *something like that*.

Just then, Julian exploded inside her, blocked by the latex sheath that separated them. He trembled slightly and then slowly lowered her leg. She held him around his neck, thinking about how it would feel to dance with him . . . really dance. Not just this sexual rumba they did here in this dimly lit hotel room, but in a ballroom . . . or a ballet.

"Where's your mind, baby?" Julian asked, grinning. She smiled at him, thinking to herself, *I came to break up with you . . . that's where my mind is..*

"Who's Kyla?" she asked smugly.

"Who?" Julian asked, pulling from her slowly, keeping everything intact. He grabbed a towel from the chair and headed for the bathroom.

"Did you hear me?" she asked.

"Yes, I heard you. She's a woman from the church I've been counseling. Actually, I've been praying with her. She's sickly. So you going home from here?" he asked, quickly changing the subject.

"Of course," she lied—again.

"How did you know about Kyla?" he asked.

"I overheard you on the phone talking to her when I came into the church."

"Oh, spyin' on me now, huh? Wow, you're acting more and more like a wife every day," he said, teasing her with the idea that she might be one day. She'd given up on that lie, so his telling it at a time like this was borderline perverse.

Glancing at her watch, she thought about Reba. She was waiting. Portia made a date with Reba for dinner, and she had now officially stood her up for Julian.

"Julian, I need some money for my Visa bill. You've been promising for weeks, now, to reimburse me," Portia began, bolder than usual. Julian noticed. He sucked his teeth in mild irritation.

"I didn't stop at the bank before coming. I uh, didn't think there'd be a fee," he smarted sarcastically. Portia grew immediately angry. This was getting old.

"Look, Julian," Portia began, only to have him walk

past her and back into the bathroom. She followed. "We had a deal about these hotel rooms," Portia explained, her tone firm and unyielding.

"You have a house. We could go there," Julian said, turning on the shower. Portia showed her anger now, shaking her head vehemently.

"You have a house, too, and a pretty big one, I might add. I wonder how your congregation would feel about you having and them having not!" she yelled.

"Keep your voice down. What the hell is that supposed to mean? Don't threaten me, Portia," Julian growled through gritted teeth; however, his attempt at intimidation wasn't working tonight. Portia had too much at stake. Maybe it was the life she wanted as a professional dancer, or maybe it was her infatuation with this man, Julian Marcum, coming to an end. Whichever it was, she wasn't going for this weak argument—his attempt to turn things around on her.

"No threat, Julian—more like an overdue promise," Portia said, leaving the bathroom and sitting on the bedside. She could shower at home, she could sleep at home, and she could be herself at home. Bottom line was, she was getting the hell out of there. Julian stepped in front of her, hovering with the towel still wrapped around him. He had turned off the water. She looked up at him and his menacing expression. The silence was thick between them.

Her imagination soared, picturing him grabbing her by the hair, dropping the towel and forcing her face into his crotch.

Instead, Julian squatted. He placed his fingertips together, making a pyramid against his full lips before he reached out with one hand and stroked her face. She felt herself flinch, though she wasn't really afraid of him.

He was strong.

He worked out.

Vanity had him doing everything to keep his looks up. And if he went off on her, he could break her bones. She knew this. Preacher or not, he was a man and human—very human.

Jacki often told her, being a dancer is like being an athlete: you have to be strong; you have to stay strong to be good. Portia believed that, and she would hold her own if Julian went off.

"Can't we come to some sort of agreement?" he asked.

"What are you talking about? You promised . . ." Portia began, only to have Julian shush her to silence. He closed his eyes like a parent who was losing patience with his child, but trying as hard as he could to hold it together. Any second she thought he might tell her to "quit talking back."

"I know what I said, Portia."

Julian reached into his pocket and retrieved his wallet. Inside the folds were three crisp, one-hundred-dollar bills. He pulled them out and fanned them in front of her.

"Let's play a game first," he said, with a wicked smile creeping onto his lips.

"What kind of game?" Portia asked. Julian's hands then wandered, tugging on her nipples, before he moved in on her.

Portia never asked for oral sex. She knew she would never want to reciprocate, and therefore never asked for it.

"No, Julian," Portia protested, only to be shushed again as Julian pulled his lips from her lower ones.

"Just be quiet," he whispered. His eyes were at half-mast as he laid her back on the bedspread her legs wide, and again lowered his face. With quick flicks of his thick tongue, he nearly drove her to an outburst of pleasure, shoving his fingers in and out of her, and then again sucking on her pulsating mound until she could feel herself swelling, moistening with readiness. Julian, again, grew wild and unrestrained—licking her, biting, dipping his tongue deep inside her. He moaned as the sounds of his pleasure-filled praises filled the room, and soon she found herself in harmonic accord with his primal song and calling his name repeatedly.

He then lifted her hips with both hands, urging her to thrust her hips harder and harder toward him as his tongue acted in place of his manhood, thrusting deep, swirling and investigative. She was nearly overcome with euphoria. With his teeth lightly closed on her, he hung on her clit, sucking it firmly until she screamed with pleasure, pulling hard on his ears.

"God . . . !" she cried out as her orgasm burst from her body.

For the first time Portia understood what the word slave meant. Julian, in just that instant, had become the master of all her desires. She was angry, yet too far gone to fight it.

Before she could recover, Julian was free from the towel and climbing up on her, pushing his thick erection between her lips. The pleasure of his hardness in her mouth was overwhelming, as she no longer could sort the sensations she felt when he moved into position to bury his face between her legs again while she had his stiff member in her mouth. While he sucked on her clit, she wanted to scream, but he filled her mouth to capacity, sexing her oral cavity as if that was where his penis belonged—deep thrusts that nearly choked her, yet, wanting this to end was not a thought to her.

Suddenly, he was pumping his hot, bitter emission into her mouth. She immediately pushed him off her, gagging. Realization hit her hard as tears poured from her eyes while she choked and spattered, running into the bathroom, sobbing in her shame.

After a short while, she heard the door to the hotel room close. She waited a little longer, until she was sure he was gone, before coming out.

A thousand dollars lay on the bed.

This had to end. She was nothing more than his whore.

This had to end.

CHAPTER SEVENTEEN

The buzz was heavy. When he got to work, Flacca had told everyone what he'd gone through at the police station the other day. "I thought they were gonna throw me in the clank-clank for murder. My God, they are like hot on this case," he exaggerated. "I all but had to call my attorney."

Deacon Fox was dead and so was Jenessa Jewel, who had turned out not only to be a woman, but also a cop.

"You don't have an attorney, lyin' heffa," Kyle huffed, knowing that Flacca was exaggerating. He'd been to the police station, too, and they hadn't tried to arrest him. Besides, he surely had more information than Flacca could have possibly given them. "Why was Jenessa here undercover? What was she looking for?" Kyle then asked, allowing his natural curiosity to come out.

"This is California. Everyone has an attorney," Flacca said with a bull-like snort following the comment.

"Break it up, queenies," Louise, the bartender, said. "Bottom line is, we got a killer out there, so I suggest we buddy up. No sense in taking any chances."

"Why?"

"Because both victims were associated with this place here, and now they are both dead. I'm sure the cops think one of us did it and that one of us is a killer. That's bad press, boys, in case you didn't realize that, and having the press down on our asses is not a good thing," Louise went on, pointing at Kyle and Flacca. "And I strongly suggest you not be running ya lips to the cops."

"It's gonna be blame a queer week—again," Flacca agreed with a smirk. Then, as if a profound thought cleared her brain, she blurted, "Why in the hell would we kill our colleagues or our customers? My goodness. Does that sound like good business?" Flacca said, sipping the cocktail that Louise sat before him.

"With all that down-low mess, you know they are going to blame us for all their little social problems," Louise explained further.

"Again," Flacca concurred.

"Please, he came in for those reasons and more," Kyle said boldly.

"What other reason? Counseling? Please, Deacon was as much a priest as you or me. Besides, wasn't he and Na—" Flacca began to question.

"Everybody back to work or leave!" Nala, the owner of the club snapped, descending the stairs from her upstairs loft. No telling how long she had been listening.

"Oh, hey, Nala," Louise said, grinning as if not having shared in the gossip session. "Been hearing the news about those killings, and well, it's just freaky, isn't it? Two people we know, both killed within a day of each other. Creepy . . ." Louise pointed the last comment toward Flacca, who squirmed nervously.

"People get killed every day," Nala retorted abruptly.

"Not like that," Louise mumbled, wiping down the counter.

"I'm surprised the cops and cameras haven't been here yet," Kyle said. "I mean, I'm ready for it." He fluffed his long wig, which most thought was his natural hair. In reality, Kyle's hair was cut short to his head.

"Yeah, right," Flacca spat. "It's not fun, Kyle. It's not fun at all. Them cop guys are scary as hell. I told you what they did to me. They all but accused me of killing Nessa, or whoever she was. I was like—" Flacca's mouth hung open as he bugged his eyes, making a goofy expression of surprise.

"They'll get here soon enough, and when they do, you guys better smile pretty, play dumb, and dance your asses off, because clientele is gonna start thinning out, and so are your checks. I promise you that," Nala explained flatly, moving quickly past them and into her office. She slammed the door.

Picking up the phone, Nala returned her friend Jacki's call. Jacki had told her about a young woman in need of mentoring. Jacki hadn't called in a while, and Nala missed her. But then again, Jacki had things going on. "Who doesn't?" Nala mumbled, waiting for Jacki to pick up. When there was no answer, Nala left a message, assuring Jacki that she would be glad to take on Portia Hendrix. That was the name Jacki left on the machine when she called earlier in the week.

Nala waited at the door, hoping that Flacca and Kyle would leave. The club didn't open for hours, and surely Kyle and Flacca had only stopped in to shoot the breeze and take advantage of the free drinks Nala offered during off hours to her employees. Not many took advantage of the offer, as most of the employees had lives and jobs, unlike Kyle and Flacca. They seemed to have nothing else going on outside of the club. It was sad in a way, but then again, maybe that's why they were her best dancers and moneymakers. The club was their life.

Nala remembered her days as a moneymaker. She was always top billing. She knew how to work her stuff like nobody's business. The memory made her smile.

Locking the door, Nala turned on her stereo. The music moved her to the middle of the floor, where she began to dance. Slow at first, and then faster as the beat dictated her next move. Slowly she began to strip, until she was nearly naked. Pulling on her hardening nipples, she licked her lips seductively in the mirror before bending over, gyrating her hips in a circular motion, and holding her butt cheeks far apart as if inviting a visit. The music ended, and after slinging her thick tresses back, she stood, giggling loudly at her own act.

"Damn, girl, you making me horny," she told her reflection, before playfully slapping her own hind end. "I need a pole in here."

She missed having a lover. She missed the closeness and intimacy of having just the right person in her life. Sliding from her panties, she stared at her body in the mirror, examining what she felt to be the most beautiful anatomy anyone on earth could have. Smoothing her large hands over her breasts, she puckered up and blew her reflection a kiss.

Just then, the phone rang. It was Jacki. Still naked, she answered the phone. "Hello darrrrrling," she said, sounding seductive and playful.

"What's your problem? What—or who—you smokin'?" Jacki replied.

"Please, you're just jealous because I work around all these gorgeous men."

"Oh my God, the day I'm jealous of a woman working with a bunch of queers, you'll know something." Jacki laughed. "I still don't see how you do what you do, but hey, to each his own.

"Yeah, true," Nala said, spreading her legs wide so as

to get a good view of her private parts in the mirror. She loved looking at her body, feeling it. She began touching herself intimately.

"I see you got my message."

"Yeah, I did. I was hurt. I can't believe that's all you called for. We used be so close."

"I've been busy, Nala. You're such a drama queen," Jacki told her.

Nala held back vocalizing how she felt as she touched the most sensitive areas on her body, causing pleasure to come up. "Aren't we all?"

"Busy or drama queens?"

"You're the one who got mad about such a stupid thing," Nala said, giving in to her orgasm quietly, licking her lips while enjoying the feeling.

"I was dealing with a lot of shit and you just didn't seem to care. It's just that simple. Friends care. Let's move on. Now you. My understanding is you got somebody over there killing your patrons," Jacki said flatly.

Nala, finished with her self-pleasing, slid into her robe, "Yeah, you read the paper or saw it on the news? Anyway, damn, if it's not truly the worst time for it. I mean, true, it's never a good time for murders and shit, but damn, I finally got this place on the map and blam, folks start getting killed right across the street. Suck rocks."

"You still serving a mixed crowd?" Jacki asked.

"Yeah, I think so. It's hard to tell sometimes," Nala said, laughing loudly.

"Girl, you are a trip." Jacki laughed.

"Good to hear you laugh, Jacki," Nala admitted now. There was silence between them.

"It feels good to laugh. Tell you what: I'ma come by some evening and spend some time with you, like old times."

"Oh? Old times?"

"No, get it out of your head. Not all the way back." Jacki laughed again. "I'm not getting on that stage! Never . . . never."

"Okay, but you're the one who said old times."

"Please, that was another time, another crowd, another life. Don't get it twisted," Jacki told her.

"Trust me, male or female, my crowd will always appreciate a nice ass," Nala told her, again giving herself a quick glance.

"Well, not mine."

"Suit yourself. The drinks are cheap, and frankly, I miss your ugly face."

"Back atcha," Jacki laughed.

CHAPTER EIGHTEEN

The week had passed slowly. It was Friday. The Appointed One hadn't called in over forty-eight hours, but his presence was ominous and Lawrence knew he would get active again soon if they didn't start getting a little closer. But everything about this case dictated a move in reverse, back to the older cases. Lawrence just knew the answers were there and he was determined to prove it.

Lawrence and Jim knocked on Ms. Shackles' door. She was a slender, quiet looking white woman. Lawrence was caught a bit off guard, having read the report and knowing that Marvin Shackles was a black transvestite. This meek looking woman just didn't seem the type to be married to a man like that. He had already presumed whom he would find behind the door. Some big, loud, bodacious woman, with maybe some gold teeth and surely a lot more attitude. But again, he was wrong about the pieces of this puzzle. He wasn't used to being wrong so often, and it was starting to drive him crazy.

Ms. Shackles invited them in and immediately opened

the conversation about her late husband. It was almost as if she had rehearsed her lines, or perhaps it was that she had been down this road so many times it was by rote she went down it again today. They didn't even need to ask many of their standard questions, as she was a faucet ready to drip. Lawrence and Jim had read the report, and Ms. Shackles was nowhere on the suspect list. However, so many little things were missed in the investigation. Lawrence and Jim just figured they'd see what might come out of a little "visit" with the widow woman.

"No, the police just sort of dropped it," Ms. Shackles told them, sitting down with her cup of tea. "You would have thought with such a terrible, terrible crime, they would have dug deeper." She caught a glimpse of the clock, noting the time. She didn't want her son to come home while these people were there discussing the horrible murder of her husband. He had never been told the truth about it all.

"Frankly, I don't know the truth about it all," she admitted. "My husband was a decent man, but the report says he had been intimate with . . ." she paused, "another man prior to the murder." She spoke calmly, never missing a beat in her mild cadence, never giving way to much emotion.

Jim cleared his throat, catching Lawrence's attention. "Did this surprise you?" Jim asked, keeping his tone even while he wrote down the notes.

"I told them they were wrong. Well, I screamed it," she chuckled, thinking back to her hysterical response to the insensitive investigator, who insisted that her husband was homosexual. "He wasn't, you know."

"Of course, but you see, Ms. Shackles—" Lawrence started.

"Mrs. Goldberg . . . I've remarried," she interjected.

"Already?" Jim asked before he could catch himself.

"Ahem." Lawrence cleared his throat and allowed the information to settle before continuing. "You see, just recently, there have been two more killings that seem to be related to your husband's."

The former Ms. Shackles' eyes glazed over, as if just hearing that other men had been mutilated took her mind to some strange place. "And you think there is a connection? You think this killer might have killed my Marvin? And now you think that some sick psycho killer who preys on . . ." she paused.

"Preys on what? Homosexuals, cross dressers like your husband?" Jim asked bluntly.

Suddenly Ms. Shackles burst into tears. "Like I say, my Marvin went to school right here in the city," she began after a moment or two of regrouping. "We married, and well . . . life was very, very simple. I mean, sure, before we met, I think Marvin's life was a bit different from the one we had together, but you would have to ask his brother about that. Marvin was far from a churchgoer before we met, and well . . ." she chuckled, at the apparently fond memory of the only Marvin she wanted to remember. "But when we married, he changed his life a lot. He was planning to become an ordained minister."

"So you're saying that your husband was studying to be a minister?"

"Yes," she answered. "He was taking lessons in counseling and personal life coaching from this minister across town on the east side, a Sal something or other. Spanish man, very nice, very sweet," she said with a trembling voice. "Mendoza. The police had many questions for me about Father Mendoza, too. I had never met him—only spoke to him over the phone, but still, it was almost indecent what the police were implying about that poor man. They found him dead a day or two after my Marvin. It was very sad." Ms. Shackles' face flushed red as she shook her head in shame and turned to stare out the window again. She regrouped, quickly regaining her dignity. "Father Mendoza was a sweet, sweet man."

"Yes, sweet," Jim said, trying to hold on to his seriousness. "Mrs. Shackles, I mean, Goldberg, the investigators working the case, did they ever come by and let you know . . ." Jim paused, trying to get the question out right, "if they located your husband's . . ." he stammered.

"Where his penis was? Are you trying to ask me if they ever found it?" she asked flatly, returning back to the woman they had met when they arrived—subdued and completely controlled. "No, and we hated burying him without it. I especially hated to do that, seeing as how he was quite fond of it."

Jim cleared his throat and coughed to keep from laughing.

"Ms. Shackles, you mentioned Marvin had a brother. We never read in the reports of a brother."

"He was in jail when Marvin died, so he never really came up in the questioning. But he's out now, and I'm sure he got a bevy of information about Marvin. They kept in contact often while he was incarcerated."

"Do you know where we can find him?"

"His name is Darius Shackles, and no, I'm sorry. I've only heard from him once, since my Marvin died. He came looking for money or maybe something of Marvin's to keep. Who knows, but all Marvin had of value was a wedding band, and well, that was missing, *too*. Besides, I'd remarried and cut off that part of my life . . . short of answering questions for the police." That comment had a sting, and told Lawrence and Jim it was time to leave.

"May we come back if something else comes up, and we need to ask you anything else?" Lawrence jumped in, handing her his card.

"I don't know what else I can tell you, but if you feel the need to come back, fine, but please call first," she said, showing them to the door.

"Too?" Jim said under his breath as they stepped off the porch. Lawrence couldn't keep the chuckle back.

Jim and Lawrence pulled into Burger King after leaving Ms. Shackles' house. They were about to make a visit on Ms. Mendoza as planned. However, the news of Marvin Shackles having a brother derailed them. Jim made a call to the station to get one of the other officers assigned to the case to pick the brain of the cute girl who ran the research computer. "Maybe you can get more out of her than what you tried to get last Saturday, okay?" Jim told him, and snickered. "Yeah, Darius Shackles."

Lawrence looked over at his partner and shook his head. "Do you ever stop?"

"Stop what? Having fun, living, enjoying my life? No!" Jim answered bluntly while looking around at the sights and eating his french fries.

"I'm just saying, we are homicide detectives, we deal with death and murder every day. It's like . . . bad what you do. You have no respect for the dead, or the living sometimes. You just treat everything like a joke."

"No, you can't tell me that it wasn't funny, listening to Ms. Shackles. She was trying so hard not to go off, not to just start puking her guts about how nasty she felt realizing her husband was probably wearing her panties the night he died. You can't tell me you didn't think it was funny, her talking about—his dick was missing, oh and his ring, too." Jim's voice rose to a falsetto. "Come on, man, that was hilarious," Jim said cracking himself up again.

Lawrence tried hard not to laugh, and in doing so, he just showed more and more irritation—aimed at himself but shown mostly toward Jim.

"Anyway, man, you just need to get laid. You've been around death so long you've forgotten what life feels like."

"Whatever."

After tossing their packaging, they headed out to Ms. Mendoza's place.

"Sure, me and Sal were having problems. We always had problems. And yeah, we fought some, too. I'd say we got physical but . . ." Sal's wife, Carmen, admitted. Lawrence and Jim sat side by side on her sofa, both trying to place the plain-looking man pictured in the file with the firecracker this woman appeared to be. Her Mexican accent was strong, but her English was perfect. "You see . . . I'm not like this . . . how do you put it . . . intellectual person, or whatever, but I do know that Sal had baggage, and that was why we had our troubles," she said. It was like day and night coming from Ms. Shackles' house to this one. The women were so different, yet their men were ironically similar. When they arrived, Carmen had been more than happy to let them in and spoke openly about the investigation that went on when her husband was found murdered.

"What kind of baggage?" Jim asked her.

"He had all these like . . . issues with sex and all that," she explained. "I told the cops that when they asked me last year."

"Issues?" Lawrence asked.

"You know, sometimes when like . . . a little boy is like . . . you know . . ." She winked, blinked, and shook her head, hoping the two officers would fill in the blanks.

Finally Lawrence did. "Molested? You believe your husband had issues from childhood molestation?" Lawrence asked, sounding like he was answering a jeopardy question.

She pointed at him, nodding. "Yeah, that. I think that

musta happened to him because he was always talking about stuff like that, and he was into like gay porn and stuff—the real kinky stuff, too."

"How kinky?" Jim asked. Lawrence cleared his throat. "I'm just asking. Was it simply run of the mill gay porn or like extraterrestrial gay porn or . . ." Jim explained, taking on her word whisker. Sal's wife chuckled. Lawrence was a little caught off guard by the two of them and how lightly they were taking the situation.

"I took a peek once and like, damn, yeah, it was kinky shit—considering he was a minister. It shocked me actually."

"So he was actually a true minister—priest, correct?" Lawrence interjected, trying to think back to remember if he read that in the report.

"Yeah, after he got out of jail he turned to God. He'd done a little time for drugs, and so I just figured while he was in the joint he got hooked on that porn stuff, you know? They get magazines and all that shit in there. . . . They can get that, ya know. Anyway, I figure he couldn't let it go, even with the Bible on his side, ya know? So I cut him some slack. I mean, it coulda been drugs still. But even still, after a while, he started to get outta hand with it."

"Out of hand?" Lawrence asked.

"I can't explain it. He was obsessed maybe . . . like he wanted to see those *people*," she made quotation marks in the air, "in person, and that's when he started going out—I think."

"Those people?" Lawrence asked puzzled.

"Yeah, those like, he-shes. You know. Cross dressers and stuff. He swore he never got up close to one, but I know he was curious about them."

"Maybe he wanted to give up Bible thumping for a little booty hump," Jim began, and again Lawrence cleared his throat.

"One more question, ma'am," Lawrence quickly interjected, hoping she missed Jim's comment.

"Call me Carmen," she grinned, flirting a little bit. Lawrence thought he might have even caught her give Jim a little wink. She'd either missed Jim's comment or it didn't matter what he said.

"Carmen," Lawrence corrected, "have you ever heard of the Rainbow Room?"

"Gay club on Mather—the east side. Funny now that you think about it, huh? He tries his best to get as close as he can to the place and ends up dead right across the street from it. He played with fire I think."

"I understand that your husband was a counselor for others wanting to become ministers. Do you know any of your husband's colleagues or maybe names of folks your husband serviced, I mean, counseled?" Jim asked.

"No," she answered quickly, a little too quickly in Lawrence's mind.

"Well, thanks for your time," Lawrence said, standing now, readying them to leave.

"Is that all you want to know?" she asked.

"Yes, but if we have any more questions can we come by and talk with you again?" Jim said, following Lawrence's lead.

"Sure, but this case is open and closed. One of those faggots killed him. I think they might have killed Deacon Fox, too. I read about it in the paper. Sal knew that guy a little bit."

"You knew Deacon Fox?"

"No, I said Sally knew him. Anyway, I think those flamers got a hold of Deacon, too . . . another decent man of the cloth trying to help the community."

"I thought you didn't know. . . ." Lawrence began.

"I didn't," she interrupted. "I don't," she stammered.

"Why do you think that the employees of the Rainbow Room would kill an upstanding straight shooter like Deacon Fox and your husband, Sal?" Jim asked, hoping to trip her up a little more; she was starting to stumble so he figured he would just help her fall.

"You said it, I didn't. Straight shooters, both of them."

"No, I asked you why you feel the way you do about the employees of the Rainbow Room."

"Because them *guys* at that gay place was after him, you know? They were after my Sally. You know . . ." she said, again winking and shaking her head, "like in the Bible when them gay guys were trying to get at Lot's sons or sons-in-law or whatever. And my Sal was not gonna fly that way. He told me that story and said that those guys at that place were sodomites and that they would all burn in hell. Besides, he was a looker but not a toucher. That I know. He did it straight. And like, if he was a faggot I would know, and I would have . . ." She began speaking with conviction and a little frustration growing in her tone.

"You would not have been happy about it?" Lawrence asked, interrupting her. Carmen realized what she was being led to say and shook her head.

"I would have divorced him, not killed him. And I sure wouldn't have cut his dick off," she answered calmly. "You need to be talking to them weirdos at the Rainbow Room; one of them killed my Sally. I just know it."

"Okay, Carmen. I think that's all for now. Can we call on you again?"

"Yes, of course," she said, standing to match their actions, readying to lead them to the door. "Oh, but I have a question."

"Yes?"

"The property guys said that Sally's ring was missing, and I wanted it back."

"Ring?"

"Yeah, he had like a . . . like a wedding ring, you know, and it was pretty pricey—gold—diamond inlay," she said, reiterating her words by motioning her fingers around her wedding band.

"His wedding band was missing?"

"Yeah, his wedding ring is missing," she said, sounding a little odd, before opening the door to let them out.

"I'll talk to the property guys. Sometimes it's those little things we forget about until they come up missing," Lawrence told her before they left.

They were hardly in the car with their doors closed when Jim spoke out. "It's just the little things?" His words were chased by the laughter that he had held in for quite some time.

"See, I knew you were gonna notice that." Lawrence laughed.

"You think she's hiding something?"

"You know it."

"But seriously, you thinking what I'm thinking?"

"Yeah, just one too many connections with this Rainbow Room."

"Yeah, let's see if maybe anyone at the Rainbow Room has any year-old jewelry," Jim suggested, "or any other 'little things.' "

"Seeing as how Mr. Sally only looked and never touched," Lawrence added.

Just then, Jim's phone rang. It was Mark Brown, another officer working on the case. He'd gotten information on Darius Shackles. They weren't far from Darius's last known address, so the two men decided on a detour.

CHAPTER NINETEEN

What a week, Portia thought to herself after reaching her house. It had been just short of an emotional disaster.

Dropping her bag, she headed upstairs and dressed for a run. Her stress level was high, with so many things on her mind. This was not the way a love affair was supposed to feel. Guilt was eating her up. Love was supposed to hit you like a brick, wake you up, not make you sluggish and lazy—miserable.

Checking her pedometer while she jogged to the edge of the park, Portia saw she had cleared two miles easily and was planning on a third when she stepped from the curb.

The tires screeched as the car's brakes burned. Jumping back onto the grassy area, Portia's heart raced. "Watch where you're going, lady," the driver yelled at her as if she had dashed out in front of his car blindly.

Grabbing at her chest, she felt the hard pumping as fear charged with anger rose into her heart. It was he who was in the wrong, zooming around that corner as if he was on his way to a fire, and she was planning to let him know this as soon as she caught her voice.

Slamming her fist on the hood of the car, she cursed the driver. The door swung open, and her eyes locked on none other than the tall, handsome Lawrence Miller, and he looked angry—again.

"What are you doing?" he yelled as he rushed up on her.

"No, what are you doing? Trying to kill me again?" she screamed, closing the space between them even more. She glanced once at his partner, Jim, who turned his head away and looked out the window, while Lawrence went toe-to-toe with her.

"You must like getting knocked on your ass," Lawrence said to her, breathing heavily. It wasn't as if he was overweight, but she could tell being easily agitated affected his breathing, as his nostrils again flared and his jaw line tightened. His eyes darkened and the heat emitting from him nearly scorched her face, but she wouldn't back down today. She was fully cognizant today.

"No, Detective, I think it's you who likes attacking me." Portia needed to look away. His gaze was too intense and his eyes too intrusive, so she began dusting off her pink jogging suit as if it had gotten filthy in the near miss. She could feel his eyes following her hands up and down her body.

Does he want me? Is this what this is all about? She looked up, only to catch him like a child with his hands in a cookie jar. He quickly looked away. Yes, he wanted her. *Well, you know what, you can't have me,* she decided immediately.

"How's your head?" he asked, his voice turning soft and caring.

"It's fine," she answered. "No thanks to you."

"Good . . . I mean . . ." he began, stammering, "how about dinner sometime?" he asked.

"Are you crazy?"

"No," Lawrence snapped. Portia then noticed his partner nodding slightly. She couldn't help it. She smiled.

"You're smiling. Is that one for me?" Lawrence asked, sounding hopeful. Portia rolled her eyes and ran off.

"Well, okay. Maybe we'll run into each other again soon," he called after her. Portia turned and jogged backwards for a minute.

"You only get one more chance, Officer Miller, just one more."

"Okay, then I better make the next time a good one and hit you like I mean it," he called out. Her face twisted slightly as she nearly stopped dead in her tracks. "That's not what I meant," he corrected. But it was too late. Portia turned and ran off, shaking her head.

"Hit you like I mean it?" Jim repeated when Lawrence got in the car.

"Shut up."

Darius Shackles was not handling life well. It was more than obvious by the looks of his home, clothes, and expression when Jim and Lawrence finally got him to open the door.

"Why ya'll harassing me? I pissed in the cup yesterday, damn," he growled, refusing to move from the doorway.

"We're here to ask you about your brother," Lawrence explained. Darius was clearly a little confused but let them in.

"Sit down if you want to," he told them, pointing at a filthy sofa that didn't look very inviting.

"Nah, we'll stand," Lawrence said, speaking for both of them.

"I understand you were in prison when your brother was killed, right?" Lawrence cut to the chase.

"Yeah, but I knew he was gonna die, messing with them freaks. I just had a gut feeling."

"Freaks?"

"Yeah, freaks. The cops never asked me nothing about nothing, but I coulda told them all of it. I know who killed my brother, but no cops asked me."

"Why didn't you go to the cops and tell them?" Lawrence asked.

"You crazy?" Darius replied.

"Well, we're asking," said Jim sitting down now, showing willingness to get on Darius's level a little bit. Lawrence looked around for something clean enough and finally spied a dinette chair. Pulling it from the table, he sat down in it backwards, facing Darius. Darius didn't seem to notice or care much about Lawrence's rudeness.

Jim pulled out his notepad and pen. "Tell us who killed your brother."

"Hollap, you expect me just to start talking? Nah, don't work like that."

Jim leaned back, showing a little bit of defeat in his body language. He had hoped it was going to be like that. He really wanted to get out of there. He knew they were on borrowed time with The Appointed One. Just this morning, Jim awoke from a dream about the killer.

Jim dreamed he had just saved a man's life. The man had jumped from a second story apartment window into a swimming pool and was presumed dead when Jim quickly administered CPR and saved his life. Sure, the man cussed, swore, and promised to sue Jim for his efforts, but Jim felt good all the same about saving his life. In his dream, The Appointed One suddenly appeared and began challenging Jim's efforts. "What are you saving him for?" The Appointed One asked in the dream.

"It's my job," Jim had answered.

"Then we have it, a standoff. You save. I kill. It's the game we play." He burst into laughter.

When Jim awoke, he was springing toward the maniac.

"What do you want?" Lawrence asked Darius. Jim's mind came back to the dirty living room and the scruffy man who probably resembled his brother. Who could tell from the condition of Marvin's body when it was found?

"I want some protection."

"Protection? Like what, some condoms . . . what?" Jim joked. Darius laughed, too, thinking the comment funny. Lawrence was always amazed at what Jim got away with saying.

"Nah, fool, from the freak who killed my brotha."

"Tell us about the freak and we'll protect you."

"Well, you gonna need to call a ghost busta or some shit like that, because from what my brother told me, this freak is some kinda alien."

"Pardon?" Jim asked.

Darius broke into laughter. "Nah, I'm kidding. But you had to hear my brother talking about the people he met fuckin' around that club on the East Side."

"The Rainbow Room?" Lawrence asked.

"Yeah, that place. Funny you say that. Anyway, yeah, that place. He used to come see me and tell me about that place...said it was fun going there. Probably was until one of them freaks cut his dick off."

"So your brother . . . was he always drawn to places like that?"

Darius leaned back on the sofa as if thinking back to their childhood. His expression took on a certain sadness for a brief moment before he again broke into a smile. "I think Marv was always a little sweet, but he hid it well. When he married that white girl I thought he was turning his life around, ya know? He'd even gotten into the church a little bit."

"And had a child," Jim added.

"That's not his child; that was her boy. My brother ain't neva had no kids," Darius explained. Jim took notes. "That's what she was so mad about; my brother couldn't give her no kids. That's why she married up so fast after he died, trying to get knocked up. Ask me, she was cheating on him while they were married. Why else would a man leave a woman like that for some alien shit like my brother had gotten into?

"You keep sounding like him being gay is outta this world. A lot of men are gay," Lawrence said, to the surprise of Jim who just looked at him.

"You gay?" Darius asked.

Jim cleared his throat.

"So your brother was above and beyond the norm, huh?"

"Yeah, man, my brother told me he had seen it all . . . men being women, women being men, and all those in between. He said he met this woman who had a dick. That's when I stopped listening to his mess. It was . . . you know . . ." Darius laughed.

"Making you sick?" Lawrence asked.

"Nah, man, turning me the hell on; I'd been locked up a long time." Darius laughed long and hard.

"Did your brother ever tell you about Sal Mendoza?" Jim asked, after giving Darius a moment of reverie.

"Who's that?"

"He was your brother's mentor . . . a priest."

"My brother wasn't Catholic; we're Baptist. He didn't have need of no priest."

"So he didn't tell you he was studying to be a priest?"

"He wadn't studying to be no priest," Darius insisted. "Hey, was there a priest in the Village People?" Darius asked suddenly, as if he had an idea.

"No, there was a painter and a cowboy. . . ." Jim paused, thinking hard.

Lawrence didn't even want to argue the point as Darius and Jim discussed the identities of the group's members. It was clear Darius had told all he knew about his brother's lifestyle, and that was enough for them to decide on their next stop.

"I gotta go see my mother first," Lawrence explained. Jim looked at his watch.

"Works for me. Drop me off and I'll meet up with you later."

"Drop you where?"

"You know where," Jim smiled wickedly.

Lawrence could tell by that expression, Jim was going to hit his favorite haunt.

Portia Hendrix stayed on Lawrence's mind. He wanted to check on her, make sure she was all right, make sure she didn't have any kind of delayed reactions to almost being hit by a car. Truth be told, Lawrence just wanted to know if she would go out with him. Lawrence wanted a good woman—one who wore aprons in the kitchen, taught Sunday school, someone who would like cuddling. Portia looked like the cuddling type.

While sighing just a little, his ex, Hannah, came to his mind. She was a driven woman who had only succeeded in driving him away. She was a powerful woman, at least that was her goal, it seemed. She was unbending and unforgiving. Surely Portia was more compassionate than that. Look at how she had tried to clobber him for beating up Mr. Stevenson. Sure, she was wrong for that, but it was the thought that counted.

He turned into the parking lot of Jenner's Convalescent Home, then parked in the lot closest to his mother's room, which was next to the lobby entrance. Inside, the smell was always stifling. Old age and infirmities were all around and hard to look at. It was hard to place his mother among this, but she was old, and soon she would not be here for him to love and to love him.

I really do need a life, he reasoned after thinking about how pathetic his thoughts sounded . . . even to him.

His mother was up and dressed nicely. She was clean and otherwise okay. Lawrence was glad. He was paying a fortune for this place. The least they could do was take care of his mother while she pretended to take care of herself.

"Hey, Mama," he greeted. She smiled at him, then went back to her meal and afternoon talk show. "I thought I would stop by and see you," he said. She nodded without looking at him.

Her silent treatment bothered him. She'd been doing this more often over the last few weeks. Perhaps she was angry with him for allowing this to happen to her—to be put away like this. It wasn't his fault. He couldn't care for her anymore. She needed assisted living, and his siblings weren't going to do it. They weren't going to come to her aid when called. And how could he? How could he simply drop what he was doing to see about her.

"Lawrence," she finally said to him.

"Yeah, Mama?" he asked, thinking she was going to confide something deep and profound—settle his troubled mind and tortured conscience.

"What time is it?" she asked.

"Five-thirty, Mama," he answered.

"Oh, shoot. My date is gonna be here in a minute, and I'm up here greasin' up and looking a mess, chile," she answered, quickly sitting down her plate. She used her cane to shut off the power button of her television set.

"Date? Mama . . . what?"

About that time, an old gentleman, barely able to lift his feet, shuffled into the entry way. Lawrence saw his mother's eyes light up.

"Oh my, Ben. You're early," she said, patting her white curls in a girlish fashion.

"Well," Ben began, before pausing to sit carefully on her small sofa, "I didn't want to be late. You know how I hate missing the beginning of Oprah," he declared. Lawrence cleared his throat.

"Oh, Ben, this hea is my boy," she introduced. Lawrence stepped over and shook the old man's hand. He had a firm grip.

"Howdy." Ben smiled politely. "You got thangs to do?" he asked, telling Lawrence that he was now in the way and that his visit with his mother needed to come to an end.

"Uh . . . yes, sir. I think I do," Lawrence answered.

"This is the cop," Lawrence's mother announced proudly.

"Ohhh, the fuzz," Ben said, slapping his leg as if that slang term was once his favorite one to use. He musta been trouble back in his heyday.

"Yeah, so, uh, ya'll don't be up in here breakin' the law," Lawrence said, in an attempt at a weak joke. Both the seniors burst into loud, giddy cackles.

Lawrence knew then he had to get outta there. Before he reached his car, his cell phone jingled from inside his glove box. It was Jim.

"Where you been, getting laid? I was, but I guess that's really not important, now, is it?" Jim said, sounding curt and irritated. "Chief wants us back at the station. Remember, we're cops, and we have like . . . cop-work to do," Jim said. Lawrence rolled his eyes and tried not to allow any more thoughts of Jim's or his mother's sex lives to seep in. "Check this out—dude left this major VM on the Chief's personal cell. She wants us to hear it."

"So, is it just like her personal life gone bad, or is the voice mail connected to our case?"

"Who knows with her?"

CHAPTER TWENTY

When Lawrence and Jim got back to the station, the chief fanned them inside her office.

"Just got this," she said, picking up her cell phone, which was sitting on her desk. Her movements suggested she'd heard the message and quickly set the phone down in hopes that she was imagining the whole thing. Lawrence could see the sense of invasion she must have felt.

"It seems as though I owe you all an apology. I've caused such a stir with this Rachel Williams, a.k.a. Jenessa the freak, matter. Sheesh, you all act like no one ever made a mistake before," the caller laughed nervously. "Anywho, I figure the least I could do is fix things on my end. Therefore, I decided that I'd punish myself for fuckin' up like I did. Here is the deal: you find me before I kill the person I was trying to kill, and I won't kill anyone else, obviously. But if you don't find me in time, I'll have to kill the person I was trying to kill, and then kill an extra person—the equalizer as it were. See, that's what I need to do to fix my situation—equalize things. Now, if you're good cops, this

long-ass message ought to give you plenty of information and a good place to start in finding me."

"Great, that was very helpful," Lawrence said, noticing the number he called from was blocked.

"Yeah, but at least he gave us the new rules such as they are," Jim said.

"Extra person? What the hell does that mean?" Lawrence asked.

"That's what you guys have to figure out and pronto. And you can start by finding out how in the hell he got my cell number!" the chief growled, showing her feelings now by slamming the small phone on the desk. "Get the location of this fuckin' call and nail this joker. I've about had it up to my ass!"

"And such a nice one, too," Jim mumbled under his breath.

"Jim! Get out there and do your job!" the chief yelled.

Jim grumbled while shrugging back into his jacket, which he had removed when arriving to her office, and tucking his scraggly hair under his beat up hat—the one that reminded Lawrence of the kind Harrison Ford wore in that Indiana Jones movie. "Find out who he's gonna kill on purpose and then who he's going to randomly kill. . . . What, like before he kills them, or after?" Jim asked, sounding sarcastic.

"Who services your cell?" Lawrence asked the chief. He was ready to get to work on this crazy case.

"Sprint," she sighed, rubbing her head. "I've got all the bells and whistles, so I'm sure in there somewhere I have something that will make it easy to trace the call.

"Well, that's where we'll start. The least we can do is find out where the call originated," Lawrence told her.

"The very least," Jim mumbled.

* * *

Nala liked the nightlife. It suited her. She loved to dance and she loved the sound of glasses clinking together behind the shadow of music coming from a well-spun DJ. It was all so romantic to her. Besides, she'd been told too many times that she looked better under a dim light.

Such is the life of the unpretty, she thought to herself.

When she bought this place last year, she had hoped to bring a little romance back to this broken down dump. She wanted to breathe life back into the joint. She wanted romance. She wanted to settle down and find herself . . . and maybe find love.

Today had been a bad day; Nala felt lonely and alone, or maybe just anxious, as if something big were about to happen in her life.

"You're just a hopeless romantic, that's what you are," Louise the bartender said as if reading her mind while watching Nala move around the empty club. It would fill up soon, and Nala's mood would change. But for now, she looked filled with melancholia.

Noting the funny face Louise had, all full of pink freckles against her dark hair—poor wig choice in her opinion—Nala just winked her eye. Louise was different from the kind of drag queen she normally staffed at the Rainbow Room. He was one that had a separate life outside of here. Maybe that was why Nala liked him so much. He was her little touch of reality, normalcy. "Yeah, but to have romance you need a lover, don't you think?" she said to him.

"I hear ya," Louise said, wiping the counter clean.

Love. Nala thought about the first night she spent with a man she thought she loved. It was like a dream come true.

* * *

He looked lost and out of place, sitting there with his hands around that drink as if it were his last. He was dressed casually for a white-collar worker, open top button, no tie. His suit slacks—looked far from comfortable.

"Hi," she said, finding herself at his table.

"Hi," he greeted with a smile showing on his full, pretty lips.

She purred seductively. It had been a while since she'd come on so strong.

"I'm Fath—I mean, uh, Bill," the man corrected—way too late. Nala laughed and so did he. It was obvious he was married by the indention on his ring finger, but Nala didn't care. He was beautiful.

"Ok, Fabill," Nala said flirtingly. "Is that short for Fabio?" She giggled.

"No," he answered, shaking his head and showing total embarrassment.

"Are you lost, or did you mean to come here?" she asked, noticing his uptight appearance. He looked her over.

"I could ask you the same question," he said, noticing her full bustline and cleavage.

The ice was broken.

What came soon after their chance meeting wasn't really an affair, not by Nala's standards; where she was from, Nala was used to a lot more action than what she was getting from this man. The men Nala was used to could get past many of the issues this Fabill could not. And he had some nerve. Mr. *Fath-uh-Bill* had issues, even more than Nala did, if that was possible, and so their relationship was pretty close to being nothing more than two confused people thrown together in a big waste of time—in Nala's opinion.

They would sit and talk. Nala would tell him like it

was, and he would walk out claiming his ignorance as to why he bothered to come, and swearing upon his Bible and other dead ancestors that he would never return. But Nala knew he would, and it was true. Father Deacon Fox always came back.

There was something about their relationship that had him hooked—like a drug. It wasn't that he was so much attracted to her as a woman, even Nala knew that. But Nala could feel the neediness, the void in his voice when he would call, rambling on and on about good and evil, heaven and hell. He needed someone to vent to and she had been picked. Sometimes it would turn her stomach, and she would simply hang up. It made Nala sick to hear Deacon's stories of how he controlled people as if he had the right to, as if he had no flaws.

Nala hated churches as well as the hypocrites who attended and or presided over them, but she was hard pressed not to hate Deacon. Sometimes Nala wished she knew someone from his church, someone she could tell the bitter, ugly truth about their sanctimonious, holier than thou Father Deacon. She wished she could let all his parishioners know about his dark side. She wished she could have exposed what he did when he thought nobody saw him. And maybe in an odd way, she had. Of course, not many had tied his death with her club—not yet anyway.

It was funny, though. Nala felt very strongly about every aspect of Deacon—everything he stood for, everything he believed in. Deacon was wrong on all turns, but in a way, Nala felt sorry for him. His stories about his past and his regrets moved her. He was like a hurt dog—in *bad* need of being put out of his misery.

Nala's mind came back to the now. She thought about her day and her plans. Her friend, Jacki, had come by the other day, and after spending a little time, asked if she would take on a client of hers—a little wannabe star named Portia Hendrix.

Jacki had issues, but they had been friends for a long time, longer than Nala liked to think back to. Jacki was someone Nala could relate to on both sides of the coin. They'd met during a time when both of them had seen the worst side of human nature. They were drawn to each other and soon became inseparable. It was Jacki who pulled back first and Nala allowed it, thinking perhaps Jacki wanted more of a 'normal' life.

Normal—something Nala had yet to find.

She'd agreed to take on Jacki's client, thinking it would be fun teaching dance again. Nala hadn't danced professionally for years, only for her own entertainment or that of the gay patrons who came to her club. And those patrons enjoyed the show, not even knowing whether they were watching a male or female on the stage. But then again, at the Rainbow Room, it didn't really matter.

Dancing made her feel good, however—pretty, despite her physical imperfections. She had an ugly scar that covered one of her cheeks. It was a reminder of a dark time in her life—a time of betrayal and most unforgivable of sins.

"Ms. Nala, someone really sexy is here to see you," Louise called, drawing her attention to the door.

This was the second time Lawrence and Jim had been on this street. But this time they needed to accomplish more than tiptoe through puddles of blood. This time they needed to question possible witnesses about the murder in the upstairs church across the street. According to Darius Shackles, here was where they would find some answers. The blocked number that called the chief's phone was tracked to a cell phone belonging to the business account of the Rainbow Room.

Nala walked over to greet her guests, picking up her cocktail on the way.

"I'm Detective Jim Beam and this is my partner Lawrence Miller," Jim introduced. Nala shook their hands weakly, as if trying to protect a fresh manicure. "We're here to ask you about the incident across the street as well as a few other things."

"Yum, it's the few other things that could get really interesting," she said, flirting and giving Lawrence a quick wink.

Can I have your full name?" Jim asked, taking out his pad and pen, pulling the tall, exotic-looking woman's attention back to him.

"Nala," she said, sipping her drink.

"Nala . . . Jim paused, obviously awaiting a last name.

"Just Nala. You know . . . there's Prince, Madonna, Mother Theresa, and Nala."

"Ohhhkay," Jim responded, with a bit of attitude coming out. "And you're the owner?" he asked, already knowing the answer. The bill was in the company name with *Nala Nala* as the contact person on the account.

"Yes, I own this place," she said, as if about to add the expression, 'duh' after her words. Jim just smiled.

"And you live . . . ?"

"You are so wasting my time . . . unless you want a date. I thought you wanted to know about the incident . . ." Nala added emphasis on the word 'incident,' "and gather clues and information about the fucking assholes who come up in my club harassing my guests and killing my neighbors. I know that's where you're going with this.

"Did the killer come into your club, Nala?"

Nala rolled her eyes.

"Hmm, let me think back." She pretended to ponder the thought. "How in the hell would I know? Do they wear signs now? And where I live fits in there . . . where?" she asked, fanning her hand over his pad. Lawrence noted her instant defensiveness. "I'm sure you already know that I own this place and I live upstairs," she answered.

"Do you own a cell phone?" Jim asked, still holding the cool tone he'd taken with her.

"My cell phone?" She looked around and then shrugged. "I have no idea if I own a cell phone, and how that fits into this equation is a serious mystery to me as well. I mean, sure I own one, but have I seen it recently? No. I'm not a phone freak."

"Well, when you had a phone, do you remember who your carrier was?"

"Sprint? I guess? I haven't seen my phone in weeks. I think somebody stole it."

"Why didn't you call the police when you noticed your cell phone was missing?" Lawrence interjected.

"Call the police about a cell phone? Um, maybe because I figured the cops got more to do than go hunting down a cell phone thief, if in fact it was really stolen. Like I said, I hardly even use it. Didn't even notice it was missing until like the other day. It's ironic you even asked about it. As a matter of fact, where are you going with your questions?" Nala asked.

"We got a call from here, stating that we would find some answers to the murder that took place across the street. The calls came from your cell phone. So, suffice it to say that . . ."

"Well, Officer . . . Beam, is it?" Nala went on, sounding totally bored with Jim, his questions, and his attitude. "Write this down. Take my report. My cell phone is missing."

"Do you know Sal Mendoza?" Lawrence asked now.

"Little twerp, pretending to be some kind of minister . . . haven't seen him in a while. Why?"

"Do you know a Marvin Shackles?'

"Stinky little man, wanted with all his heart to be a woman—never quite made it. Wanted to work here . . . uh, no. Why?"

"So they both came here often?" Lawrence asked. Jim was taking notes.

"You married?" Nala asked, throwing the line of questioning off. Lawrence frowned. Jim looked up from his notepad.

"Ms. . . . Nala, look. We are trying to solve a murder case, and we think this establishment might be at the root of the murders. Ironic, don't you think?" Lawrence explained.

"Oh, I like you. You use big words," she flirted. "Look, Colombo, this is the city, the big, bad city. People die everyday, and they usually work somewhere, live somewhere, and all that. The fact that those people might have come here, drank here, died here, is like incredible, to say the least. But ironic? No," Nala explained flatly, sitting her drink down so she could gesture with both hands.

"So, you're saying that this murder hasn't disturbed you or your patrons in the least. I mean, this is the second one of this kind in about a year."

She shrugged. "We don't live in the best neighborhood, Officer. That is unless you guys plan to do some . . ." she said and paused dramatically, fanning her hands over her cleavage, drawing attention to it, "Neighborhood watch."

"We just might," Jim began. And then with a crooked grin, parting his lips, he asked, "So you're female. Am I correct?"

Nala ran her fingers through her thick hair and smiled flirtatiously. Apparently Jim was back on her 'good boy' list, despite the tough cop game he was playing when they first arrived. "It's all me, baby," Nala bragged, patting her chest then lowering her neckline, just enough to give Jim an eyeful.

"I'm asking because, well . . . this place," Jim went on, "it's a gay joint. Am I right?"

"Yes, it's a gay club, and you expected a gay man to own it. Well, so much for assumptions," she remarked flatly, aiming no offense, yet setting Jim straight. "The men who come here expect to have their way with a weaker sex, and they think that weaker sex is a gay man. They feel a gay man is somehow beneath them, an easy mark. Well, they've come here, got out of line, and have had their hats handed to them . . . their asses kicked. I don't hire wimps."

"Yes, ma'am," Jim answered.

Just then, the phone rang.

"Nala, it's for you," Louise yelled. "It's your client. And you have a show in like an hour, hon."

Lawrence felt his eyebrow rise at the term 'client.' Jim's eyebrow rose looking at the ugly drag queen, Louise, behind the counter holding up the receiver of the landline phone.

Nala having clients was something they both needed to investigate. Lawrence didn't take anything that happened for granted, as a fluke, or just an inadvertent use of terms. *Words said by slip of tongue usually are truer than those coming intentionally from the brain,* he often thought.

"Client?" Lawrence asked.

"I teach dance lessons in addition to running this place," she answered. "So if you'll both excuse me . . ." Nala said, showing the two officers the door. "Gentlemen, I need to get ready for my show and also take my private phone call."

"We'll need to come back and question you a little more, Ms. . . . Nala." Jim scooped out a handful of peanuts out of the bowl that sat on one of the tables, as well a matchbook, on the way out.

"Anytime, boys," Nala said, winking at Jim.

The directions were clear and Portia followed them to the letter, pulling into the alleyway and parking next to the dumpster as instructed. She looked again at her notepad. This was the place. She'd taken days to make up her mind to make the appointment, but she was finally here.

The stairs went up the back of a brick building. Portia knew there were businesses along the front, but she had no idea what they were. In this neighborhood, the Palemos, she really didn't want to know. She was not from here, but as a kid, her mother talked about this place as if God needed to scourge it personally. To let her mother tell it, it was another Sodom and Gomorrah. Her father, on the other hand, now that Portia remembered, had friends here.

But as Portia got out of her car, she looked around as if she needed to dig down and search her soul for a recollection to burst forth. This place? This alley? "No. Maybe it was another corner . . . but he used to come here. He brought me here once," she said, smiling at her father's memory again. "Mama always hated his friends."

It's not that bad here, just old and a bit worn down, she thought. She'd gone through a couple of neighborhood streets on her way here today, and it actually looked rather homey. She had to admit, even her neighborhood hadn't held up all that well.

None of it mattered anyway. She had to keep her skills up. She was serious about pursuing professional dance. In the paper, she read where the Margaret Jenkins Dance Company was going to be holding auditions soon, and she was going to get in. She'd promised herself to at least try it. Her life depended on it. Maybe not her life, but surely her livelihood depended on it. Nala seemed to understand that when they spoke on the phone.

Climbing the stairs, she could hear music coming from the apartment. She knocked loudly. When the door opened, the tall woman with the heavy makeup and a large feathered head piece/mask took her aback. She looked almost frightening, as if on her way to a masquerade ball. Yet, this woman's eyes lit up with familiarity at the sight of her.

"I'm Portia Hendrix."

"Of course you are. Come in," Nala eagerly said, taking hold of her arm with her large hands and pulling her inside. "Girl, you are crazy. You act like you've seen a ghost. I'm about to do my show." She then giggled.

Her sensuality came through immediately, and Portia was a little disconcerted with the mixed feelings she had before coming to grips with the fact that this flamboyant person had to be Nala. Portia blushed. "Nala?" she asked.

"The one and only. Who else were you expecting to answer the door—the man of your dreams or something?" Nala grinned.

"What is all this?" Portia asked, pointing to the headpiece Nala wore, cautiously wondering for a second what she might have gotten herself into.

"Girl, don't even worry about it. You'll get used to it."

"I will?" she asked.

Nala removed the large headpiece she was wearing. Portia could then see the top half of her face. Although she wasn't strikingly beautiful, she wasn't as scary looking as that mask was. Portia could only hope that once all the makeup was off her face, she would be a little easier on the eyes.

"Girl, please," Nala remarked, allowing a wicked grin to creep onto her face. "Do you want to dance or not? Jacki gave me the impression you were desperate."

Portia didn't know how to take the question, seeing as how Nala's cleavage spoke before she did. Her nails were red and claw- like, her makeup was bold, and she was way too wild looking to be out in the daytime. Portia had to wonder what would be expected of her.

"I wouldn't say desperate, but sure, I want to dance." Just then, Portia could hear music coming from under her feet.

"What's below us?" she asked.

"The Rainbow Room. It's a gay club," Nala said before putting on another wicked grin, slipping out of her house shoes, and kicking them to the side.

"You're kidding me, right?" Portia chuckled. "I didn't know there were any in this city. Well, I guess in this neighborhood anything could be here. When did it open?"

"It *reopened* when I bought it. Where you been—under a rock, or should I say halo? We're headline news these days," Nala said flatly while slipping back into the headpiece, looking at her reflection, and then adjusting her wild hair. She then noticed Portia staring.

"What does that mean—the halo comment?"

"Girl, please . . . like you know about gay bars and stuff. I can tell by looking at you that you just one of those flat-backin'-it Christian women who wouldn't know—"

"Look. I know about . . . stuff," Portia protested, sounding more naïve at that second than before.

Nala burst into laughter, almost as if reading Portia's mind. "Don't claim you know what you don't. That could get you in trouble one day. Besides, I can tell by that comment alone you don't get out much."

Portia folded her arms defensively across her chest. This was not a good first impression on either part. She wondered if she had made a mistake.

"Look, we'll be fine. I'm just rushed, and you need to either stay or go, or come and leave . . . do something. I'm about to do my dinner dance," Nala explained, sounding rushed as the music grew louder under their feet.

The Appointed One watched as Nala moved about the stage. What a wicked tease she was, always giving them so much, and yet, nothing at all. Never did she strip all the way. Maybe once in a while she let them see a breast, maybe both if she'd been drinking too much before hitting the stage. Tonight she gave them nothing but wishful thoughts. Dreams that maybe one day they would be so blessed to bed a woman like her. Sexy, hot, and full of mystery—that was Nala. The Appointed One could barely contain himself as he felt his body reacting at the sight of Nala's smooth bare shoulders and the wiggle of her firm hips.

How he loved her. How he would do anything for her. Her tears were his tears. Her pain was his to share. So much they shared, he just knew they were one in spirit. She understood. Even without speaking to him, she seemed to know his pain. He knew hers and had appointed himself to teach those who had hurt her a lesson.

Spying him in the crowd, she blew him a kiss, one that promised a night of bliss. Maybe, but after noticing the tall, flamboyant drag queen in the crowd, the one with the good hair, the one called Flacca, The Appointed One realized that a night of bliss was more of a maybe not.

He had work to do. "Wanna drink?" Kyle asked. He worked the bar when Louise was off. The Appointed One looked him over from head to toe, and then smiled. He'd heard about Kyle, the one they called Kyla. Yeah, he knew all about *Kyla* and his boyfriend.

"Yeah, I'd like a fuckin' faggot on a meat hook," The Appointed One requested.

Kyle frowned. "There is no such drink as that," he said, jerking his neck.

The two of them were silent for a moment. "Is that your real hair?" The Appointed One then asked.

"Is that your real dick?" Kyle smarted off.

"You wanna find out?" The Appointed One answered, grabbing his crotch slightly. Kyle smacked his lips, holding up his palm.

"Sorry . . . got a maaan," he sang.

"Well, ain't you blessed," The Appointed One said with a sneer. His words were cold, and affected Kyle immediately. "Gimme anything with a kick," he finally said, sounding lighthearted and ready to finish enjoying his evening.

"Yeah, I got your kick," Kyle grumbled, pouring him straight bourbon and sliding his glass toward him. The Appointed One picked up the glass and emptied it in one toss, grimaced, and walked away after dropping a ten on the bar. "Keep the change, sweetie."

CHAPTER TWENTY-ONE

Both detectives knew there was no way that well preserved penis belonged to Rachel Williams or to Deacon Fox, but Marvin Shackles was as good a guess as any.

"I'da bet on it," Jim laughed.

"And lost. I could have told you it was Sal's."

"And you knew—how?" Jim challenged. Lawrence just shrugged and laughed as if he had an inner revelation and couldn't explain it.

They had gotten the news earlier that day, their first crack in the case. However, they weren't sure what the new opening in the case would bring.

"So, we found one, but like, where are the others?" Jim asked, sounding a bit more serious now, with a bit of Carmen Mendoza's accent slipping out.

All they could hope was that it wouldn't show up in a similar place as the one found in Jenessa's, a.k.a. Rachel Williams's mouth months from now, days from now, years from now.

The new murders now tied in almost perfectly with the old ones, short of the fact that Jenessa Jewel was female. If she had been male, it would have been a dead on match. Imagining her male made the connection to Father Deacon Fox and his being bi-curious or whatever the case, and would have made Jenessa a target for murder just as perhaps it had made Sal Mendoza and his homosexual lover Marvin Shackles. All of them were targets for the killer of homosexual clergymen and their lovers.

"So are you saying that maybe this guy has kept all these dicks as trinkets?" Jim asked.

"Yeah, I think he has. Remember, every serial killer keeps stuff, like Mary Mary was saying," Lawrence explained, saying Marilyn's name the way Nala said hers.

"Great, not only do you lose ya stuff, it shows up years later."

"Jim, your mind needs to be preserved and used for some future science project."

"Well, as long as my head doesn't show up in some chick's mouth. But then again . . ."

"Stop right there."

They both laughed.

"Okay, so in the older files, did the cops say they got phone calls from Mr. Appointed?" Lawrence asked.

"Well, it says they got an anonymous tip on where to locate the body . . . in both cases . . . no Mr. Appointed, but I would bet money that it was the same guy. Apparently, he didn't call the police more than once. Who knows if he called the victims, and maybe he hadn't realized he was appointed back then."

"Every serial killer had a first time, a trigger point, something that started the whole ball rolling. Maybe when he killed Sal and Marvin he decided to become a serial killer. I mean, we're the ones calling him a serial killer," Lawrence explained.

"He might just be mad at a few gay guys and knocking them off for the sake of doing it."

"And they don't just stop killing without a reason. But one thing's for sure: if The Appointed One is in fact a serial killer, he will be killing again—soon," Lawrence said. They needed to find out if the Appointed was new to the *crazy* game or if he was an alumnus of the class of coocoo.

Once the motive for the first victim was found, there would be a reason, a rhyme, a rhythm for everything The Appointed One did, and every move he made after that, would make sense. Unfortunately, finding that reason was going to take time. At any moment, The Appointed One might get his blundered assignment issues straightened out and kill again.

"Strippers, cross dressers . . ." Jim mumbled.

"Down-low preachers . . . yeah, I'd say it was all hooked up," Lawrence added in, feeding the brainstorm session that was common when they both got on the same page.

"Rachel was just a mistake."

"He told us as much."

"His first one . . ."

"Maybe."

"We can only hope that he's shaken, now, and soon make another one."

"I'm counting on it," Lawrence said, pouring a cup of stale coffee. They'd been working for hours, now, and it was past time to go home. As a matter of fact, it was almost time for their next shift to start.

"Extra person—that's a red flag right there because these guys never do impulsive things like that. As crazy as they are, they think things out completely. He's talking like he's just gonna jump out the damn bushes on somebody."

"He's getting ready to really mess up if in fact this 'extra person' is just some random schmoe who just happens to be gay or whatever."

"And he'd rather us catch him than fumble like that, my guess," Jim suggested, trying to get into the mind of a serial killer.

"Pride in his work?"

"He's been appointed. I'd say hell yeah, he's got a lot of pride in his work—God given pride."

"You thinking what I'm thinking?"

"Probably."

"Then I say we help Mr. Appointed One out."

The room was dark. It was mid afternoon, but what did he expect from a basement? Privacy was what he wanted, and that was about all he got from this space. But then he hadn't had to pay any rent on this abandoned basement, so who was he to complain. Who would have thought he'd find something so perfect in the middle of the city. All the hustle and bustle around him, and yet no one noticed his coming and going. He was sure of it.

Looking around at his collectables, he walked over to them, sliding out the 3X5 cards from under the four jars of remains from his previous victims. He also read the card under the newly filled one of Deacon Fox. "You just can't believe how I hate odd numbers. I hate everything odd, don't you?" He asked the question in the direction of the first jar that held the remains of his first victim while glancing out the corner of his eye at the sixth jar that sat empty—empty because he could not fill it with the penis of Jenessa Jewel. In instant anger, he snatched the card from under the empty jar and tossed the card in the trash, replacing it with a nameplate of his 'extra person,' his 'equalizer.' *It's really nice to be prepared,* he told himself, taking a deep breath, grimacing from the smell. "Smells like a morgue in here," he said aloud, picking up a fresh roll of duct tape and putting it in his pocket. He was due to call his favorite cops pretty soon. He was sort of disappointed that they hadn't figured out his last clue. "I mean, how easy was that?" he asked himself out loud. "But then again, it's not like they were given the insight that I have, nor are they as smart as me." Turning, he looked at himself in the full-length mirror and smiled. "Nor as beautiful."

Times were changing. He was changing. "And for the better," he said out loud to what he felt was his audience—his jars, rings, and other memorabilia taken from his victims. It was time to let it go. He knew this, but deep inside, he also knew it would be difficult to stop the killing. There was still so much rage inside, so much pain and ache. "But there's got to be something better for me out there."

He then stepped over and examined his knife. He'd spent hours this morning cleaning it. It was shiny again and ready to work for him. "Appointed to work for me," he clarified. "But today, you'll wait here. Today, I'm going to do something a little different, okay?" he said, speaking to the jars and the knife as if they were all in cahoots—alive, and willing to help. "So, I'll be back in a little while; don't go anywhere," he said, and then chuckled wickedly.

Portia knew, without Nala even having to say, that she had the right stuff—what it took to be a professional dancer, but she was way too inhibited to make it work for her on the stage of the Rainbow Room. "We need to loosen your ass up," Nala said clapping loudly as if that was going to help her stay on the mark.

"I'm loose. I'm loose enough," Portia retorted, sounding defensive and a little self-conscious, especially with the little Eartha Kitt lookin' drag queen, Kyle, snickering at her from behind the bar. "It's hard with people staring at me," she added with a huff, stopping her dance mid wiggle. She stood now with her hand on her hips.

"Honey, what do you think people are going to do when you get naked? I mean, they are supposed to look. Why, I don't know. You don't have much to see, but . . ." Kyle taunted.

"Stop it, Kyle. That was just plain mean," Nala told him, noticing Portia's inability to take a harsh joke like that and dish it right back.

"I'm not planning to get naked," Portia retorted, as if allowing the words to finally hit her. "I'm here for lessons, not a job."

"Whatever. You plan to get famous, you better be planning to get naked," Kyle went on.

"Oh please," Portia snapped.

"I'm just sayin'," he said, smacking his full lips.

"Like you can do better," Portia challenged, to the surprise of both Kyle and Nala.

"Oh, no she didn't," Kyle yelped, coming quickly from behind the counter.

He was dressed in spandex leggings that showed definition in his thighs. He was athletically built and Portia wondered what he did in his *other* life. Maybe he was a model or cyclist. With his 'different' kind of looks it was hard to place him outside of the club.

The music man started the music. The sound of the group, Cameo, singing, "Word Up," poured out. Kyle clapped his hands and jumped up on the stage, putting on a dramatic face and spinning with his back to Portia who moved to give him room. With his backfield in motion, Kyle began to move to the beat of the music, kicking high over his head and sliding down into splits. On the uptake, he slowly unzipped his shirt, tearing it away, slowly exposing his muscular chest. Kyle was small, but his body was tight. He wasn't short in the package either.

Portia noticed as he gyrated sexily, showing off his stuff and sliding his hands over his privates, drawing attention to it. Turning his back to her again, she heard another zipper and then his spandex pants went away, exposing his buttocks. His smooth, round buns were interrupted by only the thin string of a red thong. Giving her a little shake, he looked over his shoulder at her, licking his lips seductively and then flicking his tongue at her in a snakelike fashion. Portia felt her stomach tighten. She felt confused inside. Kyle was turning her on, yet she knew he was untouchable. He was gay. He was flamin'. The tease was killing her.

"Now, honey, you top that, and we'll talk," he said, sounding bitchy, as he picked up his discarded clothing and strutted off the stage.

"Now you know she can't do that. She's got way more ass than you," Nala joked, swatting Kyle's bare bottom as he sashayed by. Portia chuckled nervously, hoping her feelings did not show.

"That's cuz I be workin' mines," he remarked. "Now, let me get on outta here, cuz I have a date." He was dressing, zipping his things back together and wiggling into the tight clothing. "Flacca was supposed to meet me here, but I see he's late again."

"Date? I see you don't grieve long," Nala said. Kyle's eyes darted nervously.

"And why should I?" he answered nervously, tightening his lips, crossing his legs at the ankles with his hand on his hip.

"I'm just saying, last week Deacon was your beau, and now poof, he's dead and you move on, just like that." Nala's tone was cool and Portia caught it right away.

"Somebody died?" Portia asked.

"Murdered—don't you read the paper?" Kyle snapped, before widening his eyes and turning his attention back to Nala, as if readying himself for a verbal attack. "And no, Deacon was not my lover, thank youuuuu. It was never like that, I've told you that."

"Murdered?" Portia gasped. "Was he the guy who was found all cut up last year?" She sounded as if she was just putting the map together in her mind as to where she was, and had been for a few hours now.

"You mean last week! Somebody is going around cutting priest's dicks off," Kyle said, sounding bored. "Don't they know they'll burn in hell for that?" He began to straighten chairs under tables as if it was time to get ready for the evening rush. "They think it was a jealous lover," he continued, pointing his words toward Nala, sounding a bit accusatory.

"No, it's not, Kyle. It was just some religious fanatic, unless of course you know something I don't," Nala said, sounding a bit curt, yet a little curious.

Kyle shook his head. His lips were buckled as if she had sealed them tightly. "Don't know a damn thing about Deacon and his lovers . . . well, except maybe one or two."

"My God . . . what are you trying to say?" Nala growled now, her body language showing instant agitation.

"Nothing, Nala, I mean, I know how it is. You get caught up and fooled and all that." Kyle went on, alluding to what he perceived to be the truth. "And then rejection strikes and—"

"No!" Nala yelled. The room went silent. Portia could see the red coming up under Nala's fair complexion. She was livid and Portia didn't fully understand why, but it was an uncomfortable moment she no longer wanted to be a part of.

"Maybe I should leave," Portia said, just after the dust settled a tad. Nala smoothed her hair out of her face.

"Yes, and take Kyle with you," she said, fanning her

hand in his direction, quickly trying to get a grip on her feelings.

"Nala, I'm sorry, sweetie. That was so wrong of me to mess with you like that," Kyle said, rushing up to her. "I know you were hurt. I mean, being played is one thing, but being fucked over by a priest is like . . . big-time scorn," he said, pausing for drama and leaving his mouth hanging open.

Without thinking, Nala hauled back and slapped Kyle with all her might. He stumbled backward from the blow, falling flat on his bottom and sliding just an inch or two on the freshly waxed floor. Nala had put power behind the blow. Kyle used a chair for support while he held his face, looking a little stunned while sitting on the floor.

"Can you both just leave?" Nala said after a regrouping silence.

Portia could almost swear she'd seen Nala's eyes well up with tears. Knowing what it felt like to be made a fool of by someone you thought you loved, Portia's heart instantly went out to Nala. She wanted to embrace her, squeeze her tight—or maybe she wanted that for herself. Who knew, but if she could have hugged Nala without anyone thinking more of the situation than there was, she would have. But instead, she gathered up her things and headed out the door.

Flacca was upset. This whole issue of Jenessa had her nearly sick the more she thought about it. Jenessa being dead was bad, and the circumstances unclear and scary. Why would someone want to murder Jenessa? Why murder Deacon? Deacon was a man everyone turned to at times when they needed a shoulder to cry on, or whatever. Even Jenessa, well, Rachel, had told Flacca she often found Deacon Fox a man she could confide in and trust. "And that's so rare in our business," Flacca said under his breath, thinking of how fooled he was by Jenessa Jewel. Now she really wondered what their relationship was, considering Rachel Williams was a cop. "What would a cop and a priest have in common? Makes me wonder anyway," he went on, thinking out loud, because for Flacca, truth be told, at first she wondered what a priest would have in common with a male stripper, that is until Deacon called him to one of his private counseling sessions. The memory made Flacca smile. "Little devil." Flacca grinned at the memory of Deacon's face after receiving Flacca's sexual service. How beautiful Deacon told 'Flacks' he was. Sure, everyone who worked at the Rainbow Room figured that Nala and Deacon had a thing going on, but it was clear their relationship was convoluted, and pretty close to being nothing. Even Deacon had said something to that effect, about Nala being nothing more than just a friend. But then, what else would she be, with him being a priest and all? The thought was ironic. Deacon being a priest prohibited his relationship with a woman, yet, he bent his vows to engage in sexual games with a man in drag. "Funny how that goes," Flacca said aloud, releasing a large sigh. "God, who will hold me now?" he asked.

Flacca knew he was late, and Kyle was going to be pissy—again. Just because Kyle wanted some miraculous change of life to occur between he and this newest boyfriend and it hadn't, Kyle was taking out his grief on everybody and not being a very good friend. Kyle was getting on everybody's nerves lately with his little attitudes and snaky behavior.

Flacca had spoken to Jenessa about it once or twice and she said that Kyle was a jealous man, discontent and maybe even a little dangerous.

"Dangerous? Ha! I'll kick his narrow ass," Flacca

huffed, rushing down the stairs, heading toward the BART station. Taking the Bay Area Rapid Transit System—BART, would be the only way he would make it from the city back to the East Bay within any redeemable timeframe. The bus just wasn't going to make it in time, and heaven knows Flacca didn't want to hear Kyle's mouth any more than he had to. Kyle had said they would meet at the Rainbow Room since he had tended bar for the lunch shift and then they would head back to his apartment. Kyle wanted to introduce Flacca to his roommate. Kyle was convinced his roommate was gay, and so he was finally going to test the theory. If his roommate was straight, it was going to definitely damage their friendship, but Kyle didn't seem to care about that, only his own entertainment. Flacca figured Kyle was just looking for something to do to get everyone's mind off the situation with his own life by torturing someone else.

"But I'm up for it; a little game of chase me is always good for the soul," Flacca mumbled, looking through an Avon catalog and settling into a seat on the BART. Looking up he saw him, staring, smiling. Flacca couldn't help but smile back. He was drop-dead gorgeous.

Drop dead.

Licking his lips, Flacca hoped to seduce him into making his orientation clear, or at least question it if he already had one established. The man caught on and moved to the empty seat next to Flacca.

"My name is Wone," the stranger said, smiling.

"Wone . . . that sounds like Wand," Flacca teased, shaking his hand. "My name is Flacca."

"That sounds like . . ."

"Yeah, it does," Flacca giggled, realizing how easily his name could be turned to something obscene, nasty, or sexy, depending on how you used the term. "Just take the L out and see what's left, I always say."

"You're really pretty," Wone told him, holding Flac-ca's hand a long time, stroking it a little. "Un-naturally so," he went on. "You look just like someone I've . . . *dealt with* before. And about that L, maybe I'll take you up on that."

His stare was intense, and suddenly Flacca became uncomfortable. "Well, natural is relative, don't you think?"

"I suppose," Wone said, smiling.

"Where are you headed?" Flacca asked, as it was his normal come on line, despite his second impression of the tall, lean, sexy man leaving him a bit intimidated.

"The same place you are, you lovely creature."

Flacca grinned then, forgetting all about the fear, and thinking more about the forbidden. One night stands with customers were a serious offense in Nala's book. *But then we're not in the club now are we?* Flacca asked himself. Besides, it's not like Kyle couldn't find something else to fill his day.

Portia couldn't get Nala's face off her mind—the memory of Nala's anger when she knocked Kyle across the room. She sat in her car a long time before pulling off. She only drove around the block, and then went back to the club. When she went in, she found Nala at the bar, having already downed a few drinks and looking melancholy. Portia slid up to the bar beside her.

"What'll you have?" the bartender asked. It was a man dressed like Cher and doing a pretty good job of sounding like her, too. Portia stared before she caught herself.

"Oh, uh, a Tom Collins," she said. "Where's Louise?" she asked the man.

"He's off tonight. He takes classes on Friday night," the bartender volunteered.

"The whiskey sours are better," Nala said, holding up her empty glass to be filled again.

"You've had enough, Nala. I don't know why you don't

just fire Kyle," the bartender said bluntly before sliding Portia her unordered whiskey sour. Portia looked at it, then at him, and then at Nala.

"It's not Kyle's fault," Nala explained. "He's a whore and can't help himself."

Portia chuckled under her breath, taking her wallet out of her small bag to pay for the drink, despite the fact that she hadn't ordered it. Nala stopped her before she paid

"Please, employees never pay for drinks."

"I'm an employee?" she asked, taking a short sip.

"If you wanna be. Hey, where's my drink, Harry?" Nala said, turning her attention abruptly to the bartender.

"What did I tell you, Nala? No. People are starting to come in, and you're drunk—always a bad combo," the Cher look-alike explained.

"Sing for me, Harry . . . 'if I could turn back time,' " Nala sang, imitating Cher.

"Oh God," Harry, the bartender who looked a lot like Cher, groaned.

"But Nala, this is a male strip joint. I can't dance for shit, and needless to say I'm not male, but hey, I can clean a mean table," Portia said with a chuckle in her voice. Nala's singing was cracking her up.

"Hey, I probably fit all the above qualifications, too, but then again, I own the place, so nobody really cares what I can and can't do—right, Sherry?" Nala burst into laughter after combining Harry's name with Cher's. By now, Harry was ignoring Nala altogether and turning his attention to the couple of patrons who had stopped at the bar.

"Do you serve food here, or should we go out to eat?" Portia asked, sounding like a big sister, even though she could tell Nala was older.

"Please, folks don't come here to eat."

"Then lets go out, Nala," Portia offered, thinking Nala probably didn't get asked out often, not before midnight anyway. Plus, Nala definitely needed food on her stomach to temper the alcohol.

"Okay, fine. Just please don't ask me about my love life," Nala said, cutting her a glance out of the corner of her eye while sliding from the bar stool, snatching up her purse and Portia's drink, downing it in the process.

"Had no intention of doing that," Portia lied.

Nala looked around as if having forgotten something and then suddenly remembering it. She reached over the bar and pulled out her cell phone. Taking Portia by the arm, she led her out.

CHAPTER TWENTY-TWO

"This is where you live?" Flacca asked, as he moved past Wone into the dimly lit, shadowy basement. Flacca's eyes were wide with curiosity. Surely this basement went the full floor space of the building that sat atop it.

"Would it please you if it were?" Wone asked.

Flacca paused to eye the beautiful man as he shut the heavy door behind them. He flinched and felt a chill writhe through his body at the booming sound. "I'm not sure," he replied, swallowing hard.

Wone, who wasn't sure if this was the right moment to let Flacca know he was in fact The Appointed One, let his lip twist up into a half grin. He could see the fear lingering in the corner of Flacca's eyes—*maybe Flacca senses it already*. The Appointed One stepped close to him, bringing his lips a hair away from Flacca's neck. "Would you say I am handsome? Or beautiful?"

Flacca could feel his heart beginning to pound in his chest from The Appointed One's sudden proximity. He nearly swooned, closing his eyes, praying The Appointed

One's lips would find his neck. "Both," he whispered weakly.

The Appointed One chuckled lightly. He knew Flacca would say anything that came to mind, as long as it would get him what he wanted, and perhaps he, too, was sharing in the game of lies, for he knew beyond a doubt, what he wanted as well, and what to say to get it. "You're gonna have to choose one or the other," he explained, making his voice breathy and heavy with seduction.

Flacca shivered in the darkness, feeling The Appointed One's hands wrap around his waist. "Baby, why you gonna make me choose?" Flacca whined, feeling himself melting like butter within his embrace.

Slowly, The Appointed One moved around Flacca, keeping him within his embrace until he felt Flacca's behind pressing against his groin. "Because that's how I will know," he told him.

Flacca arched his back and grabbed The Appointed One's hands, pulling him closer as his desire threatened to burst his pounding heart. All Flacca could think of was how much he wished he could have had the boob job instead of spending the money on that trip to Bermuda last year. How Flacca wished he would give this beautiful man who was promising him so much bliss something to squeeze, fondle, maybe even suckle. "That's how you will know what, baby?" Flacca moaned, giving in to his fantasies and the growing heat of the moment.

"That's how I will determine what to give you," The Appointed One whispered.

Flacca saw the hidden meaning in his words and a chill traveled through his body at the thought of it. "Handsome, baby," he breathed in reply. "Definitely handsome."

At those words, The Appointed One felt his lip twitch. It was not a twitch born of carnal desire, but of pure, unbridled rage. The rage was brought up by the memories, the dark memories that tore at his core and pierced his conscience, ethics, and sense of right and wrong, the memories that changed him as a person, making him now, less than human—at least that's how he saw himself—less than human.

"How could you do that to me? How could you think to do that to someone as innocent and beautiful as me?" The Appointed One asked, his whisper carrying into the darkened room an air of distance, a feeling of vast space and separation from reality.

The memories . . .

Sometimes, he could simply block the memories out, but other times, like today, they consumed him.

He was fifteen when it happened, and his life was never the same after that.

Not that anyone cared about his life.

It was Saturday night. His mama was out on the town visiting her sister, and his daddy was at the church. Daddy was always at the church.

That church was not much more than an upstairs storefront, a rented room, but still, it was church and he tried to respect that fact . . . and his daddy.

His daddy, the Reverend Joseph Samuels, well, stepfather, was the worst of all evils—a full-fledged damnable hypocrite. With his well-rehearsed lectures and sermons, using the Bible, twisting the words into condemnations for the sins of others when in fact, it was the reverend, himself, who sinned more than all the congregation put together. Once, upon arriving at the church to do his secretarial tasks, the reverend was heard through the door of his office, moaning and grunting, between the crude and lascivious words he spoke. The male voice whined and whimpered until finally there was nothing but the sounds of the reverend's voice—heavy and filled with lust.

"Do you love it, Mary?" the reverend asked.

"Oh, I love it," the manly voice of Mary cried out.

The sounds of it all turned his stomach. Although he was ashamed to admit it, the sounds of the reverend and Mary going at it also aroused him. Reaching into his jeans, he felt his own hardness and was immediately confused, frightened, and maybe even a little angry.

After it was over, he hid, watching to see what would happen when the door opened. When Mary came out, with face flushed and reddened, and walking slightly impeded by what had just happened, it was clear that Mary was probably around nineteen or twenty. But even dressed in women's clothing, it was obvious that Mary was a man. The young man had on makeup and looked very pretty in the face. "You are so pretty," the reverend said, moving quickly to pull Mary into his arms for a good-bye hug. But Mary avoided the embrace.

"Now where is my money? I gotta go."

"Money? Yeah, I see what's happening. This was just a tease, right, a game people like you play."

"Us people? Please, you got your nerve," Mary said, sounding harsh and even more manly.

"Yeah, you freak. You—"

"What choo gonna do, scold me now?" Mary asked, taking out his lip-gloss from the small purse he carried and applying it. "You gonna find one of those scriptures to use on me? Look, you were curious and I satisfied that curiosity. But for long-term play, you besta appoint someone else to be your toy."

Suddenly looking around as if maybe he had sensed someone was overhearing, the reverend shushed Mary. Opening the collection box, the reverend paid Mary, who with a sly grin, kissed the reverend's cheek before walking out.

There was a moment of silence before the reverend looked around and then aimed a glance in his direction. "You can come out now," the reverend called out then.

Scared out of his wits, he slowly crept from his hiding place. "I didn't see anything," he began, before the reverend shushed him.

"I guess you heard, then, that I'm looking for another helper."

"I didn't hear anything either."

"Yes you did."

"I don't want to be your . . . your helper," he said, his words sharply edged and cracking from both the growing humiliation and the adolescent hormones that fought within him.

"Well, you don't have a choice, I've just appointed you," the reverend said sounding a little angry.

"Appointed?"

"Yes, appointed, and you're perfect for the job," the reverend said, locking the door. "Take your clothes off," he insisted.

"No. Mama said to never take my clothes off in front of you."

"Take ya damn clothes off. I don't give a damn about what your mama says."

"Call that other boy back if you want someone to get undressed for you!"

The reverend charged at him, his eyes crazed and possessed, and his determination to accomplish this perversion, clear. The newly appointed one ran toward the door, hoping for escape, hoping to get out of this nightmare before it occurred. All he could think about was getting Mary in the dress to come back, to finish what he started, to soothe the beast that he had created in the reverend.

The reverend grabbed The Appointed One around his waist, pulling at him, reaching under his heavy sweatshirt and pulling at his breasts. "I knew it," he exclaimed. "I knew ya mama was hidin' something from me, treating you special and shit. I knew you had a secret!"

"Stop! Don't touch me! You're not supposed to touch me like that! Mama said nobody was ever supposed to touch me."

Ripping the sweatshirt over his head, the reverend stared at The Appointed One, who stood vulnerable and exposed, attempting to cover himself. In the struggle, the rubber band holding his hair back broke, and his long mane fell free around his shoulders.

"But why? Why not let me touch you? You're beautiful . . . more beautiful than all the rest," the reverend said, sounding instantly awestruck as if truly seeing an angel before him.

"Stop, don't say anything to me. Please. Just give me back my sweatshirt. Let me go home. I promise I won't tell Mama anything. I won't say anything," he pleaded, reaching out for his sweatshirt with one hand and attempting to cover his breasts with the other.

"It's too late," the reverend explained, stepping toward him with lust in his eyes.

"Please don't do this to me," he pleaded, thinking of the scriptures now, the Bible story of Lot and the Sodomites who begged to have relations with the men of the house.

It was a shame to have that interruption in my process of turning into a man, The Appointed One thought as Flacca suddenly groaned in protest to having to contain his lust a moment longer. "Innocence. I think not, daddy; you're a sinner just like me. So let's get ta sinnin'. I'm more than ready," Flacca purred, answering The Appointed One's earlier question and bringing his mind back to the moment. Flacca's hands reached around to pull The Appointed One's hips forward as he pushed his behind against his groin. "You going to give it to me now, daddy?"

The Appointed One frowned in the darkness. Reaching up, he grabbed a handful of Flacca's big hair, snatching his head back violently, causing Flacca to grunt. "You'd like that, wouldn't you?" He suppressed the burning desire to break Flacca's neck at that moment and pulled his hands away.

Instead of fear, the sudden roughness nearly pushed Flacca over the edge of ecstasy. "Yes, daddy, yes!"

The Appointed One grinned evilly. "I know you would," he whispered, letting his tongue dart into Flacca's ear teasingly. "But first," he said before releasing Flacca and pulling him along by the hand deeper into the shadowy basement, "there is something I would like to show you."

Even after Flacca's eyes had adjusted to the lack of light, he still could not see more than a foot in front of his face. He let the beautiful angel lead him along through the cavernous room, wondering what it could be that this man wanted to show him. *A collection of toys to enjoy? Something to impress?* Flacca wondered. Hearing a sound somewhere off to his right, Flacca strained his eyes in that direction. A darker shadow, the size of a small cat and fast, moved along the baseboard of the wall. There was a definite squeak. Again Flacca felt a chill, but continued to wander with the beautiful stranger at the helm.

Finally, they came to an abrupt stop. Flacca nearly

tripped over the man's heels. The Appointed One scowled in the lightless area, feeling Flacca's erection brush against his hip. "Right here," he announced.

Flacca pulled his eyes from the scuttle he heard in the corner and felt around for The Appointed One with his hands. He found his strong shoulders and felt immediately relieved. There was something unsettling about this place.

"Stay here," The Appointed One now instructed.

Flacca's shoulders slumped at the command. He had no desire to be alone in this creepy place with those unknown creatures roaming about, but he obeyed.

A moment later, he felt the stranger return. "Would it be too much to ask for a little light?" Flacca asked him.

There was fear in Flacca's voice and it brought a smile to The Appointed One's face. "Are you afraid?" he asked.

"No," Flacca lied. "I just want to be able to see the good stuff you're going to give me."

"Good stuff," The Appointed One said, remembering a similar statement said to him . . . years ago.

He'd run away right after that night at the church, well, maybe not that night, but definitely after the second time the reverend raped him. He realized then that having the reverend working out his perversions on his backside was to be his fate, and it was a fact he would not be able to live with.

How could he convince this stepfather that every one had a purpose and that being a sex slave was not his? How could he tell the ignorant man that despite his physical differences he was not put on this earth to serve his sexual perversions, and that although he was beautiful, he truly was not appointed to this purpose? He knew right from wrong and he grew angry every time he saw a man in drag. He viewed the man as a taunt to true manhood. Manhood—something he craved, but felt was beyond his grasp. He hated the cross dressers and their flamboyant ways, their careless flirtations and seductions. He blamed them for his own life's situation.

It was ten years later that The Appointed One found the strength, both physically and mentally, to face the reverend again. He was grown up, true, but still there were so many mixed feelings when it came to the reverend and the part the reverend played in changing this life.

Thinking about his life, he grew angry all over again while moving in close to Flacca, turning him around and pushing him over at the waist. His erection pressed against Flacca's behind in the darkness. "Are you ready?" he asked him.

Flacca forgot about the creatures scampering in the darkness and without hesitation, he raised his skirt, dropped his panties and stepped out of them. "Yes, baby, I'm ready for you," he purred.

The Appointed One growled in annoyance, angry with himself for letting this little whore arouse him. Roughly, he shoved Flacca forward as the memory of that fateful night came quickly and powerfully, engulfing him more than ever before.

When he showed up at the church, the reverend, although appearing unbothered by his presence, shifted nervously in his wing-backed chair, as if feeling familiarity somewhere deep inside. It had been a long time since they'd laid eyes on each other.

"I need to talk to you," The Appointed One said, noticing the reverend scrutinizing him, noting the changes, the maturity . . . the beauty. "Can I call you Daddy? Reverend sounds so formal."

"I've been called Father before, but never Daddy. What

is it? What can I do for you, chile? Who are you?" the reverend asked, the façade of innocence dripping from his tongue.

"You don't know me, do you?" The Appointed One chuckled, looking away to keep the burn from his eyes. Just seeing this man bought on emotions that he could not fight, and the tears were coming before he could stop them.

"You're upset. Have we met?" the reverend asked, standing now, stepping toward him with arms outstretched. "What's got you so upset? You are much too pretty to be upset."

He was still handsome, with just a hint of grey around the temples. He was a widow, now, with no restraints on his sexuality—as if he ever had any. The reverend could now be as promiscuous as he wanted to be and according to sources, he was.

It took all of a moment for The Appointed One to realize how attracted he was to the reverend. Maybe he always had been. Maybe that was what he felt that day in the church, listening to him sexing Mary in the back room. Maybe it was jealousy. Who would ever know, for within a moment he pulled the reverend into a tight embrace.

"Whoa, girl, you strong as hell!" the reverend chuckled nervously, looking around for a possible means of escape if things got out of hand.

"So, you think I'm pretty?" The Appointed One asked before deepening his voice. "Or handsome . . . and you must choose one. You see, unlike you, I like to give people choices before I destroy them."

The reverend audibly gulped as the close proximity to The Appointed One brought revitalization to his memory bank.

* * *

Off balance, Flacca squealed and his hands shot out in front of him to break his fall, landing on the flat surface of a wooden bench. His fear and desire combined to drive him loony with hunger for sexual satisfaction. He heard what he thought to be The Appointed One's pants hit the floor behind him. "I can't see you, baby. Let me see you, please," Flacca begged, attempting to turn, only to find his face shoved down onto the wooden workbench. "Ouch! That really hurt, baby." Flacca found The Appointed One's strength to be more than he could handle, and before he knew it, his arms were pulled tightly behind his back.

"Yeah, I'm sure it did," The Appointed One said, holding Flacca's head down, and then with his other hand, reaching forward, retrieving the grey duct tape from where he had left it on the table top.

Slowly, Flacca's fear began to override his lust. He could tell a bruise was forming on the side of his face from the impact with the bench. He began struggling against the tightening tape around his wrist, weakly at first, due to his still lingering desire to feel the beautiful man deep inside him.

"Don't struggle," The Appointed One said calmly.

Flacca swallowed hard as the sound of the duct tape wrapping around his wrists echoed throughout the space they occupied. "But baby, you're really hurting me," he tried to explain cautiously.

"No, no, don't think of it as pain." The Appointed One smiled as he sat the tape down and reached for another object. "Think of it as retribution in your flesh."

Flacca heard the clamor of a chain in the darkness and felt its cold touch around his waist. He realized then he couldn't move from the bent over position. This situation was getting funky and he was ready for it to change . . . for the better. "What are you doing?" Flacca whimpered.

With a deep grunt, The Appointed One pulled the chain tightly before slipping a padlock into the links, securing Flacca to the table in a bent over position. Flacca groaned in complaint.

"Now, this is gonna hurt a litte, but please don't scream; my ears are very sensitive," The Appointed One said.

The eerie tone of his voice put panic in Flacca's heart. This was bad. Flacca winced, feeling splinters dig into his nose and cheek as he turned his head this way and that, straining his eyes in the darkness, hoping his vision would start adjusting a little better. He began to cry. "Please, don't hurt me. I'll do anything you want me to do."

"You're gonna do that anyway, whore," The Appointed One said softly. Reaching over Flacca's head again, he picked up the massive dildo he had altered for just this purpose. He grinned as he slid the huge black monster along Flacca's cheek, neck, down his back, and along his bare hips.

Flacca trembled. He'd had some well endowed men in his life before, but none came close to the size of that dildo.

"Nice ass," The Appointed One complimented, touching Flacca's smooth backside, slowly parting his butt cheeks.

That was when Flacca realized the man had yet to remove his gloves. "Oh shit," Flacca cried out, struggling frantically now against the tape and the chain, but it was all in vain. Pain suddenly shot through Flacca's nerve endings as the monster dildo lined with razor blades shoved deep into his rectum.

Sometimes the memory of the reverend's screams still

haunted The Appointed One's dreams. It was as if it was happening right then, right now.

"Shut the fuck up!" The Appointed One ordered. "That's how it felt my first time, too," The Appointed One told him.

Suddenly Flacca began to vomit and choke, but The Appointed One refused to remove the dildo from his anus. Instead he twisted it just slightly, but enough to cause Flacca to scream again.

"You must want me to really hurt you, punk. I said shut up," The Appointed One growled, ripping the dildo from Flacca's rear opening.

Flacca could only moan in delirium. Blood and feces now covered the thick dildo. "Open your eyes!" The Appointed One shouted, snatching Flacca's head upward and back. "Open them!" Flacca obeyed, blinking several times, not understanding what it was he was seeing in front of him now.

There in front of him, lined across the back of the table, were several jars filled with liquid and male members. Suddenly, Flacca's eyes ballooned. He realized what the objects in the jars were and who the man sodomizing him was. With all the strength he had left, he began to scream again.

"I told you to stop all that damn screaming," The Appointed One said, and then out of pure frustration grabbed Flacca's head, jerking it back and shoving the dildo in Flacca's mouth, ripping it in and out twice before letting go. Flacca's head fell onto the vomit-covered bench. He was unconscious.

Walking around now, pondering his next move, The Appointed One caught his reflection in the mirror. Glancing back at Flacca, whose head lay in the vomit and blood, he realized that he could still see the color of the blood, even in the darkness. Pausing for a moment, he looked at his hands and could see the liquid dripping from his gloves. Even in the darkness, he could see it, almost as vividly as he could see it that night in the office of the Reverend Joseph Samuels. He could almost feel the dampness of it on his skin, despite the fact that under the heavy fabric gloves, he wore rubber ones for extra protection.

"See how many lives you've ruined?" he said in the direction of Flacca and the jars that rested on the table, undisturbed by the ruckus that had just played out in front them.

Walking back over to Flacca, he shook his head, looking down at the pitiful sight. "Let's get you up," he said, pulling Flacca up to a sitting position on the floor. He unchained him, removed the rest of his clothing, and clamped the shackles back on each of Flacca's wrists.

Over on the wall, he found the chain and pulled it, hoisting Flacca's body into the air. He stopped when Flacca's feet were an inch or so from the floor. Then he secured each of Flacca's ankles to the wall with more shackles.

CHAPTER TWENTY-THREE

Stepping from the shower, Kyle realized he'd been stood up, and Flacca had not returned to the club either, according to Harry. Kyle could only assume why—Nala. No doubt Nala had threatened him or made him feel as though the club was off limits suddenly. Of course, in all honesty, he'd not given Flacca a lot of thought after leaving the club the way he had. He headed straight for Julian's little church. Sure enough, Julian was there. Within just a few moments, they had locked themselves in his office. "And I smoked him like nobody's business," Kyle said, seething into the mirror, thinking back on his eager performance between Julian's legs. Julian nearly cried out near the end, when Kyle released him unexpectedly.

"What are you doing, baby?" Julian asked, sounding desperate and pretty close to bursting.

"Don't you ever think I want a little, daddy?"

"What do you mean?" Julian asked.

Kyle had never been so bold with Julian. Normally he was the pleasure giver. Sure, sucking Julian's big ol' dick was damn good but, "sometimes the goose needs a little gander," Kyle thought aloud. And besides, if they were going to be a permanent item, Julian needed to learn some turnabout.

Standing before Julian, Kyle unzipped his pants and moved his erection close to Julian's face, touching it to his lips. Julian looked up at Kyle questioningly, unsure of what to do next. "Just open ya mouth," Kyle instructed.

"I can't," Julian confessed. "I'm not ready."

Disappointed but not deterred, Kyle reached into his fanny pack, pulled out a mini tub of K-Y Jelly, applied it anally, and simply straddled Julian, allowing his erection to slide down his belly while easing himself onto the tip of Julian's hardness. Julian about flipped, having only enjoyed Kyle's oral sex all these many months they'd been playing the homosexual sex games. Hunching upward, Julian showed eagerness to feel Kyle's tight hole around his stiffened member. Kyle rose up quickly. "Let me work it, daddy." Kyle purred in his ear as he controlled the amount of entry into his rectum Julian was going to be allowed.

"Okay, okay," said Julian, eager and willing, excited to let this happen. He would be willing to let Kyle say whatever he wanted to say for a chance to feel something new like this.

Easing up and down in Julian's lap, Kyle squealed and squirmed, twisting his hips seductively while toying with the thick head of Julian's penis until it exploded with molten white heat. Julian couldn't help it; he became vocal as if Kyle's performance had been the best he'd ever been a part of. Kyle then kissed him full on the mouth with plenty of tongue play.

"I love you, Julian. I love you so much. Tell me you love me," he insisted.

"I love you, too, Kyla," Julian said, hungrily eating at

Kyle's mouth. Noticing Kyle's growing erection against his stomach, Julian grabbed it. Kyle quickly stood, allowing Julian to tug at it until Kyle, too, burst forth, purring and cooing the whole time. Julian was pleased beyond belief, and Kyle knew then they would be together forever. That is until after they cleaned up in the bathroom and Julian wanted to do it again. He wanted more and this time he wanted to take the lead.

"No, we need to talk now," said Kyle moving away from his grasp.

"No, baby, I want that ass again," said Julian, grinning like a goof ball, tugging at Kyle's penis, groping at his buttocks. Kyle slapped his hand.

"No."

"Bitch," Julian growled, slamming out of the bathroom like a spoiled child.

Shaking the now unpleasant memory from his head, Kyle again thought about he and Flacca's situation with Nala. He and Flacca were friends, and now that he was on the outs, Kyle could only assume that Flacca was, too. "How dare she kick me out like that? Like I'm just some skank ho off the street. I'm one of her best dancers. She's just becoming a bitch." Kyle hated the bully Nala had become. It was only recently that she had been pushing her weight around. Kyle had thought long and hard about quitting, especially with Portia on board now. And now she was brown-nosing with the boss. "Going out to eat and shit . . . whateverrrr," Kyle smacked. "What is she doing trying to dance in a gay club anyway?" She was another freak like Jenessa was—a woman pretending to be a male cross dresser, in Kyle's opinion. And to what end? *To see how many bent men she can attempt to straighten out?* Kyle wondered. He hated women like that. Of course, he didn't feel like he was doing the same thing where Ian was concerned—forcing his orientation on Ian on every occasion. Kyle didn't even think about the fact that he was going to introduce Flacca to him in hopes of swaying him further into admittance of bisexuality. He had no thoughts that he might be wearing on Ian's nerves. "But then it doesn't matter now, because Flacca stood me up," Kyle mumbled.

He remembered his first time with a girl. He almost threw up. Just the smell of her wet cunt made him sick, even when he entered her. "Ew, I thought she would swallow me whole," he said aloud, looking at his reflection. Just then, he heard Ian moving about. He quickly washed his face and tightened the towel around his waist.

Opening the door, Kyle could have sworn he caught Ian's eyes drift to his lower half before they met. Or maybe he just wanted that to be the case.

"What?" Ian asked.

"Just haven't seen you in a minute, or so it seems, so I didn't want to miss you before I left for work."

"Kyle . . . since when?"

"Lately you've been distant." Kyle touched him on his chest, only to have Ian quickly grab his hand.

"Don't touch me like that," Ian barked.

"Since when?" Kyle smarted back, jerking his hand free. "I've touched you before, and you liked it."

"Kyle, lately you've been really pushing this gay thing, more than you have in years. I don't know why, and with what's been happening lately, I thought you wouldn't be acting like this."

"Like what? I'm supposed to what, start acting straight just because there's some psycho out there? Please, there is always a psycho out there . . . somewhere."

"None of this is funny. It's not a game either. People are dying—"

"I know, but what does that have to do with us?" Kyle asked, laying it out on the line.

"There is no us. We are not lovers. We will never be lovers, and even if I was gay, which I'm not . . . see, why do I have to even say that?" Ian's eyes suddenly dropped again to Kyle's southern region. "I hate living with you now. Ugh!" Ian threw up his hands and stormed into his room, slamming the door.

Kyle stood there naked. His towel had slipped loose and fallen to the floor.

Lawrence and Jim walked into the Rainbow Room with no hesitation. The air was thick with feminine perfume, polluted with male pheromones. It was nauseating. Lawrence was hoping that Nala would be willing to walk outside, but of course, she wasn't. It was clearly a busy evening and there was no way she was leaving her guests.

"Besides, it's cold out there," she said, shivering, waiting, dressed in too sexy of a dress for this time of year. But Lawrence had to figure she had made sure she looked as distracting as she could after getting his call. *Who knows with a woman like her*, he thought, shaking the trance her eyes attempted to put him in, off. She licked her full lips, leaving them parted slightly, the way Marilyn Monroe always did, and blinking slowly she asked, "Now Lawrence, what's this about you wanting me tonight?" Leaning back against the bar, she jutted her full breasts forward while directing the question to Lawrence.

"No," he answered quickly. "We . . ." He pointed at Jim and then back at himself. "We wanted to speak with you tonight . . . on police business." Lawrence realized now how much he hated talking to her. Smirking, she stood straight and strolled behind the bar to pour herself a drink of club soda.

"Would you both like a drink?" she asked, directing

her question to Jim now, who smiled and accepted her offer. She winked at Lawrence while handing Jim his club soda. He guzzled it down and then belched into his fist while handing the glass back to her. "A man after my own . . ." she looked Jim over, "heart," she teased. Lawrence scowled at Jim and then flipped open his notepad.

"Ms. . . . uh, Nala, we are here as a courtesy. Actually we could have just staked this place out without asking, but we wanted to let you know that our main concern here is to make you aware that we are putting your club under surveillance for a few nights a week while we complete our investigation on the murders that occurred here," Lawrence said, speaking quickly and without a break or looking at her.

"Didn't nobody get killed here. You need to get that right!" she interrupted, jerking her neck, losing all femininity. Lawrence looked up at her, caught off guard by her quick change in mood. He made a mental note to investigate Ms. Nala a little further, maybe check her—or his—record for any assault charges. She or he seemed to have quite a little temper. Lawrence's jury was still out on Nala's orientation, and maybe that's what made him so uncomfortable whenever he was around her. He felt aroused, and yet disgusted at the same time. It was an awful state of being.

"So you want to hang out here for police business, huh? Yeah, like I believe that." She laughed.

"Look, Ms. Nala . . ." Lawrence began, only to have Jim interrupt.

"Okay, you got me. I told my partner that we needed to figure out a way to convince our boss to let us come here," Jim said. Nala's attention turned to Jim along with a large smile that crossed her face. "You are just too hard . . ." Jim paused long and with full premeditation, "to resist."

"Really?" She grinned broadly. "Finally a little honesty; that's all I ask for," she said stingingly, aiming the bite at Lawrence. Reaching out, she took Jim's hand. "Come, let me show you the place. I'm sure you'll find some great nooks and crannies. Oh my God. Say that fast three times," she giggled. "Anyway, some great spots to hide out while you survey goings on." Jim looked back at Lawrence while allowing himself to be dragged off by the statuesque woman. "I'll even show you my bedroom," she went on. Jim mouthed the word *help*. Lawrence couldn't keep from laughing.

"I'll take that club soda now," Lawrence told the bartender while he leaned against the bar, watching the room fill with the crowd of gay men. It was going to be a long night.

After a day at the Rainbow Room and then an early dinner with Nala, Portia was glad to be home. "Just a little too much of the 'other side' for one day. I'm so not sure I'm ready for this," she told herself.

The week was long and emotionally tiring. Portia had so many things on her mind. Her dancing career looked all but over, her house was falling apart daily, her life wasn't too far behind—as her relationship with Julian was all but over. Even a couple of the women from the church seemed to have a sadder look on their faces last Sunday when she came in and sat as far from Julian as she could. It was obvious others had assumed the same as she had where Julian was concerned. It was clear they also thought Julian might be their perfect match. With that thought, she at least felt a little less stupid about how this had all played out.

But a stripper, Portia? Is that really going to help your life any? she had to ask herself. *Should I really be stripping in a gay club?*

After stepping in the shower, Portia groaned with the answer she came up with and let the water cover her head, wetting her hair. She needed something strong in her life—stronger than alcohol and not as addictive as sex. She needed a cleansing, a prayer—something. The water poured over her again, rinsing the sweet smelling soap from her body. Why couldn't life just be simple?

Just then, someone banged hard on the bathroom door. She screamed like the woman in the movie *Psycho*.

Reba sipped her coffee without saying anything as she watched Portia, who was still shook up from the scare. The lock on the back door was broken, and it only took a couple of jiggles for the lock to release, allowing Reba entry into the house. She had warned Portia about the door weeks ago and thought it would be funny to bust in on her, bringing the point home that she was not living safely. Reba had also hoped to dispel Portia's thoughts about moving some stranger in, but hearing the terror in her voice when she busted into the bathroom on her was beyond funny. Reba was starting to feel a little sorry for petrifying her like that and realized that maybe Portia did need a roommate—for security if nothing else.

After banging, Reba busted in and ripped the shower curtain back. Portia stood screaming with her eyes closed and then fainted. Reba was sure she would have a bigger knot on her head now than when Lawrence Miller threw her into the street, the day she jumped on him.

Speaking of Lawrence Miller . . . Reba thought to herself as she nibbled on her toast, still watching Portia regrouping in the large recliner. Reba loved Portia, but worried about her. If she were married, she would be living better, even if she had a decent boyfriend, Reba believed. Ever since her father died, Portia's life was going down the toilet. Reba knew what she had to do. She had to fix this mess—stop it before it went too far. There was someone out there for Portia and Reba was going to find him. Reba hadn't met this guy Portia was seeing, but she knew he was no good for her. He'd not done a damn thing for her, and a good man would have been over here fixing up stuff or something.

Just then, she heard a police siren in the distance. Friday night and folks were breaking the law.

"Portia, you still want me to go to church with you this morning?" she asked meekly. Portia just stared at her as if she had something far from holy on her mind and saving Reba's soul nowhere in her heart.

The phone rang. Reba answered it. "Portia, I need you to come to the club right now. Kyle is a no–show, and so is Flacca."

"Who the hell is this?" Reba snapped. "And who you callin' a fucka?"

Portia grabbed the phone. "Whose calling?"

"Harry. Nala wants you to come in because Kyle and Flacca are no-shows tonight. It's crowded and I have stuff to do, and well . . ."

"I'm sorry, Harry, but no. It can't happen tonight," Portia answered before abruptly hanging up. She didn't even care if Nala fired her at that moment. She could tell by the look on Reba's face that she had enough work in store for her tonight, explaining to Reba what she had been doing with her spare time.

After hanging up, the two women stared at each other, regrouping privately, and then with a weak smile, Portia stood. "Let's go cook something," she suggested, knowing that cooking always helped things between them.

"As if you can cook," Reba grumbled playfully, following her into the kitchen.

Reba loved to cook and Portia didn't know how. Reba

told secrets and Portia kept them. The two of them made a good team.

"So, you got secrets?" Reba asked, after hacking out her smoke and coming in from the deck. She always did that after a cigarette. It was a dirty habit, in Portia's opinion, and she wondered why Reba held on to it.

"Why do you still smoke; it's so filthy a habit."

It was a habit Portia's mother never approved of either, and it made the house less than peaceful, considering her father was a big-time smoker—always had been.

Buried knee deep in the church, and as lifetime best friends as close as sisters, both of their mothers sang in the choir, baked bread for the bazaars, and raised their daughters, Reba May and Portia Dawn, to be good girls. It was Reba who first left the church for more of a fast life, clubbing and the like. Portia had hung in a little longer, but not much. Maybe it was just because Reba's sins were more in the open that she just seemed so much more rebellious. Portia had always been more secretive . . . sort of like now.

"At least it's the only bad habit I have. Can you say the same, Miss Secrets?" Reba retorted.

"Secrets? Girl, I don't have no secrets," Portia explained, leaving out the fact that she had taken a job at a gay bar and just that afternoon had gone out on a date with a woman who was clearly a lesbian. And in all honesty, despite her earlier thoughts, it was true: she couldn't wait to see Nala again. Yes, Portia had plenty of secrets.

"Why haven't you told me who's been taking up ya time?"

"I have been at the church," Portia lied.

"Hmm, you in need of that much prayin' lately?" Reba huffed, while giving the collards another good washing.

"Reba, you're a fire starter, you know that?" Portia

smiled slyly and then burst into a full on grin. "I do have a job there."

"What the heck does that mean? Fire Starter . . . where did you get that term?"

Portia thought about the club, how often everyone there used that expression. "Just looking for trouble—that's what it means, like I don't have enough here to worry about. I told you I had a crush on a teacher I work with, and you blew that out of the water, so I give up. Look at this house; this is all that's on my mind." Portia looked around the kitchen, pointing out the cracks and deficiencies there as well as the broken lock on the back door, which Reba had blocked now with the dining room table after demonstrating to Portia how easy it was to get through.

"You gonna get money outta him?"

"Who?" Portia giggled.

Just then, the phone rang. Reba glanced at her watch and then answered it again, much to Portia's irritation.

"Who is this?" Reba answered instead of a customary hello. Portia reached for the receiver, only to have Reba playfully shove her back. "You read the ad for a room?"

Portia reached again for the phone, but Reba again resisted her. "What do you do for a living?" Reba asked crudely. "Oh, hell nah, you can't rent a room here. And I know ya'll mostly come out at night, but don't be calling folks in the middle of the night. It really doesn't help your image," Reba snapped, hanging up the phone.

"Reba!" Portia yelled staring at the phone. "How could you do that?"

"The woman was a mortician, Portia. A mortician . . . touchin' the dead and shit. Nah, she can't live here. Oh, hell nah," Reba restated plainly, while resuming her cooking duties. Portia was stunned into silence.

"A mortician?" she finally asked as the shock wore off.

"Mor-ti-shun," answered Reba bluntly.

Both women broke into laughter.

"I don't know what I'm gonna do about this roommate situation. This ad thing is not working," Portia admitted, wiping the hysterical tears of laughter from her eyes. "I'm gonna have to get the money from my boyfriend." Portia was thinking of Julian Marcum now, not Ian Randolph, the man she had lied to Reba about seeing. Portia was thinking she would have to, at the very least, get the money Julian owed her.

"Yeah, you do that. Shit. A damn mortician? I think not." Reba shook her head.

It was finally Friday night and the last class of a long week. Ian was nearly worn out—so many opinionated people. Especially one young man in particular, Louis Franken . . . Frinkin . . . whatever. It wasn't like Ian cared what his last name was; that guy drove him nuts. Maybe it was his bushy red hair and face full of freckles that caught Ian wrong. Or maybe it was the way he would call him by his first name when everyone else addressed him as Mr. Randolph. Ian didn't know, but there was something about the guy Ian found disconcerting. Having him for more than one class was even worse a feeling than that. This Louis guy had been in an earlier class that day and now he had showed up tonight for the online class. They were to meet this one time, again at mid term, and then again for the final. The rest of the term would be online. "Thank goodness," Ian thought aloud.

Finally, in frustration, Ian picked up an assessment paper to look over. He had might as well face it: the semester had officially started and this was going to be life for the next seventeen weeks. He glanced at his watch. There were several places he would rather be right now. Kyle and he had gotten into a major argument earlier that evening and Kyle ran out crying. Ian always hated making Kyle cry, but it was just getting so hard to talk to him. Kyle just would not accept that he was straight. Why was it so hard to believe? Why did people have such a hard time believing that a straight man could be celibate or that a straight man could have affection for a gay man without wanting to have a gay relationship with him? He and Kyle had been friends for years. Until just a few years ago, before Kyle started working at the dance hall, Kyle never even went out in drag. He looked like a regular guy in public, but then it all changed. Now, Kyle was impossible to live with. Ian knew their living arrangement as well as friendship was coming to an end, and it was sad to think about. During the class, Kyle had text paged him, asking to meet him later to talk.

Changing his mind about the papers, Ian gathered up his backpack for the night. Before he could get out the door, Louis what's-his-name entered.

"Louis," Ian said, showing his surprise.

"Wow, you remember my name," the young man grinned. "I never know if you really know me or not when you see me," he chuckled. Ian moved him back out of the room as he himself exited. It was getting dark.

"What do you want?" Ian asked, sounding curt and starting to walk off quickly to where he was going to meet up with Kyle. He was irritated and a little flustered over his disappointing thoughts.

"Oh, I was wondering if you would like to have a drink with me?" he asked. Ian stopped dead in his tracks, causing Louis to bump into him.

"What?" Ian asked, trying to keep his eyes from rolling to the back of his head.

"A drink," Louis repeated, pretending to throw back a couple. "You know . . ."

"A drink?"

"Yeah, I uh, want to get some help on the first assignment. I know I seem to know a lot, but no, I really don't. I got in over my head when signing up for this class," Louis explained quickly, stumbling very little, but enough for Ian to notice.

"Then you need to *drop* maybe," Ian stated bluntly, walking again, heading to the parking lot. Just then, Julian pulled in the lot, no doubt to pick up Portia Hendrix—she was his girlfriend after all. As discreet as she felt she was, it was clear that she and the preacher man were involved. Ian felt his chest tighten. He was attracted to Portia, but she just didn't seem to want to notice it. Too caught up in the game . . . too caught up in Julian Marcum.

"Julian Marcum," Louis said under his breath, with almost a sneer to his words. Ian caught it.

"How do you know him?" Ian asked. Louis snapped to attention, looking innocent again.

"Oh . . . oh, I don't. I mean, everybody does," he stammered. Now he was lying.

"Look, Louis, a drink? I'm afraid not," Ian declined firmer now.

"I was thinking we'd talk over an apple martini or something. I make a pretty mean one, people say," Louis said now, his words sending Ian into another moment in time—a time when a young, slender, dark-haired, freckled-faced drag queen approached him in the Rainbow Room, giving him the same offer. He remembered the night they met; it was back when he had a car. Kyle had just started working there and needed a ride home and Ian picked him up.

"I don't date . . . um, men," Ian tried to tactfully explain.

Louis cocked his head slightly to the side. "Then maybe you should choose your friends better."

"What does that mean?" Ian asked.

"Nothing," Louis chuckled.

"No, seriously. What do my friends have to do with who I date?" Ian asked, trying to figure out why this guy thought he was gay and why he felt he could be all up in his business this way.

"Your . . . um, boyfriend," Louis said, leading in his tone.

"Ohhh, you know Kyle." Ian accepted the assumed connection that Louis was drawing.

"Of course I do." Louis looked around cautiously. "I'm a bartender; you know I know everything."

Ian laughed out loud, "Well, Kyle is wrong if he's given you the impression that he's got a man at home." Ian made quotation marks in the air around the word *man* and then again around *home*. He then started laughing. "And as far as boyfriend, he wouldn't be my type—you either." Ian continued laughing, walking away thinking even harder about Portia Hendrix.

"Too bad, professor; we could have written the book on good times," Louis called out, sounding almost forlorn.

"Not interested," Ian repeated, calling over his shoulder. "And you guys need to quit pretending to be women; you and Kyle and your boss, too, for that matter, are all lousy at it." Ian knew he was being rude, but he didn't care.

"It's not like I always wear a dress, and at least I know when to take it off. You're the one who needs to take your mask off for a minute."

Ian stopped dead in his tracks, but couldn't bring himself to even address the statement, so he just kept walking.

* * *

That night, while sitting in a back booth at the Rainbow Room, Julian was ready to make a decision about his life. He knew he had to choose between Kyle and Portia. However, as much as he wanted to make the decision and needed to make it, it was nearly impossible. He'd gone to the school to meet up with Portia, but apparently she hadn't had classes that night. He called, but she didn't answer her phone. And he wasn't allowed at her house since the first time he went there and they made love on the sofa. That was her fault, too. Everything was her fault. It was her fault he was here—at this gay bar!

There was no way he could come out in the open with his homosexual relationship, and Kyle was getting tired of hiding it. That was obvious. But there was no way his financial backers would keep his church doors open and his cushy salary coming if he came out as an openly gay minister.

"Besides, I'm not gay," he mumbled under his breath, watching cross-dressing servers delivering drinks. Julian knew he would need another drink after this one—bad—if nothing else, to wash the thoughts of Kyle on his lap that afternoon in the church out of his mind, because that was probably never going to happen again after Kyle got the bad news. Yes, he was going to break it off—end it. He was going to choose Portia as his primary companion. Just at that instant he made the decision. Maybe somewhere along the line, after marrying Portia, thus satisfying inquiring minds, he would hook up with Kyle again, but for now, his only plans were for Portia—marrying her. She would go for it. She'd been holding out for him to broach the subject for months, like a puppy dog, waiting.

Julian felt his head shake with the thought of a clingy

woman like Portia for a wife. Downing his drink, he again thought about Kyle, and the unbelievably good feelings Kyle caused him to have. He felt his erection tighten against the fabric of his trousers. He fanned over the cocktail server.

Finally, around two A.M., Julian was just about to give up on waiting for Kyle to come in. He was going to tell him right here and now. The alcohol had helped him work up a plan of action, but without Kyle it was all for naught.

"That little pissy ass, pain in the butt," he said, thinking about Kyle and his little temper tantrum.

"Look, Julian, you are going to have to make me your number one concern, not the church or your little fake followers," Kyle began after chasing him out of the bathroom.

"Let's talk after," Julian challenged him.

"No! We talk now, or not at all! If you want more of this," he said, pointing at his rear end, "You listen to this," he said, pointing at his mouth. "I want to be your number one. I want you to come out with this thing or end it," he threatened.

"He don't know who he be foolin' wit," Julian muttered, sounding harsh and street potent. Julian wasn't thinking clearly. He'd had too much to drink. He did have a Saturday sermon tomorrow at the Boys and Girls Club, and the least he could do was try not to be too hung over for the children. Kyle was only going to be a problem for a few more hours. He had time to get in some sleep before dealing with him. Maybe he'd show up at Portia's place. Surely, if he was gonna propose she would let him in. He'd sleep it off up under her tonight.

"Yeah, that sounds like a plan," he grumbled, working himself out of the booth.

Julian got ready to leave, but just then, *he* walked in. He was tall, well-built, and exotic looking—downright beautiful for a man. They locked eyes on each other immediately. But it was when this stranger smiled that Julian felt his world rock. He felt shame and lust all at the same moment. He wanted to fight the feeling, as he could not explain the whole thing away like he had been doing with Kyle.

See, what was going on with Kyle was an experiment. He needed Kyle to prove to himself that he wasn't really gay and that Kyle was just a temporary fix to a temporary need, one that only came now and then. Kyle was just to satisfy his curiosity—nothing serious. But this man burned his loins and Julian wanted to have sex with him. He wanted him. There was something about him that touched Julian way down deep—and immediate.

Before he could stop himself, Julian sat back down and fanned the stranger over to his table. The tall, fine, sophisticated-looking man responded by strolling over confidently and sitting down.

"You're new here?" Julian asked quickly, sounding almost giddy.

"I can tell you're not."

Julian tried to ignore the comment, as it would mean admission to an alternative lifestyle to which he was not ready to acquiesce.

The barmaid, Louise, came over and didn't even attempt to lighten his voice. He was tired, and although in full drag, he was not in the mood to be womanly any longer. It was almost closing time, and he was already mentally out the door.

"What'll it be, guys?" he asked gruffly, his five o'clock shadow showing dark around his chops. The stranger looked him up and down and then giggled. It was then that his feminine side showed. Julian noticed, but still it didn't change how he felt.

"I'll have a gin and tonic with a little lime clingon," he said.

Julian ordered the same and then chuckled. "Clingon?"

"Yeah, you know the way they put it on the side of the glass. Anyway, you know what I'm saying. You just must like hearing me say it," the man flirted.

Louise sighed heavily, showing boredom. He walked away after Julian paid.

"I could have paid for my own drink," he told him.

"What's your name?"

"What's yours?" he asked.

"Bill."

"And you're a damn liar," the man laughed, smoothing back any loose hairs that attempted to escape from his tight ponytail. Julian noticed his hands, manicured perfectly as if he possibly played piano. He wondered what this man did for a living. *Maybe he's a banker,* Julian thought. *Maybe someone's husband.*

Guilt came again, but Julian pushed it to the back of his mind—his heart. The drinks came and Julian pulled off the lime and sucked on it, puckering his lips tightly and then smacking at the tartness.

"Well, that was exciting," the man teased, dipping his in the drink just before licking it, then setting it on his napkin. "I guess that tells me a thing or two," he said.

"What? Tells you what?" Julian asked, showing great curiosity.

"Oh, nothing except that . . . you know . . . I lick, you suck," he went on, before taking a long pull from the glass. When he lowered it, Julian was staring.

"Uh, I'm not gay," Julian finally said.

"Hell, I'm not either. I just like the conversation," the man retorted quickly.

"Whew, I was hoping you weren't getting the wrong impression. I mean—"

"No. I mean, why would I? We're both two straight

men sitting in a gay bar, flirting our asses off with one another. How could I get confused by that?" He let joking sarcasm show in his words. Julian burst into laughter.

"I mean, I'm even about to be engaged—to a woman," Julian confessed, trying the words on for the first time.

The man shook his head. "I'm not ever getting married or anything like that. As a matter of fact, this is my first time in a place like this. I mean, I was curious, you know . . . with all the murders—"

Julian held up his hand to stop him. "Me, too. I would not normally be caught dead in a place like this. I mean, it's like a freak palace here. I mean—" Julian stopped himself. He couldn't even finish the lie. He was feeling giddy and excited and still a little tipsy. It had been a long time since he'd felt this way about another man.

The man burst into laughter. "I feel ya on that. I was just curious about it. Nothing serious," he said. He looked at Julian's hands. "You have nice hands," he went on.

Julian looked at his hands and then back at the gentleman who had taken his hands into his, stroking at his palm seductively. "You want me to read your future?" the man flirted. Julian pulled from his gentle grasp.

"Uh . . . no."

"You have a nice ring," he said, noticing Julian's jewelry. Julian still had on his parochial school ring. He had gone to Catholic school, despite his ordination as a Baptist minister. No one had noticed the ring before, or at least no one had said anything about it. It had a gold carving of St. Marten De Porres.

"Isn't that like a saint of some kind? Are you Catholic?" the man asked.

It was one too many questions now. Julian slid the ring from his pinkie and handed it to the nosy stranger for closer examination. The man slid it on his ring finger with ease. Julian always wished he had smaller hands, but he didn't. Tall and slender, he had fleshy, large hands like his father's. Carpenter's hands, his mother called them. He hated it. He was not meant for hard labor and had never put it in his mind to work in the same field his father had. That was why he went into the ministry—cushy job, to say the least.

"I mean, I live in the city, and I see curious guys all the time. . . . Once I saw two dudes French kissing on the street. I mean, they were just . . ." the man said, after admiring the ring up close. He then stood, leaned over the table, and locked lips with Julian, sliding his tongue between them. Julian quickly joined the play, failing to catch the pleasure-filled moan as it escaped. Pulling from the kiss, the man remained standing. The kiss seemed like an impulse move and it emptied Julian's head of all he was thinking about prior to it.

"Let's get outta here," he told Julian.

His voice was deep and sultry and Julian's mind continued to spin. This was too real, too easy. This man was no drag queen. He wore no dress. He was gay and had no issues with it. This man wanted him and was willing to just walk out with him.

"Where, uh . . . where would we go?" Julian asked.

"Does it matter? I mean, you want it, don't you? And damn, I want you. I'd fuck you under a rock," the man said coolly, seething ever so sexily.

He was very direct. Julian wasn't sure he liked that. He was used to dominating the situation, not the other way around. He wasn't sure he was ready for this.

"Well, I was actually waiting for someone," Julian reneged, looking around, thinking Kyle might appear, and hoping in a way, he wouldn't. The place was thinning out. Many couples were leaving and the music had slowed to a dirge.

"Snooze you lose, baby," the tall stranger said, licking his pretty lips and batting the long lashes that protected suggestive and dreamy blue eyes.

He drew Julian's attention to his well-filled crotch area. Julian felt his body react instantly to the sight of the bulge coming up tight underneath the thin fabric of the man's slacks. As hot as he looked, suddenly Julian realized, just as with Portia, this man was too easy, and that made it all less than desirable. Julian liked the game—the chase and the tease. Pausing too long, the man walked out, all the while Julian's loins ached with desire for him.

Growing instantly angry, Julian suddenly realized the man still had on his ring, the one he'd had for years, the one that he wore for good luck. Bursting from the building, he looked this way and that way for the tall stranger, only to find a dark empty street. His heart sank. Heading back into the bar, he decided to just get his jacket and head home. That's when he realized his cell phone was missing, too.

The pain was intense. Flacca's eyes fluttered open in an attempt to return to full consciousness, although he could not pull his thoughts together.

"You're awake. Good for you. I had to run an errand, but I'm back now. You passed the first test. You're very strong. I'm surprised you've survived this long. But then again, dancers are strong people. I should know." The Appointed One reached in his pocket and then sat something small on the table. "Went jewelry shopping," he said as if being asked.

Flacca opened his mouth, releasing a blood flow that ran down his face. At first he didn't realize why he could not speak, but then it dawned on him and his head dropped.

"You're a mess."

Flacca could move his head from side to side slightly, but there was restriction. Focusing on his surroundings, Flacca realized where he was. This was no kinky sex playroom. This was a torture chamber of some kind, and he was hanging from a stake with duct tape and chains. Again, Flacca attempted to speak, but when he opened his mouth, blood gushed out. The Appointed One jumped back, missing the spray.

"Gross," The Appointed One yelped and then burst into laughter. He shook his head. "If you had stopped screaming like I asked, I wouldn't have had to do that to your tongue." Tears seeped from Flacca's eyes as he wept.

"I know you want to die, and normally I would just kill you, but see, you are going to have to live so that you can be the cops' clue to finding me. I know, I know," The Appointed One began tauntingly, with raised hand, as if to silence Flacca. "I could have just called them again and told them we were here, but hey, I'm supposed to be a psychopath, remember, so it's expected for me to act psychotically."

Flacca groaned.

"Let me start by re-introducing myself. You see, I'm the Appointed One. I'm designated to . . . oh well, what I was sent to do is rather meaningless now, considering how badly I fucked up killing that woman instead of you on New Year's. I can't believe how much the two of you looked alike in the dark and what a bad mistake that was. Anyway, it would have been so easy if I could have distinguished the two of you. I would have just killed you on New Year's and had it over then. I could have gone into an early retirement, but now I have you. However, to kill you would set me off kilter—again . . . you'd be odd . . . er."

Flacca's eyes begged for further explanation, so he offered it. "I'm not odd. I don't do anything oddly, even kill. But you have to die. You realize that, right? You defiled a man of God, and now you must be punished. But in killing you, I would be obligated to find an extra person . . . an equalizer . . . but if I let you just sort of . . ." The Appointed One opened his hands and showed Flacca his large palms, rolling one hand over the other, like the closing of a casket, "sort of just naturally die, I won't feel too obligated to straighten out the mess you caused. And this is all your fault, for dressing like a fuckin' woman in the first place and enticing men to turn against their natural use of the female, blah, blah, blah. If you're gay you're gay—find other gay men, have a fuckin' gay party for all I care. But it's the game you play, the 'let's see if he's straight, let's see if I can bend him game.' I know that's what you do. You go in and ruin the lives of men who otherwise would have just been normal! You are the reason I must do what I must do. Because of you and your fuckin' dress, my life was ruined!" The Appointed One screamed, almost losing control. He paused to regroup, to realize that Flacca was not Mary. "It's all very complex and more than I'm sure you can comprehend. Either way, you will die. But not just yet, and not by my hands . . . directly. I mean, if the cops get here in time, who knows, they might be able to put ol' humpty dumpty . . ." The Appointed One took hold of Flacca's penis, "back together again."

Flacca's head dropped. Both despair and agony overwhelmed him. He knew now who this man was. He was Deacon Fox, Jenessa Jewel, Sal Mendoza, and Marvin Shackles' killer. He had a reason for killing gay and bisexual or bi-curious men. He'd probably killed long before finding his way into this neighborhood. And now this man had killed him. It was true and Flacca knew he was going to die, just not fast enough.

He knew immediately what was going to happen next

when he saw the large knife. He could do nothing when the The Appointed One took hold of his penis, jerking at it until it became firm. Looking up at him he smiled. "See, Ruben, despite what you think, you're a true man, always ready to fuck something," The Appointed One said, raising the knife above his head and slicing downward.

"Don't worry, my dear, you'll die soon enough," he promised. "Unless the cops find you first."

Covering Ruben Garrett's, a.k.a Flacca Facina's eyes with duct tape, The Appointed One, opening the cell phone, took a picture of him.

CHAPTER TWENTY-FOUR

There was no rain promised for the day. Nala smoothed back her hair and stared at her friend. Jacki was looking tired and a little stressed. But then again, ever since she'd known Jacki, she'd been a darker kind of person, always troubled and discontented. Sometimes Nala felt bad for Jacki because she herself never felt down, well, not for very long anyway. She had her club and the stage to keep her happy and hoping. Even today, Nala hoped reigniting their friendship would help Jacki's dark mood swings.

"Well, I'm in love again," Nala blurted, thinking that might lift Jacki's spirits, but instead she only got an eyebrow raise.

"So what does this person do for a living?"

Nala, knowing exactly what Jacki meant, just frowned. "Oh, so you gonna bring up ol' stuff?"

"What do you think of these killings?" Jacki asked, changing the subject, realizing immediately she had changed Nala's mood.

"Considering the last victim was a friend of mine, I try not to think anything."

"How can you not think about it? They are occurring right outside your place of business. You know these people who are dying; why in the hell are you still there? Why do you enjoy being so close to danger all the time? Everything is a fuckin' game with you. That's your problem. You'll never change," Jacki said, shaking her head, getting it all out finally—clearing the air, emptying her chest of what she felt to be 'Nala's issues.'

"Wow, that was a mouthful."

"Whatever, Nala," Jacki mumbled, taking a swig of her strong drink. Jacki, when she drank, she drank Jack Daniels. It wasn't a sissy drink, but then again, she wasn't a sissy.

"Oh my God. Is that why you called me in the first place, because you heard about the killings and you . . . you were worried?" Nala asked, feeling the heat rush to her cheeks. Jacki looked away and then back at her.

"I just don't want you to get hurt. I love you. You are my best friend," Jacki explained. Nala and Jacki shared a moment before Jacki, after a cleansing breath, changed the direction of the conversation. "Sooo, how is Portia Hendrix working out?"

"She's great," Nala said, trying not to let her crush on Portia show, but Jacki was too quick for that.

"Oh my god," Jacki gasped, bursting into laughter, covering her mouth to hide her grin.

"Why do you do that? Why do you cover your mouth when you smile? You have a beautiful mouth," Nala said, pulling Jacki's hand down. Jacki turned away shyly and then turned back to Nala, fighting the smile that parted her lips.

"Oh," Jacki said, remembering suddenly. She dug deeply

in her pocket and pulled out a small box. "I know how much you love jewelry."

Nala squealed excitedly, taking the box from Jacki's open palms. Opening the box, a small opal ring sat in the middle of a velvet inlay. "I saw it in a pawn shop window when I was in the city last and I thought of you."

"You are always thinking of meeeee." Nala grabbed Jacki by the shoulder, pulling her into a big, loud cheek kiss, leaving her lipstick on the side of Jacki's face.

"Yeah, yeah, whatever," Jacki giggled.

After a moment of admiring the ring, Nala finally got serious. "I'm thinking of closing the club."

"I was just blowing out hot air, Nala. I didn't mean to—"

"No . . ." Nala raised her hand. "No, I'm serious. I've never really been afraid before, but some freaky shit has been happening lately and very close to me, I might add. I mean, I knew Marvin Shackles. I knew Sal Mendoza," Nala said counting on her fingers. "I told you about Deacon Fox . . . you know I knew him." Nala spoke with wide eyes. "And that woman . . . well, she worked for me, so I guess I knew her, too, so like, I'm almost thinking someone is out to scare me. I mean, this isn't funny, so it's not a joke, so—"

"Who do you think would do that?"

"I don't know, but if one of my employees doesn't show up soon, I'm gonna wonder if maybe he had something to do with it."

"Why?"

"Because he and another guy . . . Kyle," Nala said with a scowl, "Well, they hate me, they are jealous of me," Nala added dramatically.

"But to kill the people you know just because of that? I mean, Nala, you're beautiful, but come on."

"It could happen—remember Vegas?"

"Yeah, Vegas didn't go well," Jacki answered dryly.

"Oh yeah, not well at all."

"You two want anything else?" the waiter asked. Nala looked the young man up and down and then winked ever so slightly.

"Maaaybe," she answered flirtatiously. Jacki smacked her lips and snickered under her breath.

"You will never change," Jacki said.

Portia and Reba left the Boys and Girls Club, where they had spent that bright, clear Saturday morning hearing a youth church service, feeling remorseful, both for their own private reasons. Just seeing Julian again had caused Portia's mind to go where it shouldn't have. He was so very handsome up there, and powerful. She'd dreamed about him the night before, and for the life of her she couldn't help but want him again. Love and hate crossed such a thin line. Or maybe it was just heat, like Nala had said during dinner yesterday.

Nala, despite her initial refusal to divulge personal information about herself, had told Portia one interesting story after the next. Portia couldn't help but be fascinated by Nala's life and decision to buy a gay dance hall. She couldn't help but be amazed at the enticement the Rainbow Room created. It wasn't until quite a ways into one of their conversations that Portia realized the last man Nala had a crush on was a priest.

Portia thought back to their conversation.

"You dated a priest?" she asked her.

"Dated is such an archaic term, one that would imply he was my boyfriend, and well, frankly, one doesn't date a priest, and they certainly aren't boyfriends," Nala explained.

"Well, considering they usually have some kind of vow of celibacy, I would say not," Portia blurted, without think-

ing how her comment might affect the conversation. Nala just stared at her, blinking slowly.

"You have some serious issues, don't you?" Nala asked.

"With what?"

"Judging people on some miscalculated values of right and wrong?"

"Miscalculated?"

"Yeah, you and your one plus one must equal . . ." Nala counted on her fingers while she spoke.

"Nala, I'm just sayin', if he was a priest, and he was dating, then the implication is that you too—"

"Again, one plus one." Nala rolled her eyes and sipped her whiskey sour.

Despite leaving the Rainbow Room for a nearby restaurant, Nala still managed to get her hands on her favorite drink. Portia was amazed at Nala's alcohol consumption. She was a statuesque woman, but still. The more Portia thought about it, she'd have to say that Nala drank like a man. But then once more, she was probably just doing the math wrong.

Nala was a powerful woman, and maybe that was why she handled herself the way she did. Nala was seductive, yet had an air of 'can't have this,' sort of like Julian, and maybe that was the attraction they both had. Either way, Portia knew nothing good would come of the feelings she had for Julian. He was a dark man with secrets lying behind his soul dividing eyes.

Portia suddenly realized, when her mind came back to the now, while climbing in the car with Reba, that she wasn't sure she even wanted to know what Julian's or Nala's secrets really were.

"I need a cigarette," Reba mumbled under her breath as soon as they reached her car. Portia had talked her into coming along.

"Can you at least wait until we leave the parking lot?

Dang," Portia whispered, as if God would have to listen extra hard to hear their voices, let alone their hearts.

"I can't stand when preachers do that shit to me," Reba fussed.

Portia shushed her again, looking around for retribution to strike any moment. Julian's sermon was a strong one and full of reprisals and warnings for the wicked. This was the first one Reba had attended with Portia.

"Don't say that."

"No, seriously. If I have to hear how evil I am one more time, I'm gonna kill myself," Reba gasped, taking a long drag off her cigarette as soon as she got it lit.

"You're not evil, Reba," Portia assured. Reba looked at her a long time as if trying to read her tone, her repentance.

"I guess this is where I say neither are you," Reba said.

"Oh . . . um, yeah." Portia squirmed.

Reba turned Portia's face toward hers. "What is going on?"

"Nothing I want to share right now." She moved her face away from Reba's hand.

"What does that mean? We talk about everything."

"Not this, not now."

"Sounds serious."

"I'm in love with Julian Marcum," Portia blurted out, hoping she wouldn't have to tell Reba any more than that. Reba burst into laughter. "Okay, there, I've got it out."

"And that was serious? Girl, please. It's a crush. You musta broke up with that guy you were seeing. You know . . . the secret guy from your job. I kept saying he musta not been worth nothing if you couldn't introduce me to him," she said without hesitating. Reba had clearly missed the connection between Julian and the secret man Portia had been seeing. Reba took a long drag from her cigarette and again chuckled under her breath.

"How can you say that?" Portia knew how she could say that—easily, because Reba had no clue how long she'd been sleeping with Julian already. Portia was a little surprised at how well she had kept her secret from Reba.

"I can because I know how it is. Trust me. Right before I found Bradley, I thought I was in love with my college professor. Oh my gosh. I just knew I loved that man, but I didn't. I loved Bradley. You just think you love your pastor because you *don't* love that other guy."

Portia chuckled and nudged Reba hard. "Reba, there was no other guy. I have been in love with Julian all this time and . . . well, you don't understand, and I can't make you understand because I'm not you, Reba."

"Honey, I know that. If you were, you'd know how to cook. Come on, and let's get something to eat."

There was silence between them that told Portia that Reba had heard all she wanted to hear for the moment.

"Yeah, I'm starving," Portia agreed.

"Yeah, and that, too. He's a black man that has 'skinny white woman' written all over him and, well . . . you're too black and way too healthy for his narrow ass anyway."

Portia shrugged, showing that she now had heard enough, but Reba continued. "Seriously, that man don't want no black woman. He has exactly what he wants—trust me. Besides, he's got too many little funny ways."

"What do you mean by that?" Portia asked, being led into conversation about Julian anyway.

"If I didn't know better, I'd say he was gay."

"Shut up. You getting outta hand now. Let's get something to eat. Your sugar must be getting low, talking all crazy like that. Besides, didn't you see him lookin' at me while he was preaching?"

"No, I didn't. Look, I'm tellin' you, I gots me some gaydar for reals, and I can spot 'em. And honey, you don't need no booty busta. You need a man who can break you off a little sum-sumthin' straight up." Reba cackled loudly. "When's the last time you got some anyway? Please don't tell me it was the last time you told me."

Portia felt the heat rise on her face and laughed.

"Oh hell, if it's been that long, I'm not surprised you're in love with that gay preacher man. You need to be going after that cop that hit you on the head, have him hit you a little harder the next time, set your ass straight."

"Stop, Reba!" Portia was laughing hysterically now.

Despite Reba's warning, Portia knew in her heart that she did want Julian Marcum, gay or otherwise. He was what she wanted, and the more she thought about their last time together, the more she wanted him. Besides, there was no way he was gay. That thought made her chuckle under her breath.

Julian is all man, Portia thought to herself. *But then how would Reba know? It's not like I've told her the whole truth about Julian and me.*

Later that day, despite her earlier convictions, Portia stopped by the church. She dug in the files until she found an address that she knew had to be Julian's. She'd never really looked for it before, figuring one day her patience would pay off and he would simply volunteer to take her to his home. But since that wasn't happening, she drove by without an invitation.

The house in the very affluent community of Hercules was outside the city of San Francisco. The house was large, sitting on acres of fine cut grass. It gave off an air very different from the one wafting off the humble church on the east side. This house stank of money. Her anger rose in her throat. How dare he use her as he had, pretending to be unable to care for her. It was obvious he could more than provide. There had to be another reason for his lack of commitment. Maybe Reba was right about a few things. "Yeah, he's a selfish bastard and a liar. But gay—never," Portia mumbled, thinking about giving Nala a call. She needed advice on Julian.

Two single women, out for a day of girl talk—nothing more, Portia assured herself after seeing Nala at the table waiting for her. But it was a lie. She wanted advice. She wanted Nala to have all the answers to her life's problems. She wanted to spend time with Nala.

Reaching out for her, urging her to 'hurry up and sit,' Nala's bracelets were jangling loudly. Portia looked around to see if anyone noticed the flamboyant woman, but no one did. Portia was experiencing some mixed feelings and asked herself, *what am I doing here with her*?

"I feel like I've been eating all day. I had lunch earlier with a mutual friend of ours," Nala told her.

"Who is that?"

"Wouldn't you like to know," Nala ribbed and then winked. "Jacki, your old *sensei.* I explained, grasshopper, how much happier you were to be working with the mastress, if that's a word."

Settling into the chair, the waiter waited beside the table as if he had been down this road before—serving Nala. Nala smiled broadly with the face of a naughty child. She was getting ready to flirt. Portia could tell.

"Order what you want, honey. It's on me," she said, playfully taking hold of the waiter's white cotton apron. "I always tell Berry here exactly what I want, but he gets all crazy, so order what you want and make sure it's on the menu, right, Berry?"

Portia looked again at the blushing waiter, who squirmed uncomfortably. "Nala, stop . . . you're so bad."

"No, honey. I'm as good as it gets," she stated boldly. "And that's the first thing you need to recognize about me."

"I'll just have the California Comfort," Portia said, not even glancing at the menu before handing it back. She'd been to many restaurants in this chain before and knew the menu well. Not cooking had afforded her the opportunity to try out nearly all of the restaurant chains in the tri-county.

"I want the skinny salad; I'm watching my figure," Nala said, winking at the waiter who took the menu and headed off. "Big eater. I'm impressed," Nala then said to Portia.

"Well, I don't cook, so usually I eat one good meal a day out and just kinda—"

"How do you expect to get a man if you can't perform well in the kitchen? I mean, sure, the bedroom is one thing, but sheesh, it's not everything."

Nala methodically moved her silverware around. Portia watched as Nala's hands moved over her plate and napkin, switching the forks and spoons around. It was clear she was left-handed. Nala then saw the ring Portia wore on her pinky. She'd not noticed it before.

"I guess I just figured the right man would love me as I am."

Nala's eyes popped open with that comment. "You thought what? Please, I know you are not that naive."

"Nala, not everything is about sex and seduction and all that. Sometimes, life is just about living and finding your way through trials and tribulations, and relying on prayer to—"

At that, Nala's hands flew up, her jewelry chasing the sound of the wind. "Don't don't start. None of that preacher-man stuff for me. Please. I've literally had my fill of preachers, and I'm speaking in the literal and theological sense, okaaay?" She went on to shake her head in disgust at what her instant memories made her feel.

"Well, Nala, I happen to want to end up with a Godly man. I think it would be wonderful to have one love me and want me to have his babies and—"

"And fuck around on you," Nala said, nodding along with Portia. "Making you feel like somehow it's all your fault, explain it all, using the Bible, all backwards and upside down, how your shortcomings as a proverbial wife caused the problems you're having . . . yada yada."

"Nala, no. My boyfriend wouldn't—"

"First off, grown men aren't boyfriends. That's going to be your first lesson. They are not boys. They're . . ." Nala again ran her hands over her shapely bosom as if that was going to help her calm down a bit, "lyin' ass men," she huffed.

Portia giggled while watching Nala. She was scared of Nala at first, she had to admit it. Nala was different from Reba; Reba was all steam. Nala, on the other hand, was heat—fire. She knew her way around the block, Portia could tell, and she wasn't sure she wanted to learn what Nala had to teach. There was something in the way Nala looked at her—so much sensuality. It always made Portia uneasy—like now—how Nala looked at her while touching her breasts. Portia felt almost violated, yet aroused. It was very disconcerting.

The waiter came back to their table. He sat Portia's plate down and then leaned over and whispered something in Nala's ear after sitting her plate in front of her. Nala then whispered something back and the man glanced toward her lap area. Then, looking at Portia, seemingly puzzled, he whispered in Nala's ear again before quickly walking away. Nala's blush piqued Portia's curiosity as she turned to watch the young handsome man look over his shoulder only once.

"What did he say to you?" Portia giggled, taking a small bite of her omelet.

"He told me he likes dick. I told him that I do, too, and as a matter of fact, I have one—a pretty big one at that." Portia gasped and choked. "So we have a date for tonight. When he gets off at seven, he wants to see it," she said, casually taking a pen from her bag and writing the address of the Rainbow Room on her paper napkin for him to pick up when he returned.

"Nala . . . why? It's a li . . . lie . . . isn't it?" Portia asked, stammering.

"It's called a tease, Portia. A man likes to be toyed with, even gay men."

"So you don't have a penis?" Portia whispered.

Nala, taking a bite just winked. That wasn't an answer and Portia was now more confused than she ever was about Nala's sexual orientation. There was no use in attempting any more conversation with Nala, as Portia's mind was scattered. All she could do was listen while Nala rambled about one thing or another, before finally, the young waiter came and gathered their plates along with Nala's address. Portia caught his wink before he nonchalantly strolled away.

Portia and Nala got up, then walked to the parking lot.

"So where are you going from here?" Portia asked.

Nala adjusted her purse and smoothed down her ruffles. "Back to the club. I've got this . . . ugh . . . meeting with the police."

"The police? Are they still harassing you?"

"God, do they ever stop? I think its abuse, but then again, the one that wants to sniff up my skirt is hella cute, so its' all good. Where you going?"

"Oh, um, I guess I should head to the church to help

my pastor with some stuff that I promised him I would get done." Portia pulled out her white sunglasses, which looked good against her dark complexion and sassy with her new short cut.

"Oh, God yes. Run to him, my dear. Just watch your back, because if you don't, he'll be on it humping like a dog."

"Nala, it's not like that. Our last encounter didn't go well at all and I've been avoiding him, and well, I need to fix this if it indeed is fixable."

"Pu-lease, I can connect the dots better than you think, and girl, this sounds very broken to me. And it doesn't take a mind reader to know that this 'pastor' is the one you're all gaga about."

"Nala, I heard what you said, but I just know I need to talk to him. I need to find out what's really what with us."

"Don't let him hurt you, Portia, please don't. It will really piss me off if he—" Nala reached for Portia's hand. She was surprised Portia didn't move it. She let Nala cover it with her larger one. "It'll really piss me off, honey, if he hurts you."

When she spoke, Portia could have sworn she felt something between them—something that went beyond just female bonding. Nala then glanced at her watch.

"Yeah, well, I have to get going."

CHAPTER TWENTY-FIVE

Portia wanted badly to meet with Julian. She'd lied to Nala; Julian hadn't called in days and she was nearly crazy to see him. She wanted to see him, confront him face to face about everything, including Kyla and the big house, but she turned right instead of left, heading toward home instead of the church. She thought about what Nala had said to her, how she had added up the obvious and still often got wrong answers. Nala was right. She had been duped. How many times did she need it brought to her face?

"Well, I'm not wrong about you, Nala," she said aloud, voicing for the first time her true thoughts of Nala. Nala was a lesbian. Portia felt it in her bones, and if she didn't watch herself, Nala was gonna make a move on her one of these days. But then again, Portia wasn't sure how she felt about that whole situation. She'd accepted the job at the Rainbow Room with full knowledge of the company she would be keeping and yet, while there, it all just felt . . . okay. Never had she been this fickle before. Her life was a mess and getting messier by the minute.

"See, girl, now you think women are after you. You are

going insane with this imagination of yours." Shaking Nala free from her brain, she noticed the blinking lights of the phone.

"Portia," Julian said. "I would like to see you tonight. Come by our spot at eight. It's important. I think you'll agree once we uh . . . discuss . . . what I have on my mind." He chuckled seductively.

Staring at the phone as if it was a foreign object, she blinked a few times and then played the message again. It was unbelievable; Julian had called her for a date. He must have been reading her mind.

Quickly, she picked up the phone to call him back.

"Portia? I didn't even hear the phone ring. Anyway, girl, come over; I feel like gossiping," Reba said, having called right at that moment.

"You got some good gossip since this morning?"

"Maybe," Reba teased. Portia laughed. Rethinking her pride and how quickly she was losing it, where Julian was concerned, she decided to go over to Reba's house, hang out with her, and retain a little bit of it.

Julian waited for Portia for about an hour before giving up. Just then, his office phone rang—the caller's number was his own.

"Hello, Father. I—"

"You! Look, you stole my phone and my ring. And . . . and I've heard about the murder of that preacher, Deacon Fox. You killed him, didn't you? You said you were going to kill him and you did."

"Him and more. Where have you been? Oh yeah, with your dick up someone's ass." The caller laughed. "I've been calling you for weeks and you have never taken me seriously. I've pleaded with you to listen to me and hear me, but no. So now I got in your face. To let you know that I can."

"I should call the cops."

"And then what? Tell them that because you are a fuckin' faggot, men got slaughtered, because of men like you, people are dead and that you need to get straight, or you're gonna die?"

Julian covered his mouth to keep his shock inside. What could he say? Was he being reprimanded by a killer? Was he really talking to a murderer? He didn't believe it. It couldn't be that easy. Someone was playing a sick joke on him.

But how? he asked himself. Who knew his secret?

"How do I know you are the . . ." Julian picked up the newspaper. It wasn't as if the killings hadn't made the front page. "this Appointed One character?"

The Appointed One laughed at Julian's arrogance. "Ya know, I had called to tell you that I was gonna stop all this killing, that I was gonna go about finding my peace another way or at least rethink it or . . . whatever, but just keep in mind that you could easily change my mind, so tread lightly, okay? Pray. Repent. Be sorry for all the pain you've caused."

"Sorry?"

"There are some people you need to apologize to. Sometimes that's all that it takes to fix what's broken, just a simple I'm sorry."

"I have nothing to be sorry about," Julian said. "And I think I know who this is now . . . and let me just say this: I'll be sorry when I'm sorry." Julian slammed down the phone. It rang again, but he didn't pick up.

It came in on Lawrence's cell phone from a blocked number. The photo of the man, bloody and covered with duct tape, while hanging from what looked like a meat hook, was horrifying. The phone rang about two minutes after Lawrence viewed it, and his stomach instantly tightened. He had a feeling it was The Appointed One. He was right.

"Did you get your picture? It's Flacca Facina, formally known to his mother as Ruben," The Appointed One said, sounding a little snippy. Lawrence, again, pulled Jim into the call. "Oh, look, you have another body on your hands."

"Why did you kill him—"

"Oh, Flacca's a man?"

"You know he's a man. Why did you kill him?"

"Oh, so you can see that Flacca is a man? That's what I'm saying; it's so obvious they are men. Why in the hell do they wear dresses? Why do they do what they do? I mean, it's so clear to you why this had to happen, right? I mean, isn't it?" The Appointed One asked, chuckling wickedly. "Actually, no. Probably not. None of this is probably clear to you. You've never had your manhood questioned, taunted, mocked. Anyway, I don't want to talk about it. Let's do some math. I'll give you a head count, catch you up, okay? Marvin, Sal, Deacon, Rachel, and well—I—wasn't planning to count Ruben. He just did sort of died on his own. I mean, I didn't really kill Ruben, so does that mean I'm still at four, or is it really five while on your watch? What's your take on it? I mean, if you're gonna blame me for Ruben's death, then I have to re-calculate it, and that will mean another person has to go."

"You only gave us a day to . . ." Lawrence blurted, interrupting his diatribe.

"And the poor fool suffered all that time waiting. That was your bad. Get on the shtick. I mean, I would have figured out who and where I was by now. Damn! I've given you phone numbers and all that. You're just as bad as those other cops ten years ago. Hey, listen. In an . . ." there was a pause, "hour or so, you'll even be getting another clue . . . dang. What do you want, me to walk in there and sit down at your desk? I'd hate to have you on my side." There was a moment of silence before he sighed heavily. "Okay, so here is the game now. It's a race to the finish. Like I say, I've chosen my extra person, so if you can find him before I do, I won't kill him. I'm going to give you a week. You don't even have to find me. Just save the life of my extra victim and we'll call it square. It's like a two-fer, which to me says fifty-fifty. I like the sound of that. It's equal." He rambled on, not making any sense to Jim or Lawrence. He was losing it as far as they were concerned. He was breaking. "You're not going to find any prints on anything—ever. You're not gonna find out anything about me—until you find me. I've been at this way too long . . . oops, that was another hint, boys," The Appointed One went on.

Just then, a deliveryman walked in. "Lawrence Miller, Jim Beam, either one is fine!"

"Hey, that sounds like your delivery. Let me jump off here so you guys can get a clue. Pardon the pun."

"Can't we get the lab guys to open it? I mean, hell, it could be anything," Jim said, eyeing the box after the deliveryman sat it on the desk.

"Well, it's too small to be a head," Lawrence responded. "But still . . ."

"You scared?"

"Hell yeah. Quit playin' and take that to the lab," Jim said, fanning the box with a file. "Just open it. I'll stand right here."

Lawrence, in his growing frustration, grabbed the box and ripped it open. Out dropped a gold ring and chain with a St. Christopher medal on it. "Well," Lawrence said calmly holding out his hands for gloves, "isn't this special?"

"We got a trace on that call!" one of the eager officers

assisting on the case yelled out. "Phone belongs to a Julian Marcum and we have a location of the phone."

"Let's go, we can appraise the jewelry when we get back."

The blood-gorged rats scurried through the shadows when they entered the basement. The lock on the front door was broken and it appeared all but abandoned. Lawrence asked the officer again about the address of this place; it didn't look as if it had been inhabited for quite a while. Confirmed to be where the call came from, the men ventured deeper into what felt like an abyss. Perhaps the inhabitant of this place could maneuver in the dark. Maybe the dweller of this hellhole knew their way around in the dark, but the officers did not and carried flashlights. Stopping abruptly, it wasn't the rodents that stymied the men as much as what they found hanging there on the wall, his hands and feet bound with chains and his eyes covered with duct tape. Shining the lights along the length of the body, they realized they were all standing in a pool of blood and other human matter. The sights and smells ravaged Lawrence's eyes and nose, turning his stomach immediately.

"Oh my God," one of the officers sighed heavily.

Flacca Facina, a.k.a. Ruben Jefferson, was dead and had been for hours.

There were what appeared to be plenty of clues on the scene—rings, penises floating in jars, resembling science fair projects, complete with identifying name cards under each one, all the things that a maniac like The Appointed One would leave behind.

"Looks like he's moved on, sir," one of the more astute officers said, speaking up after the moment or two everyone needed to gather their thoughts. It was clear the young officer had been doing his research on serial killers and psychopaths. With his flashlight, he drew their attention to the cell phone laying on the floor. "He's left too much here to come back. He's making a move."

"We really have to find this bastard. His little game is not funny at all," said Jim, looking at the naked body of Flacca, a.k.a. Ruben, hanging there. Flacca's long hair was caked with dried blood, vomit, and feces, straggly on his head, and his mouth gaped open with his appendage dangling therein instead of a tongue.

"Not fuckin' funny in the slightest," Lawrence said, bursting out of the room to empty his stomach.

CHAPTER TWENTY-SIX

Lawrence, Jim, and the two other officers working along with them, knew as they approached the doors of the storefront church, that they were about to do one of two things; interview a potential suspect—their first, or meet up with another dead body—number six—or five, if they wanted to use the math The Appointed One did. Tracing the phone number was too easy, in Lawrence's opinion, and so he opted for the second possibility. Glancing over at Jim, he shook his head. "Where is he finding all these gay preachers?" he asked.

"I don't know, but he made it just way too easy to find this one. Do you think he's dead in there?" Jim asked, showing a little apprehension. He had to admit, two bodies in one day was a bit much, even for The Appointed One.

"You are so paranoid. Why not just take the help and be glad?" Lawrence balked. Jim all but choked on the irony of Lawrence's statement.

"Help? You actually think this guy is out to help us? If

he wants us to find this guy, it's for some sick sadistic reason. You know that," Jim told him.

"I know, you hear all that singing?" Lawrence pointed out to the others.

"Can you imagine if he's in there dead and they don't notice?" Jim chuckled, pushing open the door.

Julian Marcum, the tall, dark, and handsome preacher was charismatic, and his speaking ability was enthralling. After only ten minutes in the church, even Jim found himself nodding during the sermon, while they sat in the back waiting until it was over to approach him about the cell phone and his possible connection to The Appointed One. They were more than certain he wasn't The Appointed One, as he didn't appear to have a motive—at this moment. They weren't even sure he was a potential victim as again, he didn't look the type. But then again . . . "Excuse me, Pastor Marcum?" Lawrence greeted him formally. Still smiling from a friendly chat with church members who came up to commend him on another sermon well done, Julian turned to the two officers in uniform with a smile on his face.

"Yes, gentlemen," he said, returning the greeting to Lawrence.

"I'm Detective Miller and this is my partner, Detective Beam. We would like to ask you a few questions."

"Concerning?" he asked, raising his eyebrows in an innocent looking inquiry.

"When's the last time you've seen your cell phone?" Jim asked, getting to the point. The moment spent with God had worn off, and he was back to his old self.

"Hmm, my cell phone . . . I'm not sure. You see, I don't really use one; I'm more of a traditional man. You know, no computer, none of that Internet that kind of thing."

"But you had a cell phone, right?" Jim asked.

"Oh, of course. I think everyone gets one, but then the novelty wears off, and well . . ."

"I see. Well, apparently the five year novelty didn't wear off until you used it yesterday."

"Well, I didn't use it. So I guess . . . I think it got stolen. Why the questions? Did you find it somewhere or something?"

"Sort of. Have you been listening to the news?"

"I try to avoid it, why?" Again, Julian was smiling. Lawrence could tell Julian Marcum found himself attractive, because he was apparently attempting to charm his way through the conversation. They would get a search warrant if they needed one, and Lawrence knew that would take the smile off Julian's face real fast.

"There have been some murders of clergymen, and well, sir . . . the last call received from the killer came from your phone."

Julian swooned slightly. Lawrence couldn't tell if it was staged or real. Either way it was right on time and very convincing.

"Lord, help me . . . why would anyone want to involve me that way? Surely you're not thinking a member of this congregation?"

"That's what we would like to ask you. You see, we have a theory about that, but I don't think right here . . . right now . . ." Jim began, noticing a church member approaching their conversation, "would be the time."

"I understand completely."

"You do?"

"Pastor Marcum, you never cease to amaze me. Lawd, you don't," the woman praised. Julian's face broke into his practiced smile again, and Lawrence knew then they were working with a chameleon. "Is there any trouble?" she asked, noting the uniforms.

"No, no, my sistah. These men are here out of concern. You know I do a lot of work with the community, and well . . ." he let his sentence hang, and she, not seeming to notice the blow-off, meandered away after giving the officers an approving nod. As soon as she walked away, his expression returned to one of concern.

"If you wait just about another ten minutes, I'll be available for any questions," he told them.

"Great, we'll wait."

Stepping outside the church, the two uniformed officers headed back to the precinct to get results from the lab on Flacca's a.k.a. Ruben's murder scene. Despite the brags of The Appointed One, there would be almost no way he could have done that much damage without leaving one fingerprint. Meanwhile, Jim and Lawrence hung around waiting for all the church members to leave. Lawrence noticed the parking lot across the street. It was the parking lot of Moorman University, the school where Portia Hendrix taught. Yeah, he'd taken a minute to do a little personal homework. He wondered immediately if she was a member of this man's church. Lawrence was quick to put together a scenario, despite the fact that she was not in attendance today.

"Okay, I'm ready." Julian called from the church as soon as the last member left.

"Thank you for your time. Sir, we have reason to believe that the man we are looking for has targeted certain members of the clergy," Lawrence stated carefully.

"Certain religions or . . ." Julian asked, leading the question to an uncomfortable place, as far as Lawrence was concerned.

"No, certain clergymen—clergymen who have dealings with less appealing crowds of people," Jim took over.

"Aw, yes, I happen to know about a group of my peers

who make a habit of taking their ministry to the uh . . . Red Light District."

"Deacon Fox," Lawrence interjected.

"Yes, I know him . . . knew him," Julian corrected.

"So you do read the paper?" Jim asked.

"Well, that news was everywhere—hard to miss."

"So you know how he died?" Lawrence pressed him. "Or why he died?"

"Why he died is not in my power to guess, but how. Like I said, the news was everywhere. It was very tragic."

"You ever been to the Rainbow Room?"

"Well, yes and no," Julian answered.

"Is it yes or is it no?" Jim asked.

"I'm on a few committees that get together on occasion to discuss how we can benefit our communities better. For instance, on Saturdays I have an open sermon, outside at the Boys and Girls Club, and during this time of year, we have it in the gymnasium there. It has proven very beneficial to the homeless children and . . . and so, yes . . . we actually went there to the um, Rainbow Room . . ." Julian spoke articulately and without stammering, "once, to see if perhaps there were any souls we could save."

"Ah, the souls of drag queens, pimps, and crack heads . . . so did you happen to save any?" Jim asked.

Julian's face held to a stiffened front. "No," he answered, "And I chose to avoid that venue to those better suited and apparently, my colleagues should have as well."

"Suited?" Lawrence asked.

"How can I put it . . ."

"Truthfully would be good," Jim interjected.

Julian chuckled at Jim's comment. "Of course. You see, I would rather be a part of shutting down places such as, for instance, the Rainbow Room. I'd like to see places like that close. So preaching to those people, I feel, is a conflict. I feel it's hypocritical, because frankly, they are all gonna burn in hell."

"Strange you should mention the Rainbow Room in that light," Lawrence jumped in.

"Why? Why is it strange?"

"Just is. Can you tell us where you were two nights ago?"

"No, I can't," answered Julian flatly.

"You can't?"

"No, I'm sure I was here. . . ."

"I see, well then, I suppose you wouldn't know how your phone might have gotten away from you?"

"No."

"And I'm sure you know we're investigating a murder in the area of the Rainbow Room. A clergyman was killed. We're just wondering if by chance you knew him?" Lawrence asked, pulling out a decent picture of Deacon Fox.

"Yes," Julian admitted. "He was on the committee I'm on."

"How about this man?" Lawrence asked, pulling out a picture of Sal Mendoza.

Julian blinked slowly. "Yes," he admitted.

Lawrence could see he was not prepared for this part of the questioning, and his words were coming truer than he probably wanted them to. He'd admitted to knowing Deacon Fox, but that was all. "How do you know him?"

"Same committee."

"Hasn't it bothered you that these men are dead?"

"No. As I said, they chose to spend a good portion of their time with the wrong kind of people, and well . . . it's like war; there are casualties sometimes."

"So you would rather stay on the sidelines . . . here?" Jim asked, looking around the church.

"Something like that."

"What about this man?" Jim asked, whipping out the picture of Flacca, a.k.a. Ruben, at the crime scene.

"Christ!" Julian yelped, covering his mouth at the sight of the man hanging dead.

"How about this?" Jim said now, reaching into the file Lawrence had in his hand and pulling out the picture of Kyle in drag.

Julian looked at the photo and then turned away slightly. "No, I don't know that person either."

"Hmm, that's strange, because either you lost your phone a while ago or your lyin', because this guy's phone number was called from your cell phone over a hundred times in the last three months," Jim stated flatly. "And this guy," Jim pointed at Kyle's picture, "called this guy . . ." he pointed at the picture of Flacca that Lawrence still held, "every day. Funny, huh? And I don't mean funny, ha ha."

"Is that all?" Julian snipped, showing them he was finished playing nice. The next questions were going to preferably be answered in the presence of his attorney.

"For now. We're going to go question this guy next," Jim said, looking at the picture of Kyle and then Julian. "See if maybe he has a better memory than you do about who he knows and who he doesn't."

"Well, I'm sure that this guy has been to my church. They all have at one time or another," Julian volunteered, losing all congeniality and starting to stammer.

"All of them?" Jim asked. "They? Them? What are you meaning?"

"Those kinds comes here all the time. I am a storefront and across from a college," he said, snatching the picture quickly and looking at it again. "Like this guy. I'm sure he's been here," Julian reneged, and then nodding heartily, he changed his story. "Yes, I want to say he has, and maybe I even counseled him a few times."

"Ah, so you have met him before?"

"Seen him—there's a big difference. And that other guy, well, I've never seen him. Are you hearing me?"

"Absolutely," Jim agreed, sounding altogether serious. "And these counseling sessions . . . are you sure they weren't . . ." Jim's hand waved like a boat on the sea. "Are you hearing me?"

About that time, another young couple came into the church to speak with Julian. "Well, gentlemen," Julian began, nearly rushing them to the door with his words, "if you have any more questions, please don't hesitate to come back, but please give me time to call my attorney first."

"No problem, Mr. Marcum."

"Do you consider yourself an honest person, Jim?" Lawrence asked as they walked back to the car.

"Honest enough, why?"

"Would you admit to being bi-curious?"

"To you? Hell no. To my boyfriend, well, that's another subject," Jim said. And then, unable to keep it in, he burst into laughter.

"You are a freak."

"Yeah, but Nala likes me, and that's all that matters."

"God, tell me it's not true," Lawrence said shaking his head.

"Yeah, she called me last night, asking me to come to the club. . . . said she needed me to stake her out."

"Stop it, Jim. Stop now."

"Okay, so he hadn't called. I lied, but when I got home there was a message to come over. But I stood him up and now he's already called five times this morning. I didn't go to service because I didn't want to see him," Portia told Nala, having met her for a Sunday Brunch.

They had just finished their meal at what was becoming their favorite spot. She had decided to come clean and confess everything about Julian Marcum to Nala.

"So her name is . . . Kyla?" Nala asked, sounding cautious.

"Yes. Some bimbo named Kyla. I don't even think she's a member of our church like he said. I think she's just some bimbo."

"Well, we only know one Kyla, and hell no she ain't no churchgoer—not the Kyla we know."

"Well, Nala, I'm sure it's not the Kyla we know because . . ."

"Because what? Because the Kyla I know is a freak or something?"

"I didn't say that."

"You felt it. I can tell." Nala looked off, hurt. Portia, out of reflex, touched her cheek, bringing her face back around.

"Nala, I would never say that or feel that way. I know you have had some people be really cruel to you because of who you are and what you do, but it's not me. I would never say or do anything to hurt you. But the Kyla we know is a man, that's all I was saying."

"How do you know who I am?" Nala sniveled. Her tears were coming, although she was fighting them. "How do you know about me and how I feel?" Nala went on dramatically.

"Nala, I'm going to ask you straight out. Are you a lesbian? You can tell me. I can take it. I'll still be your friend. I just want to know."

Nala smiled then and blinked slowly. "No, Portia. I'm not a lesbian. I can promise you that."

Portia sighed heavily and sat back in her seat. And then as if digesting the words, she straightened out her napkin on her lap. "Okay, then, we got that out of the way. Now, like I was saying, girlfriend," Portia giggled, "you have to stop being so easily offended."

"You're right," Nala said laying her heavy hand on Portia's thigh. Their eyes met and Portia felt herself gulp audibly. "And you have to stop being scared of me," Nala said now, her voice growing deep and sultry as if fighting with hormones.

"I'm not scared."

Nala burst into laughter, causing a couple of heads in the restaurant to turn. "Good, then I say meet your preacher man and seduce the hell out of him, considering he's probably got a little hell in him. And I know you don't feel like slapping it out of him. That would be me." She laughed again. This time Portia did, too.

"Seduce him?"

"Yes, you already look all cute, got your hair cut and wearing cute stuff. Look atcha with your little cleavage showing," Nala said pointing. Portia unconsciously grabbed at the top of her blouse, closing it a little.

"So you want me to try to get him into bed?"

"Yes! Isn't that the name of the game? Isn't that what us girls do best, screw 'em, Jew 'em, and then in the end sue 'em." She cracked up again.

"I just want to marry him."

"Same thing. Only for the life of me, I have no idea why you would want to marry a sucka like that anyway. Finish your food, 'cause you gon' need your strength. I say, you call that man and then go meet him."

"Well, all right, if you say so."

"Yeah, don't let no Kyla get between you and the man of yo' dreams."

Portia smiled sincerely. Nala playfully hid behind her napkin, and then pulling it down, she lightly kissed Portia's cheek. Portia turned slightly and received the soft kiss on her lips.

"I'm sorry," Nala said, pulling back. Portia stared at her for a moment.

"Don't be, it was me," Portia confessed. Nala all but blushed. "You are quickly becoming my best friend, Nala. You . . . you do something to me, and I need to start being honest with myself and my feelings, okay?" Nala nodded. "It's not a gay thing or nothing like that. I can't imagine me being gay." Nala shook her head. "It's just . . ." Portia glanced at her watch. "Look, let me get this stuff boxed up so I can go talk to this crazy man. I'll call you tonight, okay? We'll talk about it all tonight."

"Okay, doll, I'll be waiting." Nala pulled her cell phone out of her purse and dialed. "I've got to make some calls, okay? You head on over to yo' . . . man," Nala said, grinning broadly, fanning Portia on her way. Portia grinned broadly.

"Okay, I'll call you after I see him."

Kyle was hot. The police had come by to speak with him. Ian was looking at him like he was a criminal, saying nothing at all, just staring.

"Julian Marcum. You're fuckin' Julian Marcum?" Ian yelled after about ten minutes of silence.

"And what of it, Ian! What the hell of it?" Kyle yelled back.

"I can't believe it. He's a preacher . . . he's a damn preacher."

"Oh, so you know him?"

"His church is right across the street from my school. Of course, I've heard of him. His flyers are all over the school. He's like some outreach kinda preacher."

"Well, he reached out to me and I grabbed hold."

"Kyle, haven't you figured it out? Preachers are getting killed because of being gay. Now you're telling me that Julian is gay and you're his lover. Hello . . . do the math on that. You're in danger."

"Like you care," Kyle spat.

"I care, but not like you think. I'll never care like you think. You have been my friend since we were kids, Kyle. I'm concerned that you're losing your grip."

"No, not me—you!" Kyle barked, while standing with his hands on his hips.

"Kyle, you're just about hysterical. I can't figure it out. What's going on for real?" Ian asked. After a moment of silence, Kyle broke down into tears.

"I'm in love, Ian. I'm really, really in love, and I don't think he loves me back. You wouldn't understand of course, because you have never loved anyone. I mean, not the way I mean. I don't know why you have no affection in you. I feel bad for you. But I'm a passionate man with a lot of feelings and . . ." Kyle cried. Ian slowly crept into an embrace. Kyle hung on tightly, sobbing. Ian slowly patted him on the back.

"I understand, Kyle. Really I do," Ian said softly.

Just then, Kyle's phone rang. He glanced around at it, sniffling and drying his eyes on his sleeve. "Maybe it's Flacca. I haven't heard from his ass in days. Let me get this call. Thanks, Ian, for caring."

"Sure, anytime," Ian stammered, moving into his room.

CHAPTER TWENTY-SEVEN

After the police left, Julian called Portia several times. He needed her to get over there. He needed to get her committed to him, them . . . he needed to confirm his manhood. He was done with this undercover life . . . down-low life, whatever the hell they called it. He needed to get straight. People were dying and he wasn't about to get involved in that. The man in the club had taken his phone. And now a man was killed and his phone had been involved somehow. "The cops were here for crying out loud, Julian!" he yelled at his reflection. He was freaking out.

Julian waited for Portia to come to the church. Finally, she had called. It was over an hour ago, but she was taking her sweet time about getting there, and it was pissing him off. Perhaps she wasn't as easy as he thought she was. Perhaps she had a little sass in her. The thought excited him. Maybe marrying her would work out after all.

Just then, she whipped up in the parking lot and stepped from the car, wearing a denim skirt, pink sweater top, and white tennis shoes. She had plenty of leg showing for such a cool day; she must have known he was going to be warming her up a bit. She pulled off her dark glasses while running her fingers through her short hair. He wondered when she cut it. Had it been that long since he'd seen her?

"Wow," Julian said, watching and stroking his manhood through his trousers, as it hardened to a point of discomfort. He quickly adjusted himself. "Dang, girl, you've done something to yaself," he called out to her.

"Hellooo . . ." she called, sounding perky and eager while coming through the back door.

"Portia, hi," he said again, working to keep the primal want out of his voice. Up close she was even hotter. What had happened to his frumpy Sunday School teacher, the one who mourned her father and showed her grief every day on her face? The one who begged for his attention and got so little of it? Something had changed. For both of them

"Hi, Pastor Marcum." She looked bright and happy. He wanted to get in on it, to share in it; her renewed zest was a total turn-on.

"Call me Julian. Girl, what's wrong with you?" he flirted. "I love you, ya know." It slipped out; he couldn't help it.

Portia just about fainted. Her mind was spinning like a wheel. Was Nala a soothsayer, or was this her own doing? Had her flirtations finally gotten her here? Now she really wasn't sure she wanted to be here. Being with Nala was exciting, thrilling actually. Despite her brashness, off-color jokes, and dirty mind, Portia was fond of Nala, fonder than she was of Julian at this moment. She wanted to end this meeting so she could go call her and find the underlying cause of the feelings she had.

"I know I can call you Julian," Portia remarked. She

moved over to her desk, which had been unattended for a while. "You wanted to see me and I think you should tell me why."

"I needed you here to um . . ." he stammered, watching the way Portia's hips were moving while she sorted the papers that sat on her desk. Moving up behind her, Julian made sure he was close enough to her backside so that she could feel his erection. She apparently did, as she stood stiff and tall for a second before turning to face him. They were close enough to kiss but didn't.

"I don't know what's come over me, Sistah, but you are affecting me today," he confessed. Portia moved from between his bodily hardness against her front and the hardness of the desk on her backside.

"Well, then I suppose you need to think it through," she said, chuckling nervously. He moved with her, taking hold of her arm, lightly at first and then a little firmer, pulling her to him. Portia was undecided and was taking way too long to make up her mind about whether this was something she wanted or not, because he kissed her, softly at first, and then slid in his tongue and forced hers into action. The kiss was hungrier than she had imagined it would be when she used to dream about this moment. He was more forceful and aggressive than she imagined him being, the way he tugged at her short hair and messed up her neat curls on the top. And she wasn't sure she liked the way he made those little moaning sounds while grinding himself into her. She hadn't even closed her eyes; she just watched him while he ate away at her face. She hoped he wasn't at the point of no return, because return . . . refund . . . was all that was on her mind right now. She had changed her mind about this whole thing. She no longer wanted Julian—gay, straight, or otherwise.

Too late. He lifted her from her feet and sat her squarely on the desk, reaching under her short skirt and ripping at her panties.

"Wait a minute, Julian!" she yelped, grabbing at his thick wrists. He covered her mouth with his large hand and shushed her. Her heart was racing and fear shut her voice up tight. The fabric tore away from the lacy thong she had just bought. He tossed it to the side and pulled her hips to the edge of the table. The desk was cool on her bare bottom.

"Lean back. If you don't like it, I'll stop," he whispered. His dark eyes were mesmerizing, hypnotizing, completely seducing. She obeyed.

When his tongue entered her, she nearly jumped from the table. She'd often dreamed about the last time he tongued and fingered her this way. She was as wet as an ocean and just in time, too, because she soon heard his zipper. Opening her eyes and focusing on his swollen erection, she had to admit, she was more than ready to receive it. Flesh to flesh, she was ready to take on Julian Marcum.

Climbing on the desk, he entered her with a force that made her cry out, only to again feel his hand over her mouth. "Shhh, Sistah, just enjoy the ride."

And what a ride. Julian put on a phenomenal performance. What he couldn't move inside her with his kisses, he rocked with his lower anatomy. He cupped her firm hips in his hands, and she held him while he pounded his manhood into her relentlessly, until finally, he dove deep into her cove, releasing his hot juices inside her. She cried out with the throbbing of her womb that contracted in her belly, causing her body to tighten around his engorgement. "Wow," he said, grinding his hips against her, making sure there was friction against her clit, which again sent her into an orgasmic fit. This was real sex, the kind she'd only read about in those books by Noire and Zane.

She gasped and panted, trying to say his name, but only managing to call him 'Julie.' He didn't seem to mind; calling him Julie was just fine by him. "Yeah, baby, say my name and turn over. I want some of that ass," he whispered in her ear, after lying on top of her for a second or two, rocking with her. Portia's eyes opened and stared deep into his. She couldn't believe he wasn't finished with her. She was finished with him. He pulled from her, still hard as ever and urged her over onto her stomach. "Just relax," he whispered.

Relax? I am relaxed, she thought to herself, not realizing that when he said her ass, he meant her rectum. Spreading her cheeks, she felt the tip of his penis and the burn as he pushed his way into her. Unable to scream, she felt her face grimace as he slid deep into her rear end as if it was the customary orifice a man would enter during copulation. "Nooo," she managed to cry out. He pulled out.

"You don't like it?" he whispered in her ear, while still positioned over her. She could still feel the hardness against the back of her thigh. "You can't tell me you don't like it. I'm good at this, baby, real good," he purred, forcing his penis inside her back door again.

"Nooo," she cried, trying to turn over, to get up. The urge to go to the bathroom was strong, and she needed to get up. He'd ruined everything, everything that could ever be for the two of them. "I've got to go to the bathroom. Get up!"

He moved off her just in time. Humiliated and thinking about Reba's warning again, she ran into the bathroom. She never wanted to see him again. Sitting there on the commode, she prayed he was gone when she came out.

"Portia," she heard him call through the door.

"You're . . . you're wrong for that, Julian," she yelled at him through the door.

"It's natural, girl. I didn't do anything wrong," he yelled back. "If you are gonna be my wife, you have to be willing to satisfy my needs, girl."

"Your needs? Your wife? Please, Julian, I can't talk right now. Please just go away so I can come outta this bathroom and go home. I . . . I have to go home."

"All right, Portia," he said, leaving the through the entrance leading into the church.

Kyle hadn't meant to be a peeping Tom, but after getting that phone call from Nala, Kyle knew he had to get over there. And damn, what he saw paralyzed him with mortification. Julian was going at her good on that desk. Kyle could do nothing but watch—and hurt.

When Julian finished with her, he left out the front, leading back into the church hall, and she stayed in the bathroom forever and forever. Portia, the little no-dancing hoochie from the club. Kyle's heart was nearly broken. Julian was his Daddy Boo and he thought he was the only booty Julian was planning on tappin'. Finally, Portia came from bathroom. Kyle hid behind Julian's truck, so as not to be seen when she came out.

Kyle was livid. All he had planned was ruined. Nala was a bitch, setting him up to catch them like this. What was she thinking he would feel?

"Bitch," he mumbled, watching Portia limping to her car as if the dick was too much for her. Kyle could only imagine what she went through, having that big ol' thing of Julian's in her ass. He was green with envy. "Oh well," Kyle finally sighed, stepping from his hiding place. "I guess I'll get you back for this, Julian. Because, I'm sorry . . . this was unacceptable behavior," he said, smacking his full lips and heading to the bus stop, pointing his finger as if fussing at Julian to his face. He was full of attitude, and ready to do just about anything.

Kyle couldn't wait to get back home. He snatched off his wig as soon as he hit the door. Ian looked at him from under the newspaper that rested on his face. "What flew up our skirt?" Ian asked. Kyle rolled his eyes at the comment and then twisted his hips in a sassy manner.

"Wouldn't you like to know."

Ian pulled the paper back over his head. "Not really . . . I was just making convo."

"Well, Mr. I'm-so-straight-it-hurts, just so you know, I've had it with all you down-low men. You and your, 'I'm not gay, I'm not gay,' when in fact, you and all your little bisexual buddies are causing some serious problems out here in the real world."

Ian sat up slowly. "I don't even wish I knew what you were talking about, but go on."

"I get this call from my boss, which makes me wonder about her . . . or him, whatever the hell that freak is. Anyway, I get there, and find the infamous pastor Julian Marcum—doing Portia Hendrix," Kyle began.

"Since when do you care about Portia Hendrix?" Ian asked, his interest piqued slightly at the sound of Portia's name.

Kyle smacked his lips loudly. "Oh, Mr. Obtuse, not so obtuse. You know Portia?"

"I work with her."

"Well, homeboy, so do I, and apparently so does Julian Marcum." Kyle began to moan, pulling at his nipples, making sexual sounds while grinding his hips. "Heffa had her legs up in the air, getting anointed with Julian's unholy oils. Yeah, he's on the fuckin' down-low and I bet she doesn't even know it."

"Kyle, stop it. Get to the point," Ian snapped, closing his eyes at the sight of Kyle acting the way he was. "You saw Julian and Portia?

"Disgusting, isn't it? I mean, I guess I can see why this guy is out there trying to rid the world of that kind of shame."

"Excuse me; there wouldn't be that kind of shame if people like you were out there."

"What are you trying to say . . . people like me?"

"Kyle, don't get me started," Ian groaned, jumping to his feet, heading now for his bedroom. Kyle ran in front of him, blocking his path.

"No, you're not gonna run away this time. You hate me, don't you? No, wait. You love me—that's the problem, isn't it?" Kyle pointed his finger at him. "You are just embarrassed because you are hiding your sexuality. Ian, this killer guy, he's after guys like you. Look at the pattern. He's kill . . ." Kyle paused as if for the first time, really seeing a clear pattern. "He's killing down-low clergymen," he gasped, "who have jilted him," he panted.

"Kyle, I don't want to talk about it. I've never wanted to talk about it, so don't even try to psychoanalyze me. Your brain will pop," Ian said, stepping closer to Kyle, who was having a moment of revelation and ignoring Ian's angry heat. "Kyle, I've had it!"

"Yeah, yeah, sweetie, hang on a second," Kyle said, pushing past Ian to go back into the living room. Clicking on the TV, he went looking for the DVD he had recorded of the press conference that was on a couple of weeks back, regarding the killer that had struck the city, taking out two people within the couple of days of the new year. He heard Ian's door slam. "I love you, Ian. I want to be with you!" he yelled over his shoulder in the direction of the slam.

"Go to hell, Kyle!" Ian yelled back.

Kyle knew Ian was getting tired of him. He was getting tired of himself. But he couldn't help it. He was lonely and frustrated, and now he was hurt. Julian was going to pay for all that. He was going to be sorry he did this to him. Kyle needed to find out if this killer was a serial killer or a happenstance one, and if so, why kill Deacon and Jenessa? Again, Kyle picked up the phone to call Flacca. No answer.

"Yes, now this crazy man was serious. He meant business. Whatever it was he had set out to accomplish, he was on a mission to accomplish when he killed Deacon, and well, Jenessa, too, for that matter. Maybe he's a hit man. Maybe Nala hired him . . . or whoever. Whatever he's up to, I need to find him, because I might have to give him another mission—of mercy. He needs to take Julian and Portia out of their misery. Yeah, I bet Julian would fly right if The Appointed One was on his ass," he mumbled, listening to the reporter speaking about The Appointed One still being at large, but hopefully moving out of the city. "Yeah, even if he just *thought* The Appointed One was gonna kill him."

The phone rang. It was Nala, calling Portia to come in. again. Flacca had not come in, and Kyle was again a no-show. "I'm gonna fire him. You know that, right? So get ready to shake your ass a lot more, honey, because you're gonna get his slot."

"Oh my goodness. I don't think I'm ready."

"Well get ready."

"But I can't come in tonight; I'm a mess."

"Girl, what is wrong with you?" Nala blurted.

"I just really can't talk about it. I'll just say this: me and Julian are through."

"You found out about Kyle?" Nala asked.

"Kyle? You mean Kyla, and no, that didn't even come

up. It's something else and I can't talk about it. Can I have a few days to get myself together? Please?"

"Sure, sweetie. I totally understand," Nala said. "I'll get ol' big foot Louise to fill in. We'll be fine," she said, chuckling a little.

After the conversation, Portia went upstairs to her waiting bath, sliding into a hot tub, where she sulked and cried over all the time and self-pride she'd invested needlessly in Julian, just for it all to end up this way. She was humiliated.

After a while, she curled up on the sofa and called Reba. "Julian and I are over," Portia told her as hot tears again streamed down her cheek.

"Good riddance to bad rubbish I say," Reba barked, taking a bite from her sausage pizza. "Now you can hook up with that nice policeman. Wit his fine ass . . . you remember," Reba growled into the receiver. "Tight ass, too . . . ummph, girl."

"Reba," Portia said and shook her head, "let me get offa here. I'm gonna watch a little TV, and I have to go to work tomorrow, so I need to pull myself together."

CHAPTER TWENTY-EIGHT

The murder of Ruben Johnson didn't escape the media. Every paper in town, and perhaps in the nation, covered the crucifixion story. The Appointed One was becoming quite the formidable game player, and with his many, many clues and still not being caught, the district attorney was quick to pay the chief a visit.

"Well, that was fun," she said, after seeing the DA to the elevator. "So, where are we now? And don't even give me that 'up shit's creek with no paddles and it stinks in here' bull crap, Jim, because I'm not buying it," she growled in Jim's direction. He held up his hands in surrender. "We have to have something, boys," she barked at Lawrence.

"Tough meeting?" Lawrence asked her, knowing the answer; he could hear a lot of it through the door.

She shook her head and blew out hot air. "I'm not even sure which matter them folks are having a fit about—Jenessa Jewel being Rachel Williams, the cop slash stripper, or Deacon being a priest and homosexual. . . . . or that little, uh . . . hanging action, or . . ."

"He hasn't called in nearly a week," Jim noted, hoping to help the tense situation that was building.

"But what do we know?" she asked again. "I was lying my ass off saying we knew a lot, but I'm like, what do we really know?"

"We have the missing penis of Marvin Shackles accounted for, thanks to Rachel Williams, and we have Sal Mendoza's ring, thanks to a Fed-Ex delivery. With that I'd say we have some closure on two of the cold files. The Appointed One has given us the other two murders—Deacon Fox and Ruben Jefferson, a.k.a. Flacca Facina."

"And try saying that three time fast," Jim chimed in as if doing that was most of the work here. The chief scowled at him.

"We know we are not looking for two crazies and that The Appointed One is no copycat; he's the killer now, a year ago and . . ." Lawrence held out a file dated nearly ten years ago. The chief took it from him reluctantly.

"Joseph Samuels?"

"Ten years ago, found dead in his church, duct taped, sodomized, missing penis," Lawrence told her.

"We found it when the guys cleared out that basement," Jim went on.

"We're still looking to ID someone to match the card named Mary," Lawrence went on. "Nala and the others were at the club the night Flacca was killed, and we were, too. Oh, and we also questioned Julian Marcum, and got little to nowhere, but he had an alibi with Kyle Matthews, the little fairy that came in here right after we found Deacon Fox."

"He's a sneaky one, and I'd say we watch him a little closer, but anywho, he gave the good gay preacher an alibi for the night Flacca was hanged. Said he was getting some counseling," Jim explained.

"I bet," the chief commented. "So are we any closer to finding this guy?"

"Well, he is definitely a cell phone lifter and a jewelry collector. From the little trinkets we found along with the many, many Rainbow Room matchbooks, we figure he might also be a regular there," Jim said.

"But like I say, we haven't heard hide nor hair from him in about a week," Lawrence told her.

"So he's killed a person a week on average, and poof, it's February 1st, and now he's gone . . . so what, we gonna call him the New Year's killer now? I mean, that's all we seem to keep getting are new names for him," the chief remarked sarcastically.

"Perhaps he's taking a break," Lawrence suggested.

"Or perhaps not. Let's stay on that Rainbow Room watch and see what happens," the chief ordered. "I mean, with all this media coverage blaming him for the murder of Ruben Jefferson, he might realize that he's still a little odd, ya know what I'm sayin'?"

True, The Appointed One hadn't killed in a week, so perhaps he had taken a break, and good thing, too, for his shenanigans were sure adding to the record breaking number of five killings within the first month of the year. But with that odd number, there was always the thought that he would return, and with the prospects of at least one more murder in the queue to even the number, they had to stay on it and not be lulled into a sense of false security. Having staked out the owner of the Rainbow Room already, Lawrence's mind was set at ease about that assignment. He could get the thought of dressing up like a girl or acting like a queer off his mind. He was trying not to wrap his brain around that thought anyway. With Nala, albeit reluctantly, okay with them just hanging out at her club for a few nights a week, Lawrence had freed his brain to think more about finding a place to live. He'd yet to try calling the number in the paper for the Room Plus Meals deal again. It sounded like a sweet arrangement, providing the meals were palatable. But he'd waited for so long, no doubt the room was rented by now.

After the briefing with Jim and the chief, Lawrence had decided to drive by the address of the room for rent on his way to work. Pulling up to the stop sign, he pondered his thoughts about the case, his life, and his mother. Moving was still top on his list of things to do.

Glancing off to the side, that's when he saw her—Portia Hendrix. She was sitting next to him at the light. It was obvious she was trying to avoid him, because she kept looking in her rear view mirror and out the passenger side of her car, as if watching cross traffic. However, it was a one-way street and no cars were coming from the direction she had her head turned. Full of play, he honked his horn. Again, she tried to ignore him. He honked his horn again and then pushed the automatic button, lowering the window on his passenger side. Rolling her eyes wildly, she rolled down her window. At least she recognized him.

"What?"

"Wanna go to dinner?" he asked, the question coming from somewhere in his sleep deprived brain. It wasn't even what he had intended to say. It just came out.

"Dinner? I just finished having breakfast—no."

"Okay, lunch?"

The light turned green.

"No, I'm on my way home," she answered, looking now in the rear view mirror at the driver honking at her. Lawrence turned around and glared at the impatient man. Portia pulled off.

Missing the green, Lawrence endured the honks behind

him and the old lady's middle finger showing clearly in his rear view mirror. When the light changed, he headed toward the address of the room for rent.

Portia reached her house and hopped out of the car. She'd forgotten her study plan for the day. "What a Monday!" she growled, thinking of all she had on her mind. Nala had called her late, nearly hysterical over the death of Flacca. Just then, Lawrence Miller pulled up behind her.

"Why are you stalking meeeee?" she groaned, moving her bangs out of her eyes.

"Girl, don't flatter yourself. I'm here looking for an address."

She stomped to his window. "What is it? Let me help you find it so you can get off my street!"

"Your street?" He raised his eyebrow while unfolding the ad. She reached in the window and snatched the paper from him. Noticing the circled ad was none other than her own, she gasped.

"Oh, heck no! My house? You want to live in my house?"

Lawrence burst into laughter. "Well, at least you know I have a job, and I'm not some weirdo."

"By who's standards?" she smarted off, slamming her hands on her hips. He laughed.

After her meeting with Lawrence, Portia went back to the college in hopes of being on time for her class. She had to accept the fact that the smile that had planted itself permanently on her face was all about him. How quickly life could change from good to bad and then back again. She'd even taken his money and given him a key. It was moving fast.

Lawrence was handsome, sweet, and generous. Above

all, he was available to move in immediately, which meant added income for repairs to her home of which he had agreed to do many, if not all. It was all too good to be true.

Passing Ian, she felt the need to smile at him. After all, he had been her pretend lover once; the least she could do was be polite. She looked at him and wondered why she had chosen him, with his soft blue eyes and fair white skin. Why had she chosen him?

"How have you been, Portia?" he asked her, stopping her mid thought.

"Well . . ." she stammered, "I've been fine, Ian. How about yourself?"

"Just fine," he nodded. "I've had some personal issues, but they've been pretty much resolved. Hey, look, do you still have that room for rent? I noticed your flyer was down, but I figured it couldn't hurt to ask."

"Funny," she chuckled. Heat rose to her cheeks, thinking immediately of Lawrence and his smile. "I rented it this morning."

"You must really like your tenant," Ian said, pointing at her, noticing her blush.

"He's . . ."

"He?"

"Yes. And he's very nice. He's a police officer and—"

"Well, at least you'll be safe," Ian said, cutting her off and glancing at his watch. "I don't want to keep you, really. I just wanted to ask about the room."

"I thought you had a roommate?" she asked as he started to walk away.

"We're parting ways. We're having a 'difference in values' issue."

"I see. Well I hope you find something. There's nothing worse than dealing with someone who doesn't value things as you do." She was thinking of Julian Marcum and his view on marriage.

"Exactly, and the values we have make us who we are. They are as important as life or death sometimes," he preached. "You can't compromise on them. Some things in life were meant to be certain ways and when we mess around with nature, well, suffice it to say, it messes up the karma, the cosmos, the—"

"Wow, you have so much conviction in your beliefs."

"Well, I try not to push my beliefs on people; I used to want to be a priest before deciding on my career and—"

"A priest? I had no idea," Portia blurted. It was such a coincidence, or maybe it was just her and her draw to religiously inclined and unavailable men.

"Neither does my roommate; that's how oblivious he is about me and my beliefs. No, it's always about him. Kyle is just—"

"Kyle? I mean, wow, that name is so popular . . . Kyle, Kyla," Portia interjected again.

"Yeah, it's popular, all right, and so is the man that owns both of those names." Ian sucked the air through his teeth. Portia's mind spun.

"Both?"

"Kyle . . . Kyla. It's the same person. Look, Portia, I see you're trying to hold on to some kind of confidentiality, but I know you're an employee at the Rainbow Room. I know this . . . don't understand it, because it's like, obvious your female." Ian pointed at her hands and their smallness. "You're just too soft."

"How?"

"Kyle is my roommate and your co-worker. He's Kyla." Ian winked—perhaps unconsciously. Perhaps it was just the sign Portia needed to put the puzzle altogether.

Suddenly, as if realizing how long he had been talking

to her, or maybe how much he'd revealed, he looked at his watch again. "I'm sorry; I've really got to run. My first class cancelled and I have enough time to make it to confession."

"See ya around," she said as he hurried off. He nodded slowly but didn't turn around. "Kyle is Kyla?" she repeated, digging in her purse for her ringing cell phone while continuing toward her mailbox. Reaching the mailbox, she saw the familiar stationary; it was another letter from Julian Marcum. She'd been shredding his mail all week. *Meet me when you get a moment. It's important! Don't stand me up this time,* the note said. "Whateverrrr," she groaned. "I've got better things to do than fool with you, Mr. Preacher Man." Suddenly it hit her like a brick. "Kyla? Oh my God."

Jim noticed Lawrence's change of mood when he reached the station. Lawrence had been nothing less than gloomy for days, but not this morning. He all but had springs in his shoes, the way he bounced in. He even spoke to hairy Betty at the front desk, and she normally un-nerved him first thing in the morning.

"What's got you grinning like the Cheshire Cat?"

"Found a room," Lawrence whispered.

"Is it a secret? Why you whisperin'?" Jim whispered back, playing along.

"Portia Hendrix . . . remember her?"

"No," Jim whispered.

"Of course you do," Lawrence said, speaking now in a regular voice. He hadn't realized how silly he sounded until Jim's last comment.

"The chick I tried to kill a couple of times."

"Ohhh . . . her . . ." Jim's eyebrow rose now and he nodded knowingly. "That little pretty-in-pink-girl."

"Oh you noticed that?"

"Who wouldn't notice an ass like that?"

"Stop, she's a church girl . . . good girl."

"Oh, pu-lease. You left Hannah to take up with a good girl. Yeah, right."

"For one, I didn't leave Hannah; she threw me out, and for seconds . . . yeah."

Jim burst into laughter.

"I quit!" Kyle spat.

Nala sipped her tea calmly, watching him throw his tantrum. "You're just being hysterical. Yes, it's awful about Flacca, but we have to keep this thing together. We're family," she finally said.

"Family! I can't believe what you did. I can't believe I let you do it!" he screamed. "Damn family!"

"Honey, look, Portia is my girl and I couldn't sit back and let you take her man . . . such as he is."

"But that was not your call and it was mean and heartless. And well . . . you're a bitch," Kyle continued.

"Kyle, you need to stop calling the kettle black. You need to get a life, one of your own, and just stay out of people's business."

"Julian was my life. You're just mad because he was never attracted to you . . . because Deacon and I had a thing going on. You're just mad because Sal wanted me not you. You're just mad because Marvin and I hit it off so well, you . . ." Suddenly it hit Kyle like a brick, and he shut up for a second while listening to his words. "And Jenessa, and Flacca . . . oh my God, you . . . you killed them, didn't you?"

"You're an asshole, Kyle," Nala said, rubbing her forehead. She moved and Kyle jumped in fear. "Kyle, how in the world did I kill them? Explain that one to me. I was here when Jenessa was killed, or do you not remember that night? Jeeesus, I was here arguing with your stupid ass about your tips while that girl was being killed! So how could I have done it? And Deacon, how in the hell could I have killed that man?"

"Easy, you cut off their dicks and . . . and you killed him!"

"A woman could never do what was done to him, and a woman could never have raped Jenessa—think about it."

"It would be a good argument if you were a woman," Kyle yelled.

"What did you say to me?" Nala was growing emotional. Her womanhood had been challenged.

"Freakanatcha!" Kyle screamed.

Nala flew into a rage, attacking Kyle instantly. They tussled on the floor, with Nala being bigger and gaining advantage quickly, pummeling him. Louise came from behind the bar, grabbing at Nala's fast moving arms. Kyle had ripped her shirt and her breasts were exposed now, but she continued to strike out at him. Soon Kyle got to his feet, with the help of Louise, now attempting to grapple with Nala. She pushed Louise off and grabbed Kyle, who, out of instinct, kicked her in the groin.

The pain was intense and Nala bent over in anguish. "Fuck!" she growled, her voice losing its war with the hormones she regularly injected into her body. Looking up at Kyle, a tear seeped from her pain-filled eyes. He watched in amazement at the swelling in her lower region. It was obvious she had a penis. Holding herself there, she limped over to the bar.

"You're a fuckin' he/she. Like a . . . like whatcha call 'em—hermaphrodite!" Kyle gasped.

"Get out of my bar and never, ever come back in here, Kyle. Trust me, if I was a killer you'd be dead a long time ago." Nala could barely speak from the pain she felt. Louise quickly filled a baggie with ice and came over to her side to assist.

"Nala, I'm so sorry. I shouldn't have gotten involved. I had no idea," Louise apologized. "Truly, I never knew."

"Well, now you do. Get your shit and get outta here, too. I'm not going to work with a bunch of cross dressing traitors. None of you make good women; you're all just men who play in dresses. Fuck you all! Everywhere I go, I'm betrayed . . . everywhere I go," Nala said, breaking down into a heap of tears.

Portia couldn't believe her ears when she got the call. Her problems seemed very small all of a sudden. She barely had time to think about Julian and the 'possibilities' before she was hopping in her car and flying to the Rainbow Room. Louise announced her when they entered Nala's office, as the lights were off and Portia couldn't see Nala's face clearly. But she could hear Nala's voice. Nala's deep voice.

"Nala?" Portia called into the darkened room.

"Come in, sweetie," Nala responded, sounding like a wounded solider. She was lying on her divan.

"Is that you?"

"Yes, it's me. God, I hate Kyle with all my being," she went on, groaning while rising up on the sofa. Clicking on the light, Portia gasped upon seeing Nala there, with her robe hanging low around her shoulders exposing her breasts, while she held the ice pack in place between her legs, cooling her testes. Portia tried not to stare at the wounded creature Nala appeared to be at this moment. Gone was her glamour, her sensuality—replaced only with agony.

"You need to see a doctor, Nala." Portia's voice peaked to an un-natural high while she pretended not to be shocked entirely.

"I hate doctors, too. I hate doctors, preachers, my father, and Kyle, in that order. Oh, hell no, I hate Kyle worst of all," she laughed, before taking another swig from the bottle. "Kill his punk ass," she grumbled.

"Nala, stop, you won't kill anybody," Portia said, after taking a deep accepting breath and looking around for more ways to make Nala comfortable. Nala grinned, the effects of the alcohol showing.

"I know you're scared of me," she said pulling the ice pack off and giving Portia a full view of her male appendage. Portia, surprised at the fact that she actually wasn't afraid, just smirked. "I'm what is known to the world as a natural hermaphrodite. I'm real. I'm natural. I was born this way. Most people like me are 'fixed' at birth, but some . . ." again she raised the ice pack for Portia to see, "are not."

"You don't scare me, except maybe that hairdo. It's crazy lookin', heffa."

Nala laughed. "I was born this way, Portia. My father didn't get me fixed . . . no, the bastard had plans for me, I guess."

"Do you want to talk?" Portia asked, sitting down on the sofa next to her. Nala shook her head, releasing the bottle to Portia, who sat it aside.

"You always want me to talk about bad stuff."

"Well, sometimes talking helps."

"Well let me start talking, then, doll . . . Did you know your boyfriend was gay?"

Portia gasped, but tried to seem unaffected. It was the second time today she'd been hit with this realization—besides what Reba had told her weeks ago. "You're just saying that because you don't like preachers."

"No, I'm saying that because who in the hell do you think Kyla is? Hellooo . . .?" she said, conking Portia playfully on the noggin. "Kyla . . . Kyle . . . Hellooo . . . ?"

"Kyle? Kyle and Julian? How long have you known?"

"Kyle told somebody who told somebody . . . doesn't

matter. Kyle is a creepy little man who seems to get off on tapping into the hearts of weak men. Hell, perhaps we all do that in our own way," she said, with a reflective sigh while running her free hand through her thick hair.

"Well, Nala, I think as *women,* we all do." She emphasized the word women on purpose. "Anyway, we're not seeing each other anymore."

"He raped me . . . my own father raped me," Nala said, after a moment shared with Portia, after realizing they truly did have a bond of trust and understanding between them. Nala's lip was trembling. "I was just a little girl . . . boy . . . I had just started developing. And you know, with my deformities . . ."

"You're not deformed, Nala."

Nala held up her large hand. "He should have had this fixed when I was born, but no, he didn't, and my mother was too scared of him to force the issue. She let him convince her it was God's will." Nala shook her head. "Like I was some kind of treat from God."

"Why didn't you do something when you got older?"

"Do you know how tricky a surgery like this is—and expensive? God, it costs a small fortune to have a sex change operation. I can barely afford my hormones that keep the hair off my damn face and chest," she complained, showing Nala her smooth chest as if it still wasn't smooth enough. "Besides, I got by. You'd be surprised how many of us are out there."

"Like maybe someone I know?" Portia asked, shoving the thoughts of Julian to the back of her mind, while pulling Nala's robe up on her shoulders.

Nala nodded with a wicked smile crossing her lips. "Maybe . . . you'd be surprised about a lot of people you know . . . or think you know. But then, of course there are a lot of people out there who are users, like my daddy. They are vicious and dangerous."

"You mean like that guy who was killing people, The Appointed One?"

"Actually, that person is not who I was thinking about, seeing as how I kinda like the mission he's on, taking it upon himself to rid the world of all the liars and cheaters that way. I should have killed my father. Fortunately, somebody else did it for me."

"Your father was murdered?"

"Yeah, somebody cut his dick off."

"Nala . . ." Portia paused.

"Oh I know, and when those murders starting happening I was scared to death. I didn't know what to think. As a matter of fact, short of a few differences, I would have wagered that The Appointed One had killed my father, too. But it was just a coincidence, I'm sure."

"Wow, that's a fantastic story."

"Who you telling, girl? I even started thinking maybe I was like . . . skitzo, and killing people in my sleep or some shit like that. Hell, I read a lot of books and well, that shit can happen, you know."

"What do you really think happened to those men, though? Did you tell the cops about your father?"

"No, I didn't tell the cops about my father . . . please. But then I'm sure if they were looking for evidence against me, they would have found out about it, but they didn't even ask me about my father. But as far as Sal, Deacon, Marvin, and even poor Flacca, who turned out to be a little snake as well, I figure those guys were getting what they deserved."

"But Nala, you had dealings with all of them."

"So what are you saying?"

"Nothing, I'm not saying anything," Portia lied.

"When you become a clergyman, you take on more responsibilities than just your sorry life. Just like my father, you take on more than just your own pleasures and needs."

"Your father was a preacher?"

"I thought I told you that."

"No, you didn't. You . . . have you ever told anybody else about your father and what happened to him?"

"A couple of people. It's not really cocktail conversation, if you pardon my pun." She laughed. "Why?"

"Just wondering."

"Portia, I was in Paris when my father was killed. Besides, if you must know, I'm impotent because of the medications I take . . . have been for years. My doctor can verify that. I couldn't have killed those men."

Portia's sigh of relief showed on her face, and Nala touched Portia's cheek softly. "I knew you would come, Portia. You are truly my little girlfriend."

"I'm very fond of you, Nala," Portia admitted freely. "I didn't want to think you were a killer.

"But it's okay to think I'm a freak."

"You're not a freak; you are a hermaphrodite. It's not a sin or a curse; it's what you are. Embrace your differences and love yourself."

"Thank you." Nala's voice cracked as was common for her when late on her daily hormones.

Reba couldn't wait to make it over to Portia's that evening for dinner with Portia's new house guest. His rent included some meals and she had volunteered to do the cooking until Portia figured out a way to get out of that part of the deal.

Portia didn't get in until much later, and Reba and Lawrence had already started eating. Portia settled into her seat, looking over the food.

"So how is your new job working out?" Reba asked unexpectedly. She still didn't know Portia was moonlighting as a stripper at the Rainbow Room. Glancing quickly at Lawrence with guilt showing like a neon sign, she gulped audibly.

"Fine," she answered quickly.

"Well, you should be able to quit now and just teach, right? I mean, with Lawrence here, right?" Reba went on.

"Where do you work besides the college?" Lawrence asked now, feeling comfortable enough to join in.

"Uh . . . uh," Portia groped. "I uh, a bookstore," she lied.

"A bookstore? Now why didn't I know that?" Reba asked sounding confused even more. "Which one? I'll come in. I love to read. You know that."

"I work at the college bookstore; there are only reference books there," she lied on, filling her mouth with the cheesy tuna casserole. Suddenly she caught Reba's eye, and confessed to her lie without saying a word. Reba nodded slightly, glancing over at Lawrence, and then continued to eat without saying more on the subject.

"Speaking of work, ladies, there's crime in the street, and it has my name on it," he said. "I have to do a double tonight."

"Oh, I like that," Reba purred. "Mr. Policeman on da job," she cackled, flirtatiously slapping Lawrence's muscular arm. She allowed her hand to linger a minute and then pulled it back. "Oh yeah, I like that."

Lawrence glanced at Portia, who looked everywhere but at him, and then slid into his jacket, which was on the back of the chair.

"Have a great evening."

"Sure will," Portia said then. She too had to get back to the club. She had agreed to dance in Kyle's place tonight. She was a nervous wreck.

She also felt guilty because she had a feeling Lawrence was working on or at least knew a lot about the case of the murdered priest, but she didn't tell him what she had found out about Nala and her past, nor what she had found out about Julian. She didn't want him to jump to any conclusions about either of them. She didn't want to either. However, she was sure Nala's physical condition was why she had been so torn when in Nala's presence. Nala had the best of both worlds and knew how to use all she had to make it through the tough life she had apparently been living. But still, Portia had to wonder if Nala might have lost some of her strength along the way, strength that would have forced her to kill men like her father. Portia knew in her heart that she wished she had the strength to appoint herself the killer of men who took God's word in their hands and twisted scripture to suit their own selfish needs. If she was a person stranded between being a man and a woman, would she kill? Maybe so, and now with that thought, did that make her crazy, too? Portia was going to ask Lawrence about it when he got home. She was gonna see what he thought about her theory of the killer being someone *like* Nala.

CHAPTER TWENTY-NINE

Portia was feeling distracted tonight. She felt as if she was being watched. She'd had the heavy feeling all day, but Nala assured her it was normal to feel that way before going on stage for the first time.

"What was I thinking, saying I would do it?" Portia wondered, holding the fans this way and that while practicing her moves. "How am I supposed to make this work?" she asked the mirror, regarding the newly acquired male appendage. She'd never even showed her breasts but tonight, even they would be exposed. Nala had showed her how to put the fake male organ in place, explaining to her that Rachel Williams had worn one and fooled a lot of people—even her—thus giving her the idea.

Portia was covered by so little, it was as if she was going to be completely naked tonight. It was a normal tradition, where normally Nala was the draw, exposing her breasts and the like. Tonight, Portia was to be up for show. "I must have been crazy agreeing to this," Portia sighed, hearing her music starting, sliding into her topcoat, hat, manly slacks, and spats. Nala knocked on the door and peeked in. "Come on, honey, it's your night." She winked. "Take it off like you mean business."

"Yeah," Portia laughed nervously.

Lawrence wasn't sure what he would see tonight. Jim had told him all kinds of fantastic stories from the night he visited the Rainbow Room alone, his one night 'freak fest' stories, only half of which Lawrence believed.

The lights dimmed and Lawrence was instantly put on guard, glancing around the crowd, hoping to spot someone who might be The Appointed One, maybe picking a pocket or slipping a cell phone off the table of some unaware, bi-curious male, a potential victim. Maybe he would see Julian Marcum and bust him flat out. But no, there was nothing, only everyone's attention fixed on the stage.

Suddenly the dancer stepped onto the stage and took a dramatic stance with her or his back to the audience. A few woof calls came from the audience from both men and women, as the sex of the dancer was undeclared, hidden under the big clothes. Lawrence didn't know what to do with his eyes as the dancer began to disrobe, kicking off the shoes, and still with back to the audience, wiggling from the trousers, bringing a roar from the crowd. Still Lawrence tried to focus on his job, looking out over the audience of people who lived alternative lifestyles and were proud of it.

Turning to the audience finally, with hat dipped low over the face, Lawrence strained to see who the dancer was. Perhaps it was his job, but he hated not seeing people's faces and unconsciously drifted a little closer to the stage. Suddenly, in one smooth movement, the hat flew off and Portia, shaking her shoulder length hair loose, broke into a wide grin, jerking the jacket open, exposing her flawless body and flashing, her sequined covered breasts. Her face was painted heavily with silver glitter, including her lips. Her eyes seemed glazed and blinded by the spotlight, as she glistened from the heat of dancing in the jacket. Lawrence's eyes popped open and his jaw dropped. As she took a dip, dropping it like it was hot, coming up into a butterfly dance move, with the male member dangling between her legs, covered only by the thin fabric of a thong, while twisting her hips back and forth, undulating seductively as the music suddenly changed into a hip-hop beat. Leaving the jacket open, exposing her mostly nude body, she began to pop her shoulders, resembling Janet Jackson, bouncing and swinging until someone tossed her hat back onto the stage. She caught it, plopping it back on her head and then jutting out her chin as if a tough guy, she began her hip-shaking turn . . . and that's when she saw him.

"Portia!" he yelled out.

"Lawrence!" she gasped pulling the jacket closed, covering herself and running off the stage, leaving her fake appendage in her wake.

Lawrence was silent when he stepped from his car. He saw Portia's car in the driveway.

Entering the house, she was sitting on the sofa with her arms folded. She wore heavy sweats and had her hair pulled up on her head. She looked far different than how she had looked on the stage a couple of hours before.

"I see you stayed?" she asked him.

"It's my job."

"Oh really . . . job or preference?" she asked him. Her words were having trouble coming from her tightened jaw line and she sounded odd.

"What does that mean?"

"You were in a gay club, Lawrence."

"So the hell were you? With . . . with . . ." Lawrence pointed at her lower half, stammering badly.

"I work there!" she yelled.

"So do I . . . for now, and why are you yelling at me?" he asked in the same volume she used.

"I don't know. I'm mad!" She jumped to her feet.

"Mad about what? You were the one showin' ya ass and ya dick . . . that I didn't know you had, by the way."

Portia looked around as if wanting to throw something at him, but instead she ran upstairs. "I'm embarrassed, Lawrence!" she yelled again. "You were not supposed to find out about that. And I don't have a dick."

"Yeah, I noticed it sort of fell off when you ran. So why are you mad?" he asked, softening his voice. Portia stopped speaking suddenly.

"I don't know."

"Portia, come down here," he requested.

"No, I'm ashamed."

"That's stupid. Come down here."

Obeying him, she slowly came down the stairs with her arms folded over her chest; she was pouting. Portia was beautiful, in his opinion, and he was tossing in his emotions right now.

"I don't think what you do is my business."

"It's not, but . . ." she paused, "but I . . . I think I want it to be. But just not right now. I mean, it's moving too fast."

"What?"

"Me, I'm moving too fast."

"Yeah," he chuckled. "Damn straight. I just got here and you and Reba feeding me like a king, and you're already hiding stuff from me like a wife and . . ."

"Don't say that, Lawrence. I'd be a much better wife. I would never hide anything from you if I was your wife."

"Promise?"

"Yeah," she chuckled.

"I'm a cop. I'm an officer of the law. I sometimes have to be in strange places doing strange things. You're a teacher and—"

"And I was broke. I was really broke and I got myself too deep in debt, and the man I was seeing was keeping me there."

"Are you still seeing him?"

"No, but the debt is still there."

"I see."

"How much?"

"No, Lawrence, I won't have you paying my bills. Me and Nala have worked out the details on that and it's working out just fine. I don't mind dancing there. This was the first time I got naked . . . really, and I won't do it again."

"You can do it again if you want. I mean . . . you dance really good," Lawrence chuckled, feeling the heat rise to his face. "Even with that thang," he said, joking about Portia's pretense at being a male stripper.

Portia covered her face in embarrassment. He began popping his shoulders. "You had that little pop thing going on like Janet, and well . . ."

"You're teasing me now."

"I'm just keeping it real."

"Well, I need to keep it real, too. I am just coming out of a really, really bad relationship. Actually, I'm just realizing it was worse than I thought. And in all truthfulness, it's not all hit me yet."

"I had a feeling a pretty lady like you was tied up."

Portia smiled. "Tied up, that's a great way to explain it."

"Portia, I rent from you. I like you. But I don't own you. Nobody does. You'll know when you are ready to move forward and when you are, I'll be here . . . fixin' something."

"Thank you, Lawrence," she said, touching his shoulder and smiling warmly.

"Well, I guess I should ask you: have you noticed anybody looking odd or weird while hanging around that Rainbow Room place?"

Portia stared at him and then burst into laughter. "Duh . . . like every night."

They both laughed.

Peeking through the back sliding door window, Kyle had seen the whole thing, or what he'd thought to be the whole thing. He'd been at the club tonight. With Nala out on sick leave nursing her nuts, he slipped in to see the show. He'd also hoped to run into Julian or whoever. He had his new plan all worked out. When he saw what happened on the stage, he knew what he was going to do next. He knew everyone's weaknesses as far as he was concerned and knew right where he was gonna put the screws. He grabbed a cab and followed Lawrence and Portia back to Portia's house.

Apparently, Julian didn't know his little girlfriend was stepping out with another man—a straight man. Despite what he'd found out about her tonight, he, being straight, would no doubt forgive her, and they'd be back to knocking boots by . . .

He looked at his watch.

"Probably right about now," he said aloud, thinking he'd seen the beginning of a romance between Lawrence and Portia.

CHAPTER THIRTY

The next morning, there was nothing to report from the Rainbow Room, at least on Lawrence's report. But then again, Portia had pretty much ruined his stake-out. She was a total distraction for him, and seeing her naked hadn't helped his situation at all. He ran out after her so fast that if The Appointed One had been there, he wouldn't have seen him or cared if he had.

"How did it go last night?" Jim asked.

"Aiight," Lawrence answered, sounding so vague that Jim couldn't help but notice.

"So you spent the first night in your new place—how did it go?"

"Aiight."

"Aren't you Mr. Conversation today," Jim noted.

"I can't really talk about it right now. Suffice it to say, I think I found THE one."

"Ohhh . . . 'the one' again . . . okay."

Lawrence chuckled.

The phone rang.

"Hello there, slackers," the voice said.

"Yeah, whatever," Jim said, knowing the voice belonged to The Appointed One.

"Whatever?" The Appointed One laughed. "Okay, sour grapes are permitted at this point in time. I won the game; I get to kill the extra person. Admit it—I win."

"I'm not going to admit to that," Jim told him. "We're not done hunting your ass."

"Aw, Jim, you're such a poor sport. Look, I'm not even gonna kill the jerk, but still I could have if I wanted to. I have the right—you lost."

"You mean, Julian Marcum," Jim confronted boldly.

Lawrence tied in to the call. The trace began.

"Shit, you have been doing your homework."

"Yeah, and as soon as we find out what issues you had with Joseph Samuels, we're gonna get your crazy ass."

"Deal."

"I can't believe you," Jim chuckled at the arrogant man.

"What? I'm working with you on this. I have a job and you do, too . . . you do yours and I'll do mine, and if the two cross, then let's call it cosmos."

"You think you're gonna get away with this, don't you?"

"Ah, Joseph and Mary . . . I remember them well. I can't believe you dug up so much stuff on me. You guys are wiz kids over there. Speaking of name-calling, I mean, did you hear the news, and like, what they are calling me? They all but called me an . . . an animal."

"And you disagree?"

"I thought we were friends."

"I don't really have friends that are like . . . killers, but anyway," Jim told him. The Appointed One laughed.

"And stick to those convictions, too . . . good for you. I like the way you don't pretend to like me."

"Whose phone you steal this week?" Jim asked boldly. And why not? He figured he'd won The Appointed One's respect by now, if nothing else.

"Oh, the phone. Well, it's a hotel phone," The Appointed One giggled.

"Oh really?"

"Yes. I don't feel like killing anyone right now, so I don't have anyone else's phone. I'm thinking of just retiring. Some personal things have come up that I really need to tend to, and well, you know how that goes, right?"

"He's in Paris," one of the engineers tracing the call mouthed. Lawrence sighed heavily. Jim rubbed his head.

"Why didn't you tell me you'd left the country?"

"Who knows . . . oops, I guess only me, huh?" The Appointed One laughed. "Damn, you guys are really getting good. Looks like I got outta there at just the right time, huh?"

"You love to tease, don't you?" Jim asked.

"To death." He hung up.

Shaking their heads at the insanity of the situation, Lawrence took a sip from his cold coffee, "We finally get him traced within ten seconds and the som-bitch is not even in the country. Is there any chance the call came from here and just seemed to come from there?"

"No," the engineer guaranteed. "He was in Paris when he made the call."

"Damnit!"

"There has to be a reason he stopped with Ruben," Jim mumbled.

"Somebody give me a Bible. Why would this creep have issues with Jesus' parents, Joseph and Mary?" Jim blurted, grabbing the ten-year-old file and flipping through it.

"That can't be it. Calm down, Jim, you're letting him get to you," Lawrence said.

* * *

"Okay, here is the deal, Sparky," the caller said. "You better quit seeing that woman or else," he said.

"What woman?"

"Portia Hendrix. I'm gonna kill her if you don't," he went on. "I hate that kinda stuff."

"Why would you hate a man and woman being together? I thought that was what you wanted—men and women to do what God intended," Julian said, trying to stay calm. He'd had so many things going on in his mind and heart he was exhausted. He'd not had a call from this killer in a while and after the last conversation, he'd all but figured the killer had given him a reprieve. Now here he was calling again. Or was it him? He didn't sound the same; there was something less than articulate in his diction, less than uncanny in his tone.

"You wouldn't know what God intended if he started speaking to your dumb ass right now, spelling it out and shit."

"Look, I don't have to listen to this abuse."

"Sure you do, because you know what I did to those other men. I cut them up really bad and I killed them dead!"

Julian thought about what he'd read in the paper. He had to admit he hadn't thought about ending up dead that way. As a matter of fact, his fear was decreasing since the last call he'd gotten from the man—The Appointed One. This caller's threats seemed less than real. As a matter of fact, this caller sounded less than convincing.

Suddenly it came to him that perhaps this was a game, a sick game on someone's part to scare him. "Look, you don't scare me, not at all."

"I'll tell everyone you're gay."

"I'm not gay. As a matter of fact, I think you are. I'm a

straight man with a few issues. And I plan to resolve them soon. I'm going to marry the woman I love and there's nothing you can do or say to stop me."

"You go near her and I'm going to tell everyone you're gay."

Julian hung up.

Kyle wriggled in his seat, excited in his mind to have thrown Julian into a tizzy, or at least that's what he felt he had done.

Blackmail. It was going to be so easy.

Watching Julian from the coffee shop, Kyle could see him moving about at the church, as if trying to figure out what to do. Unblocking his number, he called him.

"Hello, boo," he purred, making sure he sounded more like himself than he had when he called just a few moments earlier. "How is your day going?"

"Crappy. What is it, Kyle?"

"You sound snippy. Want me to come over and rub your . . . you name it, baby, I'll rub it," he giggled. "Besides, I don't think you've properly thanked me for helping you out with the police."

"What did you do?"

"You don't even know. I gave them your alibi."

"What? You did what?" Julian yelled.

"I told them you were counseling me, helping me with my identity issues," Kyle lied. "Have they come back?"

"No, apparently what you told them worked."

"Sweet. So when do you want to see me?"

"I don't."

"You don't?"

"No, I've been trying to talk to you, Kyle, but with all that's been going on, I've not had the chance. I think this little whatever it has been is over with us."

"What?" Kyle squealed loudly. A couple of patrons in

the Starbucks coffee house looked at him. "You're kidding, right?"

"No, I'm not kidding."

"It's that damn woman, isn't it?"

"How do you know about her?"

"I know a lot of stuff about her, and other things, too, buddy."

"Kyle, don't get all crazy now," Julian said, walking around the church, wishing he could give Kyle a good shaking.

Kyle stood up from the bench and quickly moved out of the window, just in case he looked over at him.

"I want to see you," Kyle growled.

"I don't think it's best."

"I'll show you what's best." Kyle hung up.

Nala couldn't believe Portia was really going to leave the club. "Can't you like, help me manage it?" Nala asked. Portia shook her head. They had ordered dinner at their favorite place. They hadn't been there in a while.

"I don't know what I was even thinking, coming there to meet you. I just wanted to dance so badly. You said the truth that day. I was desperate. And I made a mess of everything. I'm just so mentally whipped it's not even funny."

"Well, I understand that, but who is gonna dance for me? I lost Flacca, Kyle is running around like a crazy man, having some kind of breakdown . . ."

"You're kidding me."

"No, honey. Ever since he came in and went off, he has been calling and talking crazy and threatening folks. His roommate even came in looking for him once, said he hadn't been home. It's a mess."

"Well, we can't worry too much about Kyle. He's a big boy and can handle his own dirt."

"I guess. It's sad though. I used to really like Kyle. I mean, that's why I hired him. He used to be so sweet. But he fell in love with Julian and I think that was enough to take his mind . . . I mean, who am I telling? You know that."

"God yes," Portia sighed heavily.

"So tell me about Lawrence. I heard about last night . . . your knight in shinning armor. He all but got up on the stage and carried you off. How romantic."

"It wasn't romantic. It was humiliating. Oh my God." Portia giggled.

"You are just so cute," Nala said, touching Portia's face. Portia grabbed Nala's large hand and looked at it.

"Nala, I have to quit the club. I have to stop seeing you, too."

"Why? Oh my gosh, why?" Nala whined.

"I think you know."

"No I don't, tell me."

Portia looked off. "I can't sort my feelings for anybody right now, you included. I really like you."

"I like you, too, sweetie."

"No, I mean . . ." Portia felt the heat come to her face, "I'm like . . . having feelings."

"Ohhh . . ." Nala gasped and then giggled. "Those kinds of feelings . . . oh my."

"Yeah, and well, I know I'm not gay. I know I'm not. Its just . . ."

"Portia, I'm a woman. I really am. It's not an act. Just like Julian, no matter how much you love me, you'll never love me into being a man."

Portia looked down at her plate and then back up at the exotic looking woman. "I think I understand."

"Some things are just the way they are. Find a guy who desires you, honey. He's probably waiting right under your nose. That cop for instance. He's fine as wine from what I've seen . . . you know when they were here abusing me . . ." Nala giggled. "Personally, I like that little white one." She wrinkled her nose. "I like him a lot."

"You are just too fast." Portia slapped Nala's arm playfully.

Lawrence was beat when he got home that night. Portia was in her room. No doubt feeling a little humbled by the incident at the club. Lawrence wasn't sure if she'd quit working there or not, but he could only hope her being home was a good sign that she had.

Reba was in the kitchen finishing dinner.

"Hey there, Reba. I see our girl is home."

"Yeah, I heard about what happened. I finally got it out of her. Oh, my god, I wanted to tear her behind up. I can't believe all this time she was dancing in a gay joint and taking off her clothes like that. What was wrong with her head?"

Lawrence smiled. "You just say it like it is, don't you, Reba?" Lawrence told her, taking a bite of the potato salad from the big bowl.

"Hell yeah, and she should have told me she was dancing at that damn gay club . . . told somebody."

"Well, I think she's gonna quit. That owner of the club, Nala, is very persistent, and if she wanted Portia to stay, Portia might not be able to quit. And I think she and Nala are friends. I'm not one to tell someone who they should be friends with but . . ."

"Now about this Nala . . . who is she, and what's her story?"

"Well, she's a little different and I can't describe her. My partner and I think she's . . . she's a man."

"Oh my God! Portia and her friends. I wonder if Portia knows if she's a man or not." Reba sighed. Lawrence laughed. "Now about that big case on the news . . . how did all that come out? You know, the one where that guy was killing the gay men. That was kinda scary. He was hangin' 'em and cuttin' off their private parts," Reba said, and then shivered at the thought.

"Well, apparently he retired."

"So you never caught him?"

"But the case is like . . ." Lawrence sliced the air, "right there," he lied. "We're like really close."

"Coo-coos like that never retire; they just go underground for a while. He'll be back."

"Let's just hope I'm retired when he does."

"Amen to that."

CHAPTER THIRTY-ONE

That weekend, Portia watched as Lawrence hoisted the heavy piece of awkwardly shaped lumber up onto his broad shoulders. He was wearing a thin T-shirt that outlined his muscles clearly. She couldn't help but stare.

"Now, when are you supposed to get back into dancing professionally?" he asked, taking the sandpaper and with quick light strokes, smoothing the nicks out of the repaired railing, his muscles flexing with each movement. He bit his bottom lip as he worked out the rough spots.

The banister was looking good. It had been in need of repair for so long she had forgotten how beautiful it could be.

Lawrence had done a lot since moving in. He seemed happy to be living here; heaven knows she was glad he was there.

"Well, I don't know now. I mean, with the club closing and all that, I don't have a stage." She laughed. "But I'm still taking lessons from Nala. But she's been busy lately."

"Oh really?"

"Yeah. I guess she met somebody and so . . ."

"Really? Nala has a boyfriend?"

They both laughed. "Or whatever," Portia said, snickering under her breath.

"I like hearing you laugh," Lawrence confessed. She turned away slightly. But he moved her face back to his. "I like hearing you laugh. It's just that simple."

She grinned. It had been a long time since Portia had met a real gentleman. And she had to admit, she didn't know what to do with Lawrence. "Well, your moves at the club were pretty special, so you need to get back on the stage real soon," he said, showing the laughter in his words.

"Stop, you're embarrassing me, Lawrence." She giggled. His heart leapt.

"No, really. I mean, I'm not some backwoods hick or nothing like that. But I've never seen anything like that before. It was like, wow," he went on.

Unable to resist, she moved the furniture and clicked on the stereo. Soft, sensual music began playing.

"Hold your arms up like this," she instructed, to which he obeyed, watching her circle him in graceful movements.

"What's this song?" he asked, trying to keep his concentration off her long leg which flew up beside his head—trying hard to keep his body from reacting. Her finger lightly touched his lips as she shushed him on her way by.

Holding onto his arm for balance while executing a difficult stretch, bringing her leg up behind her and touching the back of her head with her foot, she said, "This is real dance."

Turning her back to him, she put his hands on her small waist. "Lift me," she instructed.

Lawrence felt the sweat on his brow as he carefully

lifted her light body from the ground. As tall as she was, he just figured she would be heavier, but before he realized it, she was over his head.

Sliding down the front of him, she then turned and cupped his face, bending her leg high over her back, touching the back of her head with the opposite foot this time. Lawrence couldn't help but stare, wonderingly. "Wow, you're beautiful, Portia," was all he could say.

Portia's eyes locked on his for a moment. Her heart swelled with emotion.

Just then, Reba walked in with an arm full of filled Tupperware containers.

"What is going on here, Swan Lake?" she asked. "Shucky Ducky quack quack!"

"That would be Duck Lake, Reba," Portia said. They all broke into laughter.

The day was more than pleasant. Lawrence was feeling more and more like things might work out, until later that night.

Later that night, there was a knock at the front door. Portia could hear it, although her bedroom door was shut.

Lawrence had been good about handling any night callers, maybe because he never went to bed before three or four A.M., and even then, she wondered if he slept.

Insomnia. Portia recognized it right away. Her father suffered with it for years. Lawrence reminded her a lot of her father. Though she was having a hard time facing the realities of it, she liked Lawrence a lot.

Licking the taste of Reba's fried chicken from his fingers, Lawrence headed to the door. This arrangement was better than he could have ever imagined. Reba was a funny woman, old school sexy, wide hips, thick legs, a gold tooth, immaculate weave, and long, claw-like acrylics. She reminded him of one of his aunties. Her husband,

Bradley, was a quiet man, content. It was clear he loved Reba a lot.

But then, cookin' as good as she does, who wouldn't? Lawrence figured, setting the plate on the entry table that he had fixed the other day. The legs were weak, and he knew they would soon give way. He couldn't have that. His next project would be the broken-down deck. The house needed a lot of repairs. He had already put over eighteen hundred dollars of his own money just this week, into fixing it up. But he was happy to do it. Just seeing Portia smile after a hard day of working was worth it all to him. Her pride wouldn't allow him to take care of her extra debts, but he couldn't wait for her to quit that second job.

Lawrence opened the door without even a thought of looking through the peephole. Julian was eye to eye with the man who answered Portia's door.

"You? What the hell are you doing here?" he asked bluntly.

"No, better question—why are you here, Pastor Marcum?" Lawrence volleyed, his tone heavy with sarcasm.

Julian regrouped.

"I'm sorry, you caught me off guard. I'm not used to anyone being at *mah* girl's house this late," Julian remarked.

The comment came full of arrogance and proprietorship, but still Lawrence wasn't impressed, seeing as how he knew a lot about the man Julian Marcum.

Not much of a boyfriend, he'd say.

Surely, Portia wasn't one to have been played like this. Surely she hadn't fallen for a man like this.

"Yeah, well, it is late, and uh, I am here," Lawrence said, thinking about his chicken and potato salad waiting for him.

This joker had better get to the point real quick.

Julian pushed his way in as if he was accustomed to being in her home at this hour. If he acted with confidence, perhaps this fool detective wouldn't know that he was more than likely not welcome here—not after what he'd done to Portia. It was obvious that Portia hadn't told the detective anything about their relationship.

Julian looked Lawrence over with a new eye. Big. That was all Julian got out of his assessment of Lawrence Miller.

"She's in the bed," Lawrence told him. Julian glared at him, as if he suspected a deeper meaning in what he just said.

"It's late . . . she's in the bed," Lawrence repeated.

Julian stammered for a moment, visibly frustrated.

"Can you tell her Julian is here?" he requested. Lawrence was through now.

Who does this punk think he is?

"I'm not the butler."

Just then, Portia appeared at the top of the stairs. Her face was hard to read. At least Lawrence wondered what her expression meant.

Considering she was Julian's *'girl'* as he put it, she didn't seem overjoyed to see him here at this hour.

"Can we talk?" Julian asked, glancing at Lawrence out of the corner of his eye.

"Look, I was just trying to have me some dinner," Lawrence said, picking up his plate and heading toward his room.

"Wait, Lawrence, don't leave. This fool won't be here long."

"Fool, what'd you call me?" Julian asked.

"Look, Julian, you must be a fool to think you can come here and talk to me about anything. You must think I don't know. You must think I don't know how gay you are."

Even Lawrence was surprised she knew. He hadn't told her.

"How?"

"Remember, Nala is my friend. She may be a little different, but she's still my friend. She told me about you and your little boyfriend, Kyla, and how Kyle did nothing but brag about his down-low boyfriend all the time, I'd even heard him braggin' a couple of times. I just had no idea it was you."

"So you know about Kyle?" Julian began. "So now you and Kyle are teaming up to blackmail me?"

"I'm not trying to blackmail you. I have so many better things to do besides bother with your sorry ass. How dare you try to make me into your make-believe wife, after treating me like . . ." she glanced at Lawrence who was listening intently now, "after doing what you did to me," she said, editing her words.

"I see."

"No, I don't think you do, because if you did, you would be seeing your way out."

"Look, I told you about that. It's natural and you . . . you're the one with the problem. But then I guess you know that, huh?" he asked Lawrence, insinuating much. Lawrence just stared at him.

"Whatever, Julian. Get the hell outta my house," Portia jumped in, keeping Lawrence out of the argument.

"Well, Sistah Hendrix, I think you just got yourself fired as my Sunday School teacher."

Portia burst into laughter. "You are gay and lame, and being your Sunday School teacher is so not on my mind right now. I had no idea you were so crazy."

"I got cho crazy!" Julian snapped.

"Is that a threat, Mr. Marcum?" Lawrence interjected now. There was no way he was letting that one go.

Julian growled audibly and pushed past Lawrence on his way out of the house.

Lawrence closed the door and locked it after Julian left, and then turned to face Portia, who had come down the stairs now. They stared at each other for a long time before Portia finally kissed him. "Mmm, tastes just like chicken," she flirted, before bouncing up the stairs back to her room.

Julian was furious and didn't know what to do. Portia had rejected him. She was his only choice for salvation now, and she had rejected him.

"Bitch," he grumbled, thinking about Lawrence Miller being in her home. Oh yeah, he remembered the cop that had come to his church, questioning him about the psycho who had stolen his phone and involved him in his sick set of serial killings. The psycho who was now calling him and trying to scare him. But he was not afraid of some punk faggot. He would take this creep on, and now he had put two and two together and realized who it was. "It had to be the guy from the club. He's the one who stole my phone, so . . . yeah," Julian pondered. "Gosh, it's amazing how we don't think when stuff first happens, but I've got it under control now.

Julian thought about the news reports and the pictures that had slipped onto the Internet of the men who had been slaughtered by this crazy man. "Unbelievable," Julian sighed, shaking his head of the visual. "So sick."

Fear came up in his heart. It was hard to believe he'd met The Appointed One. It was frightening, actually. Maybe he wouldn't take him on . . . now that he thought about it.

Noticing the phone on his desk, he clicked the button next to the blinking light.

"You're going to die like the others. I'm going to cut your dick off and shove it down your throat and hang you from a meat hook like Flacca. You better end this thing with Portia or you're going to die," the message said. The caller had left another message, and Julian was immediately shook, that is until he noticed that this time the number wasn't blocked. Quickly, he pulled out his new cell phone, pushed the code needed to block his number and called it. He had no intention of speaking to the man, but he wanted to hear his voice. He needed to in order to conquer the fear that was building up in his heart.

"Kyle here, whose calling?" he hung up.

"What? Damn that Kyle." His libido reacted at just the thought of Kyle playing such a sick game. "Stop it, Julian," he said aloud. "You need to get a grip on yourself; you need to deal with this. This is no love play. This is serious. Kyle is trying to blackmail you and this is not cool. He almost caused you to make the biggest mistake of your life. Who knows, Kyle may be a killer, and here you have been messing around with him, putting your life in danger." Julian paced the room. "No, he's not a killer; he's a fool and he's about to be taught a serious lesson about playin' a playa."

Julian paced his office until finally, retrieving his gun from the safe he kept under his desk, and tucking it in the back of his pants. He suddenly thought about Portia. Maybe she was in on it, too. Maybe they all were. Maybe they all sat around that Rainbow Room and plotted sick games like this. Julian's mind wandered. They all needed to be taught a lesson.

CHAPTER THIRTY-TWO

It was a hard decision to close the case of The Appointed One. The whole idea of closing the case was wrong. The case was unfinished, as The Appointed One's job was still incomplete. Despite the month of silence, it constantly felt as if he was right there, in their face. Lawrence knew they were missing something, but he couldn't put his finger on it.

"Who were the other people he was planning to kill? Why didn't he kill them? That will always bother me," Lawrence admitted.

"Why?" Jim asked.

"Doesn't that un-nerve you, thinking that you could have been the target of a madman, for reasons only he knew?"

"It would have bothered me more if I *was* the victim of a maniac for whatever reason," Jim admitted, taking another big bite from his donut. "But what bothered me were the riddles. They drove me nuts. The Joseph and Mary thing drove me nuts. The guy was a lunatic."

"He felt he was doing a service."

"Speaking of ass . . . let me tell you, did you see that honey I was with the other night?"

"Nobody, and I mean nobody, was talking about ass, Jim. And when in the hell did you find time to go out?" Lawrence began, unable to keep the chuckle from his words. Jim was a certifiable idiot. Why he even bothered with him beyond their job was past understanding, or maybe Jim was, in all reality, a good friend.

"Little speakeasy down on Hulsey Street . . . open all night. But seriously, dawg, she got me home and oh myyy . . ." Jim groaned, taking a vicious bite from what was left of his donut, smiling with the powder still around his mouth. Lawrence just shook his head.

"Why do you tell me shit like that?"

"I didn't tell you nothing. You got a dirty mind," Jim joked, wiping away the mess the donut made from his lips with a napkin. "I was gonna say she got me home and cooked me up some finger lickin' chicken."

"No . . . no, no you weren't," Lawrence insisted, pointing his finger accusatively at him.

"Speaking of finger licking good, how are things going with you and that roommate of yours?"

"Good," Lawrence answered with all the mystery he could muster. In reality, things were getting pretty friendly between him and Portia. He had hoped things would move a little faster. However, he had to realize that his moving in was not for that purpose, and besides, he was fairly sure she wasn't completely over the man she had been involved with, although she claimed she was.

Ian watched as Portia looked through her mail. He had to wonder if she was still involved with the same man as Kyle. Ian was very observant and knew a lot more than people gave him credit for. He watched humans closely, as they were curious sorts that never added up evenly. They were pretty much odd for the most part.

Portia was at the root of Kyle's pain these days. He'd been obsessing over her for a long time. Ian feared Kyle was about to do something stupid where she was concerned. But what would he say to warn her? What could he say without making himself look foolish and paranoid? There wasn't a night that went by that Kyle didn't come in with a report on Portia and her new man.

She noticed him, standing there staring at her, and she smiled. "How have you been, Ian?"

"Great. You?"

"I've been terrific."

"So, it's been working out with you and your new roommate, huh?"

"I've only had one for a coupla weeks. Why would you ask?"

"No reason, being nosy I guess," he said.

"Well, I guess I should be getting to class," she said, hoping to ease away without being rude. Ian could tell that's what she was trying to do. He touched her arm. Feeling her tense, he made sure not to grip her tightly. "Be careful, Portia. Not everyone loves you," he said.

"I realize that," Portia said, not understanding him at all. He could tell she didn't understand him.

"What I mean is . . ."

"I think I know what you mean, and like I said, thanks for the warning." Portia shook him loose and strutted away.

Ian felt foolish, but his gut was telling him he'd done the right thing.

After arriving home from work that day, Portia thought about Ian Randolph and his strange behavior. "Maybe he is a weirdo. I mean, bad association can spoil . . ." Without finishing the scripture, she turned on the water and began to undress for her shower. Thinking about Nala, she didn't notice that someone was in the house. She showered a long time, rolling everything through her mind.

Yes, she and Lawrence were getting along swell. There was no love connection on her part, but that was because of her feelings for Julian. It was going to take a long time to get over Julian. She'd fallen for a man who was homosexual, and like it or not, she, too, had given into homosexual tendencies where Nala was concerned. "Or maybe it was the man in Nala that attracted me?" she asked herself while shampooing her hair. Her cut was growing out, and she was going to soon have to decide what to do with her hair. "Maybe braids," she hummed. She'd ask Lawrence what he thought about women in braids. She enjoyed having him around. He was great company.

Portia stepped from the shower, wrapping the towel loosely around her and dashing into her darkened room. Suddenly, grabbed from behind, she was held tightly around the mouth.

"So you like the freaks, eh?" the man asked, his voice just above a whisper. Portia knew it wasn't Lawrence; she knew this was no lover's play. This was a violent act. She attempted to break free of his grip, but it was to no avail.

"You smell really good, baby. What scent are you wearing?" he whispered in her ear as he bent her forward, pushing the back of her head toward the floor.

She fought to scream while trying to free herself, but he pulled her hands together tightly while binding them with what felt like rope, and then covering her mouth with a strip of duct tape.

"So you like pretending to be a man, huh, baby? You

like playing games, huh?" he asked, still whispering and wrestling with her while she squirmed, until finally he tripped her onto the floor. Sitting on her back, he tied her kicking legs together. She tried to cry out from under the tape, but with that and the thick old walls of her home, there would be no way she would be heard. She wanted to recognize the voice. She wanted to know her attacker. But before she could think it all out, he was pressing his hardness into her—sodomizing her. "Too bad you're not a man, Portia, or this would be a whole lot better," he said between grunts, "for me."

Feeling weak, she nearly lost consciousness while he pulled her hair, biting the back of her neck, pleasing himself, riding her like a pony, until finally, he finished with her. It had to be Julian, Portia thought. Who else had this much hatred for her?

"Not everyone loves you," Ian had said just that afternoon.

She lay on the floor, sobbing pitiably, when he pulled away from her. She refused to look at him, for fear of what he would do next. "Don't ever say The Appointed One never did nothing for ya," she heard him say, his voice ragged, strange sounding—different. It didn't sound like Julian, but how could he sound like himself with this crazy demon having taken over him this way?

Now he had taken from her what he had always wanted. The stench told her she lost control, but she couldn't care about that now. "Now for the coup de grace," the man said, introducing his next perversion before suddenly, without notice or care, he hit her with what felt like a belt, allowing the buckle, a heavy one, to hit her repeatedly, until she felt nothing.

At that moment in time, she wanted nothing more than to die. She finally lost consciousness.

* * *

Lawrence came in late and was surprised to see the light off under Portia's door. Despite her early hours, she was good about at least pretending to wait up for him. Tonight she must have given in to being tired. She must have gotten tired of the game he was playing. Lawrence didn't feel in his heart he was playing a game. However, it must have appeared so. After the kiss, Lawrence needed time to think. There were so many issues that needed resolving—Julian Marcum, for one.

Julian Marcum had been the primary person of interest in the murder case, even though they had put the case to bed—for now. An alleged killer had used his phone, even though Julian Marcum claimed no knowledge of that fact. And by all indications in the case, Julian was bisexual. Lawrence had to wonder if Portia knew. Was this her preference? It was obvious to Lawrence she was involved with that woman, Nala, but how involved was the question. He wanted to move further with Portia, but she had issues, and perhaps they were ones he could not get over. The kiss was wonderful, but the one thing he had to remember was what his father always told him: when you bed down a woman, the last thing you need to know is how many people are there. In Portia's case, it didn't seem like many. However, it was who they were that was just as important.

Lawrence looked out the window to see if lover boy's car might be up the street, hidden from immediate notice. The feeling of 'being watched' was always with him. The street was empty. Lawrence reprimanded himself for his momentary insecurities, but it killed Lawrence, the thought of Portia falling prey to such a loser like Julian Marcum. And Julian was a loser, big time.

He had managed to get out from the light of that hanging murder, but still, Lawrence didn't trust him.

"He ain't right bright," Lawrence mumbled under his breath, thinking about his conversation with Jim earlier that day.

"And Portia was with that undercover queer," Lawrence finally told Jim after forcing his brain to accept where all the evidence was leading. There was no way Julian could be so close to all this mess without stankin'. Even if he hadn't murdered those two men, he was just a little too familiar with the Rainbow Room and the clientele who patronized there.

"Yeah, that counseling thing did not fly," agreed Jim.

"I like her. I like her a lot," Lawrence admitted, lowering his voice and looking around to make sure their conversation was private. Jim nodded his understanding. "But she's into like . . . really weird people, ya know?" Lawrence hesitated, realizing how his words sounded full of sour grapes and jealousy . . . maybe even a little prejudiced, too.

Jim smiled but tried to hide it, seeing as how Lawrence hardly ever talked about liking someone. Since Hannah, Lawrence had all but sworn off women—sort of. This Portia Hendrix must be something special.

"Should I tell her what I think about her friends?" Lawrence asked, closing the file on the Rainbow Murders—again the case had a new nickname.

"Yeah, that'll make you look like a big manly man, homophobic that you are," Jim teased. Lawrence's eyes widened. Jim shook his head, holding back laughter. "Just messin' with you, man,"

"Look I said quit callin' me that," Lawrence grumbled.

"Lawrence, homophobic means . . ."

Lawrence raised his large hand again. Jim just shrugged. "Anyway, I don't think I need to know all that right now."

"Even after all these killings and knowing how close he is to the case, she's still seeing him?"

"I don't think so. He came by and made an ass of himself a few days ago, but since then . . . I don't think so."

"Then I say, get over your fears, Lawrence, and jump right in." Jim's eyes twinkled wickedly.

Lawrence frowned. "I can't do that." Lawrence was letting his shyness show.

"Stop being so damned polite. You want that woman, you get her—hook or crook . . . if you want the nook. You hear me, right?" Jim winked. Lawrence couldn't' help but smile.

Portia was someone he wanted. He cared about her. He was hopelessly infatuated with her.

Okay fine, he loved her.

Coming back to the now, he listened close at her door to see if he could hear her moving about. He knocked again. "Portia, ,are you up?" he called through the door. "I want to talk to you." Hearing a crash, he then heard a slight groan. He knocked harder. "Portia, you okay?" he called again. Instinct took over now, and he turned the knob and opened the door, turning on the light. She was on the floor under a table that she had used her head to push against, knocking the lamp onto the floor. There was no telling how long she had waited for just the right time to make that move, as it seemed to take all the strength she had left.

When he saw her battered face, he rushed over to her, ripping the tape from her mouth. "Did Julian do this?"

She could not open her eyes completely and her mouth was opening, but no words were escaping. Portia was broken, destroyed, and barely alive. She was bleeding heavily from open wounds on her skin.

Lawrence looked around the room and then back at

her. He could see that her bruises were dark and ugly, and they covered her upper thighs. Working vice had taught him many things, and Lawrence knew the signs of rape. Someone had done a number on her. He then noticed the blood and the word APPOINTED painted on her thigh in lipstick.

"I've got to get you to the hospital, Portia," Lawrence said, gathering her up into his arms. She groaned in pain at his attempts to move her. With one hand, he pulled the comforter off the bed and covered her while cradling her. He knew he was destroying evidence, but he could not let the authorities find her naked and devastated this way. Reaching in his pocket, he pulled out his cell phone and called 911. His eyes burned as he fought growing emotion. Her tears drained her eyes onto her cheeks.

"Somebody is gonna pay for this, Portia. Dude is gonna pay for this."

Lawrence felt his temper rising.

Jim met Lawrence at the hospital.

"Lawrence, it's not his style, man. This guy's only worked one way," Jim tried to explain, knowing Lawrence was past the boiling point—he was beyond thinking rationally.

"He made a mistake once, so . . ."

"A mistake. Listen, whoever did this meant to do this. I think they wanted to trip us up and take us off track of who he was. My wager is it's the bisexual boyfriend, and who knows, maybe he's our guy for the other killings, too. Maybe he's a copycat."

"Copycat? Why would you even think we were dealing with a copycat now?"

"I wanted to tell you about this later on today, but this morning I got another cold file."

"And?"

"Well, the more we worked the Rainbow Room, the more I got . . . ya know," Jim blushed slightly, but shook it off quickly, "thought about Nala and stuff, and so I did a background check and come to find out, her father was killed the same way as our victims were killed."

"You telling me Nala is our man . . . or what?" Lawrence blurted, immediately changing the direction of his growing rage.

"Noo, she wasn't even in the country when her father, Rabbi Marai," Jim said slowly, making sure Lawrence heard the religious reference placed on Nala's father, as well as the pronunciation of the name *Marai,* "was mutilated."

"Mary?"

"You're hearing me now. Nala was in Europe for medical reasons."

"What medical reasons?" Lawrence asked.

"She's a hermaphrodite?"

"What?"

"You were right about one thing: she's got a penis, but according to the doctor's subpoenaed reports during the investigation, it's just an appendage, dead for all intents and purposes."

"Wow."

"But, I think The Appointed One has a copycat. Maybe he was a copycat and now we have a copycat of a copycat," Jim tried to explain to Lawrence, who was no longer listening with the ears of a police officer, but of a man whose second chance at life had just been taken.

"No, I think The Appointed One has been around a while. Don't ask me why I think that, but I do. And I think Nala knows more than she's told us. Her father being a victim just about syncs that for me."

"But she didn't kill Portia."

"Yeah, I don't think so either, but I have to know who did."

Reba was beside herself and had wept uncontrollably when coming from Portia's room. Lawrence's heart ached for her, as he watched her standing with her husband, Bradley, baying at the moon, and calling upon God and all the angels to tend to the pain she was feeling.

The chief called Lawrence later that day to take him completely off the investigation of the murder of Portia Hendrix. In his emotional state, he went ballistic, proving her point and starting an extended leave of absence.

CHAPTER THIRTY-THREE

The news quickly got wind of the killing and labeled it a rebirth of The Appointed One. With the year starting out in this same way, its ending with the death of a female who stripped in a gay club seemed fitting to blame on The Appointed One.

Jim had a feeling The Appointed One had nothing to do with the killing of Portia Hendrix, but he couldn't prove it. There had been no phone call, no warning or preparedness. It just wasn't his style. And besides, Portia was a woman.

Lawrence was still in a deep depression. He had moved back into his mother's house and was all but despondent. It wasn't that he loved Portia so much as his life in general. Jim had to wonder if Lawrence would ever return to police work. He just didn't seem to have the stomach for it.

Just then, Jim's cell phone rang; the number was blocked. "Detective Beam here," Jim answered.

"I am so disappointed."

"Who is this?"

"I thought we were friends, or at least had an understanding."

"Mr. Appointed One, I thought you had retired."

"I did . . . sheesh. Do you know how much last minute flights are? My God!"

"Yeah, I've had to buy them like on standby before, the price is like . . . outrageous."

"You're so real. You know, I actually believe you aren't even tracing this call."

"I'm not."

"Good, and I believe you. Don't lie to me and I won't lie to you. Besides, I would never lie to you, not like the others."

"Who? Who lied."

"Have I ever even attempted to have an alibi? Have I ever tried to get out of what I did? I'm not a liar. Also, think about it. I'm not that vain; why would I put my name on her leg? Come on, that's so not me."

"Who is it then? You sound like you know who killed her?"

"I do, and the next time I call you, you call me back, okay?"

The Appointed One hung up.

Julian's hands shook. "What started out as just a scare had gone too far. I had no idea I could get so angry," he explained. "But she deserved it!" he screamed out loud. But The Appointed One didn't want to hear any lame excuse for why Julian had tried to blame him for his own stupidity.

"So you just decided to be me or what?"

"No, no, it's not like that."

"I think it's very much like that, and I think you better fix what you've broken."

"What are you trying to say?"

"Turn youself in."

"Never. You of all people should know that is not how it works. I won't. You're a vicious killer—I'm not. What is one more body added to your list."

"I kill for a purpose, much higher than your petty jealousy."

"You're just a freak, just like all the rest of them. I know who you are and I'll turn you in myself. I—"

"Okay, here's the deal then. You come where I am and we'll talk."

"Me come to you?"

"Sure, it's fair. I'm a fair man. I mean, we've kissed. . . . Don't you trust me?"

"Fuckin' freak!"

"Now you're getting all nasty. You come meet me at 445 Grand Avenue, apartment 3. Do you know where it is?"

"Yeah, yeah, I know."

"Yeah, it's right next to a porn shop—figured you would know."

The Appointed One hung up.

"How dare he think he can blackmail me," Julian grumbled out loud.

Julian needed to rethink this whole thing. Had he made sure he'd traced his steps carefully to make sure it looked as if she was a victim of the killer who had murdered many of the Rainbow Room patrons? He hoped so, because he was going to kill The Appointed One and make it look like a suicide. He felt emboldened, now that he'd taken a life. He felt like a pro.

After she went unconscious, he just knew she was dead. He didn't dare touch her or anything, but he just knew she was dead, so he had to think fast on his feet. He hadn't intended to kill her, just scare her, but he feared he had gone too far, and now he had to think . . .

had he made the scene look real. "She had to be breathing when I left . . . she's not dead," he fussed at himself, knowing that she was. He'd heard the news. "How dare she or anyone think they can just treat me like I'm nothing more than a second thought? The Appointed One had the right idea," he said aloud, thinking about the killer who had gone out on some vigilante mission. "I felt very appointed to teach that bitch a lesson. And now, Mr. Appointed, I'm going to have to kill you."

Just then, he noticed Portia's cell number come up on the phone. It had to be The Appointed One, playing games again, but how he got Portia's phone was a freakish mystery. Was he there? Did he watch? He let the call go, and then, flipping open his cell phone, he called Kyle. He was going to need an alibi. There was no answer. He reached the address and noticed the man from the club coming from the apartment. He quickly stepped from his car, but before he could say anything, fear came over him and he hesitated. What if that guy was indeed The Appointed One, and not just another gay patron of the Rainbow Room, making a porn stop at this particular store at this particular hour? This wasn't a game. Julian was terrified. All his brave thoughts went right out the window. It was true he was a coward.

After the man stepped on the bus, Julian decided he would see what was really going on, and ran up the stairs of the next door apartment—445. Trying the knob, he found the door open and entered.

"Oh my God!" he gasped, seeing Kyle on the floor, naked and bound with rope, covered with blood with the word The Appointed One written on his leg, just as Julian had done on Portia's leg. A chill covered him. His cell phone rang. It was Portia's number again. Out of reflex, he answered it.

"Okay, think about this: I happen to know you have no

alibis for any of the murders this year, and the only one you could have had is this little gay guy who is dead, so now you're a serial killer. You . . . asked for it, you got it, Toyota . . . remember that commercial? I always liked that jingle."

"I didn't kill him. I . . ." Suddenly Julian noticed on the floor next to Kyle's body was a small gold band. That's when Kyle's cell phone rang.

Jim had quickly redialed the number that had sent the text page. It rang and rang until finally the voice mail came on. "You've reached Kyle, exotic dancer and female impersonator. If you need a party, I'm your man. . . ."

"Shit!" Julian gasped, diving for the ring. He was panic-stricken and dropped his new cell phone. While attempting to pick it up, he'd grabbed Kyle's instead. Not noticing, Julian hurried from the apartment, before anyone saw him.

CHAPTER THIRTY-FOUR

Nala was beside herself, lonely and sad after hearing about Portia. She had called the house and got the message from a relative of Portia's that the serial killer had killed her, just days after it happened.

"Don't you read the paper or listen to the news?" Reba barked at her before hanging up the phone. Nala didn't dare call back and went immediately into a depression. She sold the club and moved into a small apartment in Height Ashbury, living off her savings. After nearly a year, money was tight for Nala, and she was unable to do the things she'd always wanted to do. She refused to dance on the stage, stripping for perverts who threw dollars at her—gawking and staring, pointing at the woman with the male appendage. Her life as a hermaphrodite had been hellish, and now it was as if life wanted to repeat itself. Only this time, she would have to go through it alone, without new friends and old.

It wasn't until she heard from her best friend, Jacki, that she remotely started feeling better again. Jacki had been tying up a few loose ends in Paris for the last year, but had come running as soon as she heard the sadness in Nala's voice.

"Why would this *serial killer* wanna kill her?" Nala asked, regarding Portia's murder, gesturing quotation marks as she put emphasis on serial killer.

"Is that what the cops think?" Jacki asked.

"Oh, I don't know. Maybe it's what I think; the serial killer guy did it because of the tape thing and the sodomy . . . just like the first woman he killed."

"I don't think he would have changed his way of doing things over one little mistake."

"Mistake?"

"Yeah, why would he change his plans, his appointed mission for one mistake? Everyone is entitled to one, don't you think?"

"I guess, but I've never heard you ever accept weakness in someone."

"I have compassion . . . from time to time. Like poor Portia—didn't I send her to you when she had no money? I knew I was about to be busy for a while, so I sent her to be your friend. I had no issues with her, so why would I . . ." Jacki paused, "why would anyone kill her? People only kill those who need to die. Like your father and mine, they deserved to die . . . they did."

"True, but I mean, a person may feel that way, but who gives them the right to kill?"

"I think people who kill the wicked are appointed by God to do it. I just think sometimes there has to be an equalizing."

"Like a cleansing."

"Exactly."

"You are so profound," Nala said, sounding in awe of her friend. "I mean, even when it came to Portia, you just knew she would be my friend, and what a terrific friend she was, but for such a short time. I'll be honest. I did have a crush on her. I thought you might be jealous when you found out."

"You have a crush on everyone, Nala. But I've always loved you anyway," Jacki chuckled. Nala smiled.

"So true, but then I'm so damned loveable."

"True. But really, I would do anything to keep you happy. Have I ever let anyone hurt you?"

"No. Even as kids, you would beat anyone's ass who messed with me. You've always had a stronger male side."

"Exactly, and I will always be your friend, Nala. That's my appointment," Jacki said, with a surreptitious smile crossing her lips.

"And I do love your new look, too; it's very handsome, very . . . you," Nala said, with much flirtation in her tone. "I'm impressed. Paris was good to you."

Jacki smiled shyly, and then with a look of excitement crossing her face, she burst forth. "Oh," Jacki said with excitement in her voice, reaching in her pocket, and pulling out a box. Nala grinned.

"Not another ring for meeee," she squealed. Opening the box, she gasped at the sight of the St. Martin de Porres ring. "It's beautiful. I don't think I've ever seen a ring like this."

"I got it from a . . . a preacher who didn't need it anymore. It's a St. Martin de Porres ring. He was a saint; humble and good. He's a curer and tender to the poor," Jacki explained. "I guess the preacher realized he was none of those things, so . . ."

Nala laughed. "You hate preachers anyway."

"Don't we all."

Nala stared at the ring a little longer. "Yes, I love it!" Nala said, reaching over and pulling Jacki into a kiss on the cheek. "And I love you." This time Jacki turned and caught Nala firmly on the lips. They shared a long kiss filled with mutual admiration.

Pulling apart, they both looked at each other, silently assessing the moment.

"So, how does it feel to be . . . whole, complete?" Nala finally asked, sounding almost shy now.

"Feels great. The doctors in Paris say the hormones have been working marvelously, even after all those years of not taking them. My body responded right away. Can't you tell?" Jacki leaned forward for Nala to stroke her face.

"Ohhh, sexy," Nala purred, noting Jacki's five o'clock shadow was filling in nicely.

"You like that, huh? Been growing it for a month now. I actually was growing it before I left but hid it from you." Jacki grinned, showing her flirtatious side, smoothing back her ponytail. Nala leaned forward and kissed her again.

"Well, I love it."

"Listen, Nala, I know we had issues before . . . like in Vegas," Jacki began, her voice deepening more and more. "But I promise I'm not going to stop the hormones this time. I promise. I was confused about us . . . sexually, and you know how I felt about—"

"It doesn't matter, Jacki. You know how I feel about you. Sex just isn't that important with me anymore," Nala explained. "And I'm sorry if I pressured you to do things you didn't want. You're a man and I should have respected that—impotent or not, and now look. I'm not able to do anything sexually but wish." Nala sighed.

"No, it was me; You loved me and wanted to show me, and I was still having all those issues with my stepfather."

Nala shook her head. "I regret so much. I almost wished sometimes that guy had made his way to my house and cut my dick while on his little spree." Nala chuckled sadly.

"Don't say that, Nala. Those men lost their manhood, because they didn't use it for good. They didn't use it for its natural purpose. You've always used yours for . . ." she winked, "good."

"Well, I have no need for one now," Nala assured.

"Well, I guess you won't be needing this then." Jacki quickly moved Nala's hand to her midsection, where Nala felt the growing erection.

"Well, well, you're full of surprises."

"Aren't I, though?" Jacki giggled. "I told you I was done playing the middle, that I was going to be a man—completely. I'm devoted to you and always have been. You made your choice long ago to be a woman, and short of that little fiasco in Vegas, you stuck with it. I'm sorry I took so long to finish this process on myself. I just had so much unfinished business . . . things in my life unresolved." Jacki struggled with the words. Nala took Jacki's hand and squeezed it.

"I know, baby, the thing with your dad. I always understood that. I'm just glad you got it behind you."

"But listen, darlin', I got plane tickets and we can leave tonight . . . if you want. It'll be just the two of us . . . and forever, man and wife—natural, the way God planned it."

"What?"

"Married, you and me. I'd want nothing more than to have it like that, if you want it. I mean, I'll take you with it or without that little troublemaker between your thighs, and if you want it gone, it's nothing but a word. I can make that happen . . . I love you."

"Jacki . . ." Nala paused and then looked at the ring again on her hand. It shined brighter than all the others Jacki had given her through the years. "I'll do it. I'd love nothing more," she agreed, squeezing Jacki tightly, and then sitting back in her, chair admiring her rings. Stretching out her long, muscular legs until her bare feet touched Nala's, Jacki then engaged her in a little game of footsy, until finally she dragged an even bigger smile from Nala's full lips.

"Man and woman," Jacki said. "One or the other, one and the other . . . you and me, complete, for the first time in our lives."

"Man or woman . . ." Nala sighed. "I never thought I would ever get to choose one or the other, Jacki. We've been both our whole lives . . . of course I want it. I've lived for this." Nala burst into a giggle, until suddenly she leaned back and looked at Jacki sternly. "You wouldn't tease me, would you?" Nala asked, barely hiding her excitement.

"No way, I'd never do that. Teasing can be deadly. . . ."

EPILOGUE

Jim and Howard, Jim's new partner while Lawrence was on leave, went to the little church. Again, they heard the singing before they entered. Jim took the lead when they marched up the aisle to the podium. Julian Marcum held to a tight smile while attempting to question their presence in his church, and in the middle of what was probably his best sermon of the year.

It was sure to be his last one.

It only took a couple of days to get the okay to pick up Julian Marcum. There would be no alibis this time. There wasn't enough charisma on the planet to save him from this arrest.

"Gentlemen, please. We're in the Lord's house. Take a seat." Julian held up his hand.

"We have a search warrant," Jim announced, knowing he would find Kyle's cell phone somewhere, as well as all the other bits of evidence The Appointed One told him they would find in Julian Marcum's possession.

Jim knew Julian hadn't killed all the victims. Maybe he hadn't killed any, but The Appointed One had done a great job of framing him, and no doubt Julian was going to do a lot of jail time. But Julian was not a good person, and in that sense, The Appointed One, again, had served the purpose of 'right'.

"No, sir. We can't do that, because see, you're under arrest for the murder of Portia Hendrix and Kyle Matthews."

The church broke into frenzy, with a couple of the women breaking into praise and songs, lifting their voices. Howard looked around, as if missing the day when he used to sit quietly by his mother in a church similar to this.

Julian didn't fight Jim; it was as if he knew better. There was something about the way this little white cop came at him, ready to put those cuffs on him. Stepping back from them, he reached under his robe and pulled out the gun. There was screaming and hollering, but nothing matched the loud cracking sound of the gunshot as Julian, aiming the gun at himself, fired one time into the side of his head.

About the Author

California transplant Michelle McGriff now writes using the lush green backdrop of the Great Northwest as her muse. Known to her family as the 'best of storytellers,' Ms. McGriff spins intelligent, poignant, and touching yarns, with a poetic voice and writing style that has become hers to keep, holding her readers captive from start to finish. Having more than 25 novels and short stories under her pen (16 currently in print) in 1998, she excitedly became a part of the Kensington Publications imprint (Q-Boro Books) in 2004, with hopes of entertaining a new audience with her rule-breaking, cross-genre writing style that is sure to entertain the enlightened reader.

Using her PhD in Organizational Management, Ms Mc-Griff is currently completing three non-fiction educational projects: **The Business of Writing, Caution: Boss is Volatile Upon Interaction, Warning: This Job Is Fatal If Taken Seriously.** These guidebooks will become part of a set of online seminars facilitated by the author. You can also look for these as well as all her fiction projects wherever you find good reading material.

LOOK FOR MORE HOT TITLES FROM

DARK KARMA - JUNE 2007
$14.95
ISBN 1-933967-12-9

What if the criminal was forced to live the horror that they caused? The drug dealer finds himself in the body of the drug addict and he suffers through the withdrawals, living on the street, the beatings, the rapes and the hunger. The thief steals the rent money and becomes the victim that finds herself living on the street and running for her life and the murderer becomes the victim's father and he deals with the death of a son and a grieving mother.

GET MONEY CHICKS - SEPTEMBER 2007
$14.95
ISBN 1-933967-17-X

For Mina, Shanna, and Karen, using what they had to get what they wanted was always an option. Best friends since day one, they always had a thing for the hottest gear, luxurious lifestyles, and the ballers who made it all possible. All of this changes for Mina when a tragedy makes her open her eyes to the way she's living. Peer pressure and loyalty to her girls collide with her own morality, sending Mina into a no-win situation.

AFTER-HOURS GIRLS - AUGUST 2007
$14.95
ISBN 1-933967-16-1

Take part in this tale of two best friends, Lisa and Tosha, as they stalk the nightclubs and after-hours joints of Detroit searching for excitement, money, and temporary companionship. These two divas stand tall until the unforgivable Motown streets catch up to them. One must fall. You, the reader, decide which.

THE LAST CHANCE - OCTOBER 2007
$14.95
ISBN 1-933967-22-6

Running their L.A. casino has been rewarding for Luke Chance and his three brothers. But recently it seems like everyone is trying to get a piece of the pie. An impending hostile takeover of their casino could leave them penniless and possibly dead. That is, until their sister Keilah Chance comes home for a short visit. Keilah is not only beautiful, but she also can be ruthless. Will the Chance family be able to protect their family dynasty?

Traci must find a way to complete her journey out of her first and only failed

LOOK FOR MORE HOT TITLES FROM

NYMPHO - MAY 2007
$14.95
ISBN 1933967102

How will signing up to live a promiscuous double-life destroy everything that's at stake in the lives of two close couples? Take a journey into Leslie's secret world and prepare for a twisted, erotic experience.

FREAK IN THE SHEETS - SEPTEMBER 2007
$14.95
ISBN 1933967196

Librarian Raquelle decides to put her knowledge of sexuality to use and open up a "freak" school, teaching men and women how to please their lovers beyond belief while enjoying themselves in the process. But trouble brews when a surprise pupil shows up and everything Raquelle has worked for comes under fire.

LIAR, LIAR - JUNE 2007
$14.95
ISBN 1933967110

Stormy calls off her wedding to Camden when she learns he's cheating with a male church member. However, after being convinced that Camden has been delivered from his demons, she proceeds with the wedding.

Will Stormy and Camden survive scandal, lies and deceit?

HEAVEN SENT - AUGUST 2007
$14.95
ISBN 1933967188

Eve is a recovering drug addict who has no intentions of staying clean until she meets Reverend Washington, a newly widowed man with three children. Secrets are uncovered that threaten Eve's new life with her new family and has everyone asking if Eve was *Heaven Sent*.

LOOK FOR MORE HOT TITLES FROM

OBSESSION 101
$6.99
ISBN 0977733548

After a horrendous trauma. Rashawn Ams is left pregnant and flees town to give birth to her son and repair her life after confiding in her psychiatrist. After her return to her life, her town, and her classroom, she finds herself the target of an intrusive secret admirer who has plans for her.

SHAMELESS- OCTOBER 2006
$6.99
ISBN 0977733513

Kyle is sexy, single, and smart; Jasmyn is a hot and sassy drama queen. These two complete opposites find love - or something real close to it - while away at college. Jasmyn is busy wreaking havoc on every man she meets. Kyle, on the other hand, is trying to walk the line between his faith and all the guilty pleasures being thrown his way. When the partying college days end and Jasmyn tests HIV positive, reality sets in.

MISSED OPPORTUNITIES - MARCH 2007
$14.95
ISBN 1933967013

Missed Opportunities illustrates how true-to-life characters must face the consequences of their poor choices. Was each decision worth the opportune cost? LaTonya Y. Williams delivers yet another account of love, lies, and deceit all wrapped up into one powerful novel.

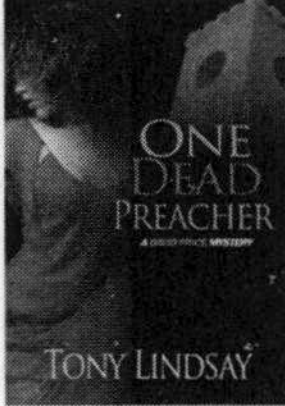

ONE DEAD PREACHER - MARCH 2007
$14.95
ISBN 1933967021

Smooth operator and security CEO David Price sets out to protect the sexy, smart, and saucy Sugar Owens from her husband, who happens to be a powerful religious leader. Sugar isn't as sweet as she appears, however, and in a twisted turn of events, the preacher man turns up dead and Price becomes the prime suspect.

LOOK FOR MORE HOT TITLES FROM

DOGISM
$6.99
ISBN 0977733505

Lance Thomas is a sexy, young black male who has it all: a high paying blue collar career, a home in Queens, New York, two cars, a son, and a beautiful wife. However, after getting married at a very young age he realizes that he is afflicted with DOGISM, a distorted sexuality that causes men to stray and be unfaithful in their relationships with women.

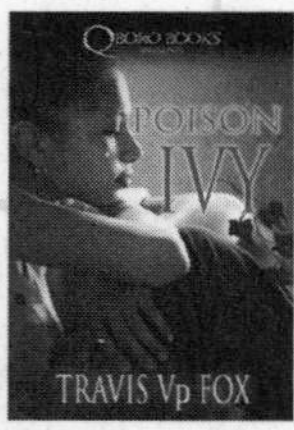

POISON IVY - NOVEMBER 2006
$14.95
ISBN 0977733521

Ivy Davidson's life has been filled with sorrow. Her father was brutally murdered and she was forced to watch, she faced years of abuse at the hands of those she trusted, and she was forced to live apart from the only source of love that she'd ever known. Now Ivy stands alone at the crossroads of life, staring into the eyes of the man who holds her final choice of life or death in his hands.

HOLY HUSTLER - FEBRUARY 2007
$14.95
ISBN 0977733556

Reverend Ethan Ezekiel Goodlove the Third and his three sons are known for spreading more than just the gospel. The sanctified drama of the Goodloves promises to make us all scream "Hallelujah!"

HAPPILY NEVER AFTER - JANUARY 2007
$14.95
ISBN 1933967005

To Family and friends, Dorothy and David Leonard's marriage appears to be one made in heaven. While David is one of Houston's most prominent physicians, Dorothy is a loving and carefree housewife. It seems as if life couldn't be more fabulous for this couple who appear to have it all: wealth, social status, and a loving union. However, looks can be deceiving. What really happens behind closed doors and when the flawless veneer begins to crack?